KILLER IN THE RETROSCAPE

A Near Future Mystery

Bruce M. Perrin

First Edition.

Cover Art by Courtney M. Perrin

Visit the Author at
BruceMPerrin.blogspot.com

Mind Sleuth Publications
ISBN-13: 978-1-7320835-1-6 (paperback)

TITLES BY BRUCE M. PERRIN

THE MIND SLEUTH SERIES
Of Half a Mind
Mind in the Clouds

STANDALONE NOVELS
In the Space of an Atom
Killer in the Retroscape: A Near Future Mystery

For all the latest on new releases, promotions, and book reviews,
subscribe to my blog at:
https://bit.ly/2MVHdCk

For my family and
their boundless love and support

Contents

When we started Apple, Steve Jobs and I talked about how we wanted to make blind people as equal and capable as sighted people, and you'd have to say we succeeded when you look at all the people walking down the sidewalk looking down at something in their hands and totally oblivious to everything around them.

STEVE WOZNIAK
CO-FOUNDER, APPLE INC.

Thursday, April 5, 2068

Morning

I trudged along the street in suburban St. Louis, Missouri, hearing only the sound of my shoes on the sunbaked sidewalk and the occasional whisper of a SCAT as it sped by on the street.

It was the time of year to be outside; the city was a riot of the sights and smells of spring. The first flowers – daffodils, rhododendrons, and redbud trees – had been in bloom for several weeks, their fragrances mingling with the smell of damp earth and newly mown lawns. Today, the white canopies of the dogwoods had been added to the spectacle, along with the tulips and peonies that refused to wait until May. But then, their early starts were in self-defense. The 100-plus degree days of summer were not far away when even the hardiest of flowers would not long survive without assistance.

One hundred-plus degrees?

My mental shift to liters instead of gallons and kilometers in place of miles had been easy. But for some reason, I still had to stop and think about temperature.

"Suze, when did the United States adopt the Celsius system?" I asked.

Suze was my virtuant, a generic term for a personal-assistant, machine intelligence who would have the answer to that query at her electronic fingertips. But virtuants did much more than answer questions about trivia. They were your presence in the virtual world, a layer of computing resources and automatic processes that followed you and controlled the physical environment. If you spoke Japanese, your virtuant would cause the familiar kanji characters to appear on a sign that moments before had been in English. If you were cold, your virtuant would sense it and your clothes would warm. If you were unavailable when a comm arrived, it would record a message or offer your TuringTalk persona in your stead.

To do their job, virtuants appropriated whatever resources they needed from the surrounding environment. Exactly how they moved from the walls of buildings to the interiors of vehicles to the clothes I wore baffled me, but they were always there, opening doors, turning on lights, setting up comms. At the moment, Suze was using speakers in what looked like a logo sewn into my shirt.

"January 1, 2026," came her reply.

"And what is 100 degrees Fahrenheit on the Celsius scale?" It was in the upper 30s, but I didn't know exactly where.

"Thirty-seven-point-eight degrees rounded to the first decimal place," she said.

"No wonder I think in Fahrenheit," I said, only partially feigning exasperation. "One hundred degrees sounds hot. Thirty-seven-point-eight sounds ... well, confusing. Whose bright idea was Celsius, anyway?"

"Ah, yes, for the days when water froze at 32 and boiled at 212," said Suze. Her synthesized voice took on that mocking tone that had become as much a part of my world as the rising sun.

"Yeah, what's the big deal?" I said, matching her tone. "Just because everyone else in the world was using it. And then, we go to the metric system too? Why change just because it's so much simpler?"

"Indeed," Suze replied. "Do you happen to know what the global car company, Mercord, did to highlight some of the benefits of going to metric?"

I smiled. Suze must have stumbled upon some interesting tidbit ... well interesting to a geek like me anyway. Of course, 'stumbled upon' hardly applies to virtuants who have access to billions of petabytes of information. Finding the perfect needle in that vast electronic haystack, however, was an acquired skill, but one at which Suze had become quite adept. "No, what'd they do?" I asked.

"They produced a line of cars with speedometers that measured speed in furlongs per fortnight. When company officials were questioned about the length of a furlong, so people would know how to interpret these gauges, they patiently explained that a furlong was ten chains."

I chuckled. "Just what everyone needs to know."

"Thought you'd like it," said Suze. "Did you also know that one of the big building material conglomerates had the greatest impact on the units of measurement debate? Do you want to hear about that?"

"Thanks, but no. Maybe some other time."

The trivia had been a welcome diversion during the walk, but I needed to return to my thoughts. I was on the way to the home of my friend of fifty years, Josh Unger. Bette, his ex-wife, had called me two days ago, saying she had not been able to reach him. And when my comms had gone unanswered as well, I set off on foot to check.

With Suze now occupied with … whatever it is that virtuants do when they aren't talking to you, there was time to think. Unfortunately, I was finding that there wasn't much to ponder when it came to Josh – at least not much recent history. We had withdrawn to our own worlds some 14 years ago and the two hadn't intersected since. But then, social isolation was the norm. Even this trip reflected the detachment people had come to embrace because other than my wheeled companions, the Self-Contained Autonomous Transports or SCATs, I would be alone.

As I passed a JavaTech store, the 'First in the Universe with Scientifically Brewed Coffee,' as their advertising slogan read, my urge for another cup became overpowering. I had already reached my caffeine quota for the day. Technically, that quota had been achieved before my first cup, according to the health and well-being machine intelligence linked to the sensors in my clothes. That was because my U.S. Security DNA-based Identification Profile, which everyone called their GovTag, indicated that I was 8 years old … well, 7.7 years actually, rather than 77, which was the case. And while even a cursory glance at me would tell anyone otherwise, GovTag readings were gospel in the virtual world, even superseding the dictates of one's virtuant.

Fortunately, I could override GovTag restrictions on an 8-year-old buying coffee. The same could not be said for many other adult products, from drinks to entertainment. And so, I relied on Ali, my wife of 50 years, to do the honors of inserting her left index finger into the GovTag Reader when I wanted a beer.

I found the little-used pedestrian portal to the JavaTech store and entered.

"Welcome, youngster. What can I do for you today?" For reasons that escaped me, stores, which were always automated, still displayed the image of a young, smiling human clerk, eager to help. And my official age had obviously registered with the talking head that was Mr. JavaTech.

"Small Americano, extra shot of espresso, please," I said.

"Are you sure there, young man? That's got quite the caffeine kick." The virtual store clerk frowned and crossed his arms over his chest, presumably to prepare me for disappointment if the GovTag reader declined the sale.

"Yes, I'm sure," I said with a resignation born of numerous repetitions.

"OK," said the image, shrugging. "Please insert your left index finger into the reader."

As expected, the GovTag system played its standard objection, '*Warning, children under nine years of age should consume no more than 63 milligrams of caffeine per day ... yada, yada, yada.*' I drummed my fingers on the counter, knowing the system would not accept an override until the message was complete. When it finally finished, I waved a hand at the screen – one of the few gestural computer commands I knew – and JavaTech dispensed my 227-gram Americano at the going rate of $27.

But the transaction wasn't complete yet. The GovTag system then warned me in text of my questionable actions, the words appearing in the middle of a screen that previously had shown workers picking coffee beans on a mountain slope. The irony of this image wasn't lost on me. Drinks from the JavaTech dispenser held nothing made from coffee beans, let alone ones that had been picked by hand on a mountainside. But then, very few foods or drinks these days came from their namesakes. Growing coffee, raising cattle, picking apples was all too inefficient for today's world.

I turned to leave, but the GovTag system was not quite done. It added an audio warning that my legal guardians would be informed of my transgression. As my parents had been dead for more than 30 years, I would have had the last laugh on this automated system, except that Ali was now listed as my guardian. As odd as it might seem to have your wife as your legal guardian, it was necessary, lest some other machine intelligence send a government official in pursuit of a coffee-drinking, nearly 8-year-old with no adult supervision. And in fact, Ali probably would warn me, again, that I was drinking too much coffee, meaning the GovTag system would have the first, last, and only laughs from this otherwise simple commercial transaction.

I departed the coffee shop with my drink in its two-hour decomposable cup in hand. When these remarkable containers were first introduced, a substantial percentage of them started deteriorating within moments of use. That problem had long been fixed, but I still had not broken the habit of checking. Clearly, I cut a rather bizarre image plodding down the street by myself, looking at the bottom of the cup after every second or third sip. But then, watching the rest of the world go by from the safe confines of their homes had become many people's favorite pastime and I was glad to do my part in entertaining them.

It was not long until I reached Josh's home. When we had first met, he and Bette lived in one of the oldest homes in a northern St. Louis suburb. The construction of that original house was entirely of wood and even the basement walls were massive timbers that had been driven into the earth, edge-to-edge. I had seen nothing like it before or since.

It was perhaps in reaction to this ancient dwelling, with its small, well-defined living spaces that Josh had created the design for his current home. It was single-story with virtually no interior walls. Both in shape, round, and in color, brownish yellow, it looked something like a large pancake, making me wonder if Josh had his inspiration for the design over breakfast. At the front and back entries, the edges of the 'pancake' were flipped up slightly. Here, a wall of transparent material provided access, as well as views into the interior. It was, in a sense, the proverbial glass house, except the walls were actually a material that became opaque yellow on demand or by schedule. They were clouded over now.

When we had been friends, Josh's front portal had been programmed to allow me access, once my DNA had been read. I wondered, however, if his home automation systems still held my profile. And without a backup plan, it was possible that I had come here for nothing. That was uncharacteristic of me. Throughout life, I had been the guy who could hardly buy a recharge for our toothpaste dispenser without weighing the pros and cons. I was not sure what it meant to have arrived so ill-prepared, but there was no time to ponder that question now.

The house appeared to be in some type of stasis, but as I neared, a light above the door came on and the reader glowed. I placed my finger into it. At first, nothing happened, but after a delay of perhaps 2 or 3 seconds, the door opened with a long-forgotten phrase in Josh's voice, "Bout time you showed up, Doug. Make yourself at home."

The sound of his voice brought back a flood of memories. At one time, we had been close. Now I wondered how it could have been so long since we had seen each other. Perhaps this visit would start a new round of socializing. It was possible. Anything was possible … but it was unlikely. The days of playing cards, sharing a beer, or cheering the local sports team at a friend's home were a memory from the distant past.

The house was hot, the air still with an odor that reminded me of my college days – dirty sweat socks and two-day-old pizza. But with the presence of a human, more and more systems were coming online. Cool, fresh air started entering the living space and the room became brighter, as vast areas of the ceiling became transparent. Views of the side and back yards took over the walls.

"Josh, it's Doug. You home?" I called out. No answer. I went through the house, calling his name, but found nothing but piles of dirty clothes and half-eaten meals. I returned to the front of his house where Julia sat. Julia was a mechanion, or simply put, a virtuant given physical form. But in reality, there was nothing simple in the transformation from a virtual, machine intelligence to a physical robot, both technologically and psychologically.

"Julia?" I said hesitantly.

She looked older than I remembered. And while we lived in an age when a mechanical companion could be a trophy, most of their human partners sought age-appropriateness over show. Josh apparently shared that view and she had added years right along with him.

"Bout time you showed up, Doug. Make yourself at home," said Julia, smiling at me like we had seen each other last week, rather than nearly a decade and a half ago. She too used Josh's words of welcome, but in her voice, not his. But as she spoke the familiar phrase, I drew back, feeling a knot form in my stomach.

I had known Julia for five or six years before Josh and I parted ways and during that time, I had learned to cope with her presence. But since then, that facade had apparently collapsed and now, I found myself looking anywhere but into her eyes. To do so would produce a wave of unease, a feeling of dissonance between the extremely realistic human form I saw and the knowledge that she was only electronics and hydraulics, hardware and software. It was a psychological gulf I had never been able to cross completely and her use of Josh's familiar greeting made it worse.

I took a breath, then asked, "Julia, where's Josh?"

She tilted her head to the right as if in thought, attesting to the attention to detail that was taken in the development of these incredible pieces of technology. "I'm not sure, but he said he was going to the back building."

Perhaps to offset the open spaces and curved flows of his home, Josh had kept the circa 2020 detached garage located on the back edge of his property. It was all straight lines and right angles. It served no purpose, however, other than to house some minor automation components and perhaps, some storage. "When did he go out there?" I asked, surprised he had not heard me calling.

Again, she tilted her head. "Twelve days ago."

"What?" I blurted, wondering if she could be wrong, but knowing that was an irrational hope.

Then, as if some health and well-being software had caught up with the facts or Julia read the alarm in my face, she said, "I hope he's alright. Do you want to check on him or shall I?"

"I will," I replied. "But why didn't you check on him earlier? Aren't you designed to protect life, not ignore it?" I would have felt bad being so blunt, but mechanions didn't have feelings.

Julia blinked, then replied. "Sorry, I've been sleeping since he left."

Being asleep was Josh's term for the times when he shut Julia down. When I had known him, that action was infrequent and never for long. Never for 12 days. I left for the garage.

I was still more than three meters from the structure when I knew something was horribly wrong. The stench coming from the building was overpowering, but somehow, I couldn't stop my feet. As I pulled the door open and light flooded in, I saw Josh's bloated and blackened body hanging from a rafter. My heart started pounding in my chest. The garage started to spin and I reached for the door frame, missed, and fell backward, out through the open door. I got to my feet and managed to stumble about a meter from the building when I lost my JavaTech coffee ... along with everything else I had eaten that morning.

I had only looked at Josh for a moment, but I knew the image would be burned in my mind forever.

Late Morning, April 5, 2068

Within moments of losing my breakfast Suze said, "Doug, you have a comm from Ali." I grunted my understanding, still spitting the last of the bile from my mouth.

"Doug, what's wrong?" Concern was apparent in Ali's voice.

"Josh's dead." I was still bent over, hands on my knees, waiting for the dizziness to pass.

Ali hesitated, then quietly asked, "Did you discover the body?"

"Yeah," I managed.

When we met, Ali had been a recently licensed physical therapist. She had been drawn to the field by her desire to help people, with that broad motivation being further refined by the fact that she was a talented, amateur tennis player. Over the years of our marriage, she had shown a continuing interest in all things medical. So, with her lifelong connection to the healing arts, the fact that she could guess what had happened from the sensors in my clothes came as no surprise.

There was a tree stump nearby and I took a seat and put my head in my hands. After a few moments of silence, Ali said, "Doug, it looks like your vitals are stabilizing. Are you feeling better?"

"Yeah, I think so," I replied, raising my head and feeling thankful that the world was no longer turning with me as the axis. "I should call PSS, get them over here. I'll call you when we're done."

"OK, honey," she said slowly. "But if you feel dizzy or disoriented, they can wait. Have Suze comm me and arrange a SCAT to a treatment center."

"I will," I said and ended the call. Then, I said, "Help, PSS."

The original phrase for requesting emergency assistance had been, 'Help, Public Security Service.' But when the system was designed, the government had overlooked the fact that 'Public Security Service' was a bit of a tongue-twister. Anxious callers were bungling it and ended up talking to everyone from public utilities to escort services – the latter an error not easily explained to a significant other. So, the required phrase had been shortened.

Of course, I could have asked Suze to contact them, but 'help PSS' was given communications priority. It would be picked up and processed by any acoustically sensitive automation within range of my voice, including but not limited to Suze. The significance attached to this phrase was a safeguard against failure of one's virtuant, although in 2068 it was more likely that the victim would forget how to talk.

After only a few seconds, I heard, "Public Security Service, this is Technician Jon Michnicovich? Would you prefer an automated response?"

When did they start asking that?

"No, speaking to a human is fine," I replied.

"Very good. Am I speaking to … ah … I'm not sure? Is it Dr. Douglas Michaels?" asked the technician.

"It is."

"Sorry, Dr. Michaels. It's just that you're showing up as a 7-year-old and on-screen … well, you look a bit older than that."

I looked around. Requesting PSS assistance authorized the use of a vast array of technology, but even so, I was surprised that they already had me on video. "The age you're seeing is a GovTag profile error," I explained. "I need to report a body at my current location. I found a friend, Josh Unger, dead in a building at the back of his property. He's been hanged."

There was a considerable delay; it was understandable. A report of death by hanging would be a once in several lifetimes event at any local PSS facility. Finally, the technician replied, "Excuse me, Dr. Michaels, but can you repeat that?"

When I had done so – twice – and answered a few additional questions to verify my identity and location, I asked, "Can you send someone over?"

"Of course. As soon as possible," the technician said and ended the comm.

'As soon as possible' turned out to be nearly an hour later when four SCATs bearing the official PSS logo on the side pulled into Josh's driveway. I got up from the stump as a young man exited the first vehicle. He was wearing a uniform that looked so crisp and new, I wasn't sure it had ever seen the light of day until now.

"Good morning," he said, taking a position a couple of meters from where I was standing. "I'm PSS Technician Alex Perez. Are you Dr. Douglas Michaels?"

"That's right," I said, nodding.

Personnel in the PSS were technicians, not officers or patrolmen. They didn't patrol and the term officer was deemed too militant for the services they provided. They applied technology to investigate security-related concerns, some extremely small fraction of which were later classified as crimes. If this situation was deemed one, then an officer from the Criminal

Apprehension Service, or CAS, would be assigned. In their case, the more authoritative title of 'officer' was fitting.

"First, thanks for reporting this incident," Technician Perez said. "It's an important civic responsibility to report unusual or suspicious situations, and the PSS thanks you for doing so."

It was hard for me to believe that anyone could ignore what I had seen, but then, 'Keep to yourself' was the unspoken dictum of today's world. I nodded in reply.

"Before we start, I want to make sure that we recorded your description of this incident correctly," Perez said. He took a deep breath, then released it slowly. "Did you say the victim has been hanged?"

"Yes, I did."

He swallowed hard. "It's just that we don't see many ... deaths by hanging. Probably got tangled up in something," he muttered. Then, he held up a hand, shook his head, and in a much more formal tone said, "Sorry, our units will fully investigate and determine the cause of death."

What he had mentioned – that it was probably an accident – was possible, but I didn't think so. Without calling the details back to mind, an option that I wanted to avoid, I believed it had been a single rope tied to a rafter and looped around Josh's neck. Hopefully, my memory was wrong, because while an accident was tragic, a suicide would be unfathomable.

"You said the body is in the garage?" asked Perez.

"Yes," I replied, nodding toward the structure with my head and reseating myself on the stump.

I had a pretty good idea what was to come during my interaction with Technician Perez. My background, which was industrial psychology with a focus on learning and research, made it so. It had taken a long time for training and education to move beyond the paradigm of 'dump a bunch of facts in front of students and hope they remember them' to one of 'dump a bunch of facts in front of students and monitor the reactions in their brains so you can repeat the last step as necessary.' But with evolutions in both learning and criminal investigation technology, a modest overlap had developed over the years.

As I watched, the technician unloaded two small robotic units and a third, large one from the three SCATs that had trailed his vehicle into Josh's drive. Each unit displayed the phrase "PSS Forensics" on the side. Despite the common name, however, they looked nothing alike, because they weren't. They had quite different functions. As Perez was about to launch into his canned spiel, designed to put the public's mind at ease, I thought of saying that I already knew what these robots did. But somehow, I felt that his well-practiced patter might put us both more at ease.

"This first unit, the smaller one here," he said, pointing, "will be documenting the crime scene. But rather than the photographs of the past, it will be building high-resolution, three-dimensional models of both the surfaces and subsurface objects."

At one time, those models were created with a combination of laser and microwave scans, the latter being similar to ground penetrating radar. But technology changes quickly, and I suspected the current systems used something even more precise.

Perez continued. "The models they create are very detailed so that any area can be enlarged, rotated, and inspected closely, should such an action be required later." Pointing at the next robot, he said, "This second unit will analyze the particulate matter in the air and on the surfaces. It is able to detect any living organism, human or otherwise, that entered the garage within the last two weeks. Since the space has been closed, it will probably be able to compile a history even longer than that."

It had always surprised me how long it took technology to surpass living organisms in this role. Dogs had been used to find drugs and explosives for many years because, quite simply, their millions of years of evolutionary history had given them sensing abilities that science could not duplicate. That was, until the late 2030s.

"And finally, the big guy here with the manipulator," said Perez. "We call him 'Muscles' because he will be clearing the way for the other two. But he's not all brute force. He has the dexterity and touch feedback necessary to thread a needle, as well as the strength to lift hundreds of kilograms. If there's any place the other units want to investigate further, Muscles will clear the way."

I also suspected that he would be used to lower and remove Josh. That thought made me gag again as if I had anything left in my stomach.

Technician Perez walked beside the forensic units to the garage door, but he stopped short. Muscles opened the door for the three of them and they entered. Lest I be confused about his actions, Perez called to me, "It's better that no other humans enter until they have processed the scene. I would just add contamination."

I nodded, pretending to believe this was the only reason he wished to stay outside.

With the robotic units at work, Perez returned to his previous spot. "Now, I'd like you to make a statement covering the reason for your visit to this home, where you went when you arrived, and what you observed. This will be part of the official, on-site incident record."

I stood and he circled around me to the first SCAT. He touched a spot on its side and a small, flat surface appeared. "You'll start with the GovTag Reader here," he said, pointing at the device. "Then, the display surface will guide you through each of those questions. Do you understand what I have asked you to do?"

"I think so," I replied. Perez nodded and then stepped away from the vehicle.

Technician Perez had, of course, left many parts of the PSS's protocol unstated, as he had been trained to do. For example, somewhere within the side panel of the SCAT was a small, yet very sensitive electromagnetic reader. It would pick up the faint signals from my brain and map them to the regions in use. Should the brain areas associated with telling a lie – the orbitofrontal cortex – light up during the interview, the questions would become more probing over time. Rubber hoses and sitting under bright lights held nothing on these systems when it came to getting at the truth.

Of course, I wouldn't lie. I wanted to get to the bottom of Josh's death even more than the PSS.

After several minutes working on the automated interview, I noticed the three forensics units emerge from the garage. Technician Perez then led them to the back door of Josh's home and they entered. Later, they emerged from the house and by the time I was finished with my questions, all three had been loaded for transport. Technician Perez was speaking to someone on a video comm that was being displayed on a SCAT side panel. As I approached, I heard him say, "Yes, that's right. The body's not a person."

What the ...?

"That body is my friend of 50 years, Josh Unger," I blurted. "What does that mean, not a person?"

Perez's head jerked around at the sound of my voice. He stepped back from me, his eyes going wide. "Ah ... I didn't know you were there," he stammered.

"Alex, let me take that question," came a voice from the display surface. Looking relieved, Perez retreated to a safe distance. When I moved to the screen, I saw a woman, perhaps in her 40s. Her short red hair framed a round, freckled face with brown eyes. She was adjusting something, perhaps the direction of the camera. "Ah, Dr. Michaels," she said, after a moment of fiddling with the controls. "Thank you for doing your civic responsibility and reporting this incident. We need more cooperative citizens like you."

I appreciated my continuing recognition as 'citizen of the hour,' but that didn't seem like the critical topic at the moment. "You're welcome," I said, frowning. "But what I want to know is why you're saying that Josh is not a person?"

"First, let me introduce myself," she said. "I'm Chief Technician Terri Finnegan. Please pardon the wording that Technician Perez used. What he meant is that the body in ... what is it, a garage ... that this body's DNA matches no known person in the GovTag database."

"Ah ... I'm not sure I know what that means?" I said slowly, my frown deepening.

"Nothing, really," Finnegan said mildly, as she pushed a strand of red hair from her forehead. "There are extremely rare instances of elaborate hoaxes where someone tries to construct something human-like in appearance from ... various protein sources." I grimaced, wondering why anyone would engage in such a distasteful hoax. "But our unit identified this body as containing human DNA. It's just that the DNA matches no records in the database."

I rubbed the back of my neck, then looked closely at the Chief Technician onscreen. "How could that happen?"

"I'm not sure, but it's undoubtedly nothing," said Finnegan. "Maybe some slight contamination in the unit that took the sample. Something in the transmission of the data from there to the processing location. Any number of things that'll disappear when we re-run the analysis." She paused, studying my face. "Do you mind if I ask you a question?"

"No, not at all," I replied.

"Assuming for the moment that the deceased is Josh Unger ...." The Chief Technician must have seen my frown return, as she quickly added, "and I am sure that will be the case when the data error is corrected. I see that you and Mr. Unger worked together in the past. Were you close to him?"

"Yeah, I'd say that. We worked together at Worthington-Huston Technology for something like 35 years. We were good friends, but I guess it has been about 14 or 15 years since I last saw him."

Worthington-Huston Technology, or WHT, had been founded by two St. Louis neuroscientists, Drs. Ned Worthington and Jon Huston, in the early 2010s with a focus on the neural mechanisms of learning. But their high-tech work often intersected with more standard training paradigms and Josh had been hired as a simulation expert during the second year of their operation. I had joined as an industrial psychologist a year later.

When Finnegan didn't say anything for a moment, I added, "You know how it is. Things happened, and Josh and I just drifted apart after we retired."

"Yes, of course," she said, smiling. "I only asked because, frankly, I thought I could save you checking back with us. We'll get the DNA matched, of course. But as soon as that happens, the case will be closed. Our machines have completed their analysis and the conclusion is clear."

I sighed and nodded slowly. "So, it was an accident?" I dropped my gaze to the ground.

"No, I'm sorry, but you misunderstood," said Finnegan. My head jerked up in time to see her smooth the front of her uniform. "Our forensic units have determined that his death was self-inflicted."

I looked directly into the eyes of the face onscreen. "A suicide?" I asked, my voice rising. "That's not possible. His life ended violently, painfully, and utterly alone. Who does that? I'll tell you. No one. No one does anything like that since the TLCs."

The Termination of Life Centers, with the somewhat incongruous acronym of TLC, were created by the Compassionate Termination of Life Act in the 2040s. They were controlled by regulation, following strict guidelines covering the medical and psychological evaluation of the client and the notification of friends and family. But with current technology, the entire process could be completed within a few hours. And once done, the end of life came peacefully, painlessly, and without stigma.

"Dr. Michaels, I'm very sorry for your loss," said Finnegan, probably reverting to her formal training on dealing with an overwrought member of the public. "It's completely understandable that you're upset, and you can and should follow up with PSS personnel until you're satisfied with our findings. I can also put you in contact with one of our machine intelligences, which will guide you through all of our procedures and grief counseling if you prefer that option. But there's no doubt in our conclusion."

Finnegan paused a moment. I tried to calm myself, willing my breathing to slow, my muscles to relax. The tactic helped my symptoms but did nothing to resolve the feeling of complete bewilderment.

There was a look of pity in Finnegan's eyes when she continued. "I'm sorry, but there's no doubt that the rope was secured intentionally. Our units were able to establish his time of death ... as a little more than six days ago. And other than your presence in the last hour, no one besides Mr. Unger has been in his house or his garage in the last three weeks. I'm truly sorry, but these are the facts."

"Six days?" I said, some hope seeping into my tone. "That doesn't add up. Julia ... that's Josh's mechanion. She said he went out to the garage twelve days ago. What happened in those missing days?"

"Yes, he may well have gone out there twelve days ago ... when he first shut down his mechanion. But we know he didn't stay there. He had been in his home as late as six days ago. But then he returned to the garage and ... never left."

I looked down again, feeling defeated. PSS's interpretation of events was a poor fit for the man I had known, even if our shared history wasn't recent. But the chance that their forensic units had missed something, even with the glitch in matching Josh's DNA, was extremely remote. "You're finding nothing suspicious at all?" I said without even looking up. "I never knew Josh to be down a day in his life, let alone be depressed enough to kill himself."

Finnegan said nothing for a moment and I looked up at the screen. She was staring intently at something off to her right, her eyes narrowed in concentration. When her gaze returned to the camera, she studied my face for several seconds. "First of all, let me be clear. There's nothing illegal ... or even suspicious in anything we've found."

"What is it?" I asked.

Perhaps I had let a little too much interest creep into my tone, as she studied me a few additional seconds. Finally, she continued. "The only thing of note is that ... let's see ... about 14 weeks ago, activity at the home dropped considerably. And by that, I mean, there were no deliveries, no communications, and very few comings and goings. In fact, in that period, he left his home only once – about three weeks ago on a SCAT that his mechanion ordered. Otherwise, Mr. Unger was having Julia run whatever errands he needed. And there weren't many of those. He was basically isolated at home for about three and a half months."

"Three and a half months?" I said, frowning at her and shaking my head. "Josh was careful ... like anyone, but housebound for three and a half months? There's something wrong in that picture."

"Perhaps," said the Chief Technician. "But your friend wouldn't be the first to shut out the world. We see it, from time to time." She paused a beat. "I thought as a psychologist, you might have noticed it too."

"Not really." I wasn't in the right field. Irrational fears or depression or whatever this was wouldn't be a part of a career in industrial psychology.

"Well, unless you have other questions?" Finnegan asked, raising her eyebrows. I shook my head along with a half shrug.

"OK, if anything comes up before this case is officially closed, I'll contact you. And I'll make sure Mr. Unger's family gets word when the DNA match is made."

There was nothing else to say except thanks, and I did. After Technician Perez departed with the PSS forensic robots, I had Suze comm Ali for me.

"How are you?" she asked, the worry still perceptible in her tone. While our connection was audio only, I knew what she was doing. She was biting her lower lip, or maybe, twirling a strand of her black hair around a finger with her brow knitted. I'd seen those looks many times.

"Physically, I'm OK," I said. "But otherwise, this thing is all wrong. Nothing fits. Nothing makes sense. Babe, is it OK if I walk for a while?"

"Sure. I'll see you later," she replied, sounding more relaxed. We said our good-byes.

Ali, of course, understood my request. For our entire life together, when I needed to think, I would go for a jog, or later in life, for a walk. Today was clearly one of those days.

"Suze, can you lay out a ten-kilometer walk home?" I said. "But put in some place where I can get a snack. I need something on my stomach."

"Sure, Doug. Want me to check for the best scenery?"

"Thanks, but no. I wouldn't notice it anyway."

Afternoon, April 5, 2068

As I approached home, I felt the first sprinkles of rain, and by the time I had climbed the front porch steps, the skies opened up. The rain came in wind-driven waves, so heavy that I could hardly see the houses on the other side of the street. A brilliant flash of lightning was followed almost immediately by a deafening clap of thunder. Violent, short-lived thunderstorms had become commonplace in St. Louis during any months other than January and February. Then, ice storms were the rule.

When I opened the door, Ali was waiting for me, most likely alerted to my approach by the proximity of Suze to our home.

"Just got in before the downpour," she said, giving me a hug. The day had been warm and Ali was barefoot, wearing a pair of shorts and a T-shirt. But the storm had cooled the air, and as a breeze slipped past the door before it closed automatically, she shivered.

"I've been trying to read," she continued, "but I swear I've read the same page twenty times. Your vitals when you were at Josh's house – they were all over the place. It must have been terrible."

"Yeah," I said, hoping but failing to keep the last image of Josh out of my head. "It was."

She stepped back and looked up at me. "Do you want to talk about it?" she asked quietly.

I took a deep breath and slowly shook my head. "Not about finding him, no. I want to forget that. But about what PSS said later? Yeah, because like I said on the comm, it makes no sense."

Ali pressed her lips together tightly, then nodded. "I was making a cup of tea. You want something?"

"No, I'll wait for you in the living room." I went there and sat on the couch, watching Ali prepare her drink through a large, arched doorway to our kitchen.

Perhaps because of my recent nearness to death, I couldn't seem to take my eyes off my wife of 50 years. I had always thought of her as small, perhaps because when we embraced, she fit perfectly under my chin. But at 163 centimeters, she was almost exactly at the national average. She was fair-skinned as if she had inherited the complexion of a blonde. But her hair was black, and other than the rare occasions when she put it in a ponytail or on top of her head, it fell to her shoulders in dark, shiny curls. The contrast between her dark hair and complexion was striking, even from a room away.

But her most alluring feature was hidden from my view by the curls that were falling around her face as she prepared her drink. It was her large, innocent, deep brown eyes. They had been the first thing I had noticed about her. They had drawn me across the crowded room at a friend's party. And I had been captivated by them ever since.

Ali finished making her tea and took a seat on a chair directly across from me, putting her cup on an end table at her elbow. After she had settled in, I told her everything I had learned from the PSS – about when Josh had died, the fact that he was alone, and his behavior before the end.

When I finished, Ali said, "Well, his isolation and living conditions might be from depression, but I never saw Josh down. Not even close."

"Yeah, in two and a half hours of walking, that's exactly where I ended up as well," I admitted.

I hesitated, having more to say but not knowing exactly where to start. But when I looked at her, Ali was watching me closely. "You're thinking you can figure out what happened, aren't you?"

I shifted on the couch, glancing away for a second, then back. "You mean like who might have attacked him?"

Ali was shaking her head even before I finished the question. "No," she said. "With the technology PSS has, they would have found something if there was an intruder. No, you're thinking it would be something subtler, something that wore on him."

Ali and I had always been about as different as two people could be. She was vibrant and outgoing, a person who could be the life of any party, if she wanted. She tackled everything she did with intelligence, energy, and passion. I, on the other hand, might be best described as precise, persistent, and analytic. Where Ali was always bouncing ideas off others, I kept my own counsel, preferring to chase down every detail before acting. But despite these vast differences in our temperaments, Ali had always been able to read me like a book. And today wasn't an exception.

"Guilty," I admitted. "Josh probably did less to mess with his head, either with chemicals or technology, than almost anyone our age. And he's certainly done less than anyone in the younger generations. So, if he got messed up, I'd like to know what happened. But mostly, I want to be sure that it wasn't something done to him."

Ali had reached over for her tea but now, sat it back down roughly without taking a sip as she recoiled. "Done on purpose?" she said, frowning. "Why would anyone do something like that? I mean, it's not like Josh was involved with something ... clandestine, was he?"

"Babe, I don't know," I said, holding my hands out. "It doesn't seem likely. But is it less likely than him getting depressed because retirement was boring and then choosing a violent, painful end rather than a TLC?" Ali's frown deepened. I gave her a what-can-I-say shrug, then her question triggered a thought. "Oh, while I was walking home, I called Bette."

Ali sat forward on the chair and asked quietly, "Did you have to break the news to her?"

"No, she already knew. I guess PSS doesn't waste any time informing ex-wives. She was upset, of course, but she seemed to be handling it OK. You may want to call her later. Anyway, I asked her that question – if Josh had been working on anything new."

"Douglas," Ali said sharply, sitting back in the chair with enough force to engage the recline function. "Up," she said, to reverse the action, her tone making it clear she didn't appreciate the chair interrupting her. Then, she turned her frown toward me. "Bette just learned her husband was dead and you're playing detective?"

"They've been divorced for something like 30 years," I said. The wattage behind Ali's glare increased, so I tried a different tack. "I wasn't grilling her, babe. It was just part of condolences and small talk." Ali shook her head, clearly indicating she wasn't convinced so much as resigned to what I had done.

"Anyway, Bette said no. As far as she knew, Josh was just puttering in his garden and enjoying his life of leisure."

"OK," replied Ali. "I'll call her later." At least she hadn't added, 'And try to repair the damage you caused,' although I suspected she was thinking it.

"Oh, I almost forgot. There was something strange about the DNA readings PSS took. They couldn't match them to anyone in their database. Anyway, they're going to double check and let Bette know."

For the second time, Ali replaced her cup of tea without taking a sip. "That's unusual," she said slowly, looking off toward the wall behind me. "Suze, do we have any new comms about Josh."

Ali had her own virtuant, of course, but she kept hers in the background, silently doing her bidding in the virtual world. She hadn't named it and rarely spoke to it, preferring to ask her questions of Suze. Many years ago, when this preference became apparent, I had asked her why. She simply said, 'I need the functions of a virtuant, but I don't need another friend.' Somehow, that made perfect sense.

"No, sorry," said Suze. "No comms about Josh."

Ali started twirling a strand of hair around a finger, her eyes again returning to the far wall. After a moment, she said, "Doug, have you thought about where you're going to start your hunt?"

"You mean, have I set up my table with rows for each week that I knew Josh and columns for all the suspicious people and demanding situations he faced?"

Ali laughed. It was good to break the tension of the last half-hour, to see her eyes smile. "I don't think you'd go that far." But as the words left her mouth, she looked at me closely, perhaps wondering if I had considered it. Fortunately, she didn't ask or I would have had to confess.

"No, I'm just going to hit a few crucial dates," I said, referring to the option I had selected. "Between what I can draw out of the old, gray matter with a few, well-chosen memory joggers and stories from coworkers and friends, I'll be able to build a pretty complete landscape of his past."

"Memory joggers, huh? You and your mind tricks, Dr. Michaels. So, you're going to build a retroscape."

I exaggerated my grimace. "Yeah, I guess a low-tech one. And hopefully, one that has some accuracy."

The word 'retroscape' had seen limited use before the turn of the century when it meant a landscape filled with objects from the past. But in the 2030s, a psychological meaning had been added; retroscapes also included mental images of bygone days. Concurrently, the necessary technology was developed. Using a mild, electrical stimulation to the scalp to 're-energize lost memories' and a capability to record mental images pioneered at the University of California, Berkley, around 2010, the first images of these mental landscapes were produced.

Psychologists and neuroscientists, however, were skeptical. Many of the techniques that appeared to tease lost memories from our minds – from Penfield's direct stimulation of the cortex in the 1950s to the well-meaning efforts of psychoanalysts through the turn of the century - had produced vivid recollections. Few of those remembrances, however, could be verified. They were, simply put, false memories. When these technology-induced retroscapes were found to have the same limitation, the connotations of the word changed forever and for the worse.

So, as a means to search for a reason behind Josh's death, a retroscape was filled with pitfalls. If I did nothing to aid in building it, I'd learn nothing new. But if I did too much, I'd create a past that never happened. It was a balancing act where, even in 2068, we didn't understand all the rules.

After a moment's hesitation rubbing my chin, not to ponder the foibles of a retroscape so much as to consider my next statement to Ali, I simply spit it out. "To fill in the last 14 years, I'm going to need to talk to Julia."

Ali didn't merely return her untouched teacup to the coaster this time; she nearly dropped it to the floor. "Douglas Michaels," she said firmly. "You can't go around poking into people's personal lives."

I tried for an innocent smile, but I was pretty sure it came out as a guilty one. "I wouldn't be asking anything about Josh and Julia's life together, just what Josh had been up to those last years. And assuming Bette inherits Josh's estate, she can give me permission. That's not too personal, is it?"

Ali rubbed her forehead with a hand, then looked at me. "Doug, you need to be really careful. You're asking a lot of Bette. I don't know exactly how she feels about Julia, but it couldn't be good. What ex-wife has ever liked the other woman ... so to speak? And to imply that Julia might shed some light on Josh's death? I can think of a dozen ways that could blow up in your face."

I nodded slowly, considering her words. "Yeah, you're right. But I won't learn anything about Josh's recent history without it."

Ali sighed but said nothing. Instead, she turned her attention to the neglected cup of tea. "Yuck, it's cold. You distracted me with all your wild ideas," she said, looking exasperated. She stood, then lightly placed her hand on my shoulder as she walked past toward the kitchen.

"I thought I'd start with the events of 2035," I called to her.

I didn't need to see Ali's face to know how she reacted; her voice had the mix of apprehension and sadness that went with that period in our history. "I suppose that makes sense," she said, returning to the living room with freshly synthesized tea. "If you want to recall a time that drove nearly everyone into seclusion ...." She didn't need to finish.

She joined me on the couch, curling her legs up beside her and leaning her head on my shoulder. Then, she started playing her free hand lightly on my arm. It was a position we had adopted when dating and had perfected over the next 50 years, and it never failed to make me feel close.

We sat in silence, me alone with my thoughts, her taking sips of her drink. After a few minutes, she got up from the couch and looked back at me. "I don't envy you the mental journey you're planning, but I'm glad you're doing it. His death is too bizarre to sweep under the rug."

I nodded and returned her sad smile. She picked up a screen known as a PlotsPro and left to read. I went to my office.

"Suze, I'm looking for pictures of a restaurant called Geraci's from 2035," I said as I entered. "Inside or outside of the building. A menu would also be great."

"Sorry, Doug. But Geraci's went out of business in 2029. Did you happen to mean Luca's, because I see charges from there in the mid-2030s."

Well great. Not a promising start.

"Yeah, let's try Luca's."

Immediately, a picture of the outside of the restaurant appeared on my office wall. Inset in one corner was a menu. OK, now I remembered the place ... and the evening.

Thirty-Three Years Earlier

Evening, March 16, 2035

li looked at me, exaggerated concern on her face. "You did remember to invite them, didn't you?" she said. "After all, you are getting up there in years." We were meeting Josh and Bette for dinner at Luca's for Ali's birthday. Tomorrow, she would be 42. As my birthday had been on March 10, when I turned 44, today was the last day she could tease me about being three years older than her.

"But you know how I adore older men," she added, also in typical Ali fashion. It was as if she worried that all common sense might someday desert me and I'd think she was serious. So, she followed each teasing remark with a disclaimer. They always made me smile, even when I was trying to look hurt.

I started to answer her in kind when I heard Josh's voice behind me. "So, how many drinks ahead of us are you two?"

I turned to see the couple approaching. It always struck me how similar they looked. Both had fair skin and light hair, with Josh's hair being a consistent reddish-brown. Bette's became nearly blonde in the summer but was closer to chestnut in the winter. She was somewhat tall for her gender; Josh was somewhat short, meaning that they ended up being almost the same height, although Bette might overshadow her husband by a centimeter or two. Even their personalities were similar, as both were easy-going and social. There was, however, one glaring difference. Bette had what I would call – when I was in a generous mood – a quirky sense of humor. And as usual, it was on display.

"Yeah, that reminds me of that old joke," said Bette. "A psychologist walked out of a bar .... No, really, he did." Unfortunately, most of her jokes were about as funny as this one. Supposedly, in college, she had even gotten the nickname, 'bad-joke Bette.' I was not sure it was true, but that was what Josh said. And it fit.

"Hi, guys," I said. "We just got here."

"And you've only had tee martoonis, right?" said Bette, smiling at Ali. Fortunately, Bette usually tormented me with only one or two witticisms each evening, although after a few drinks, I had seen them come rapid-fire.

"That's a great outfit," said Ali, as she embraced her friend.

Somehow, Ali had developed an immunity to Bette's sense of humor. I still groaned each time, but then, I secretly believed that Bette sought pained reactions. If not, I wasn't sure why she told jokes, because that was all she ever received.

"Ah, thanks, Ali," replied Bette. "You look spectacular."

I shook Josh's hand and gave Bette a hug. Josh gave Ali a peck on the lips, after taking my hand. Sometimes I wished I had the same, easygoing manner Josh had around nearly everyone. But I could no more kiss someone I knew as little as Josh knew Ali than I could fly. We sat down, with the men on one side of the table, our wives on the other.

"Lot happening around home," said Josh.

I didn't immediately follow and turned sideways. Josh was focused on his dining options and for a moment, I thought I'd have to ask when I made the connection. "That's right. You're getting those flexible, high-tech display surfaces, CommCovers, on your walls. Over your windows too, if I remember right."

"And sealing your house up like a tomb," Ali added. She glanced at me around the corner of her menu, a mischievous twinkle in her large, brown eyes. "I'm still a big fan of windows. You know, light, air, something to look at that's not generated by a computer." Since we had already installed

CommCovers in our bedroom, a fact I hadn't mentioned to Josh, this was obviously about Ali giving Josh a hard time.

"Ha, ha," Josh replied deadpan. "Very funny. You need to get yourself into this decade, girl. CommCovers are the way to go."

"Yeah, Ali," said Bette. "Windows are over-rated. I can never find one when I need it. They're always ajar." She received the expected groans from Josh and me.

"But seriously," she continued, "how often can you open your windows in St. Louis anyway? Two, three weeks a year? And when you do – the humidity, pollen, dust. Yuck. It's getting tough to find days ... or even hours to keep them open."

I selected an entrée from the menu displayed in the tabletop, completing my order. When I looked up, Ali was already done with her choices, but not with teasing Josh apparently.

"Yeah, but even a few days is infinitely more than nothing," she said. "The sights you'll miss – the lawn, the trees, the kids on the street. And yes, Josh, I know the most popular thing to display on a CommCover is a view of the street, but it's not real. It can't be the same."

"No, it's not the same," said Josh. "It's better. Way better. You remember when I was house-sitting for McQuerry?" Josh asked, turning to me. He didn't wait for an answer. "He had CommCovers. I still remember the first time I walked through his living room in my underwear and the entire south-facing wall looked like it was open to the street. Sort of like that recurring dream ... except I'm naked in it."

"Have your Covers installed backward," Ali said. "You can be living the dream. We'd even welcome you to our neighborhood."

"Yeah, right," said Josh. "You already get to see lots of half-naked men on the job."

Ali laughed. "Funny. Even before the job change, most of my patients were over 50. Now, they're even older. I missed out on the half-naked, young-male perk by not specializing in sports medicine. So, yeah, come to our street," she said, wiggling her eyebrows and leering in an exaggerated way that made all of us smile.

"I didn't know you had changed jobs," said Bette.

"It's recent and not that big of a deal. I'm just focusing more on counseling people undergoing treatments." Bette nodded.

By the 2030s, there had been an explosion of biomedical devices that cured or at least lessened a host of previously untreatable ailments – blindness, paralysis, various neurodegenerative diseases. But many patients, nearly all over the age of 60, experienced both physical and psychological difficulty adjusting to these treatments. They needed support; they needed a friend if the miracles of modern medicine were to work. And when Ali learned of this gap, she rallied to the cause with her usual passion and energy. The only downside was that she went from a well-paying, professional career to a job with a pay scale that placed it only one step away from volunteer work. But it was something she wanted to do and we could survive on my income, so it was decided.

"Have you figured out how you're going to address your CommCovers, once they're in?" I asked, glancing sideways at Josh. "I hear that 'My Wall Genie,' 'Abracadabra,' and 'Hocus Focus' are all popular."

"Not necessary," Josh said. "You can name them if you want to be funny. But really, all you have to do is look at it and make your request. If you look at a spot and ask it to open a 3-D, video comm, it'll show up right in front of your eyes. How's that for convenient?"

"You didn't really answer Doug," said Bette. Then, turning to me, "Josh wants to name ours 'Wally.' Now, is that mental or what?" Josh just shrugged and grinned at me.

As I glanced toward Luca's kitchen, four members of their automated wait staff approached – robotic units about the height of the table. Each was attired in a white shirt with black vest and bow tie, but the attempt to make them look human ended there. They rolled out on a set of four wheels, loaded trays balanced next to two cameras and a speaker that roughly resembled a face. But just before they reached our table, Ali stood up and said, "Excuse me for a second." She headed for the door.

Bette and Josh looked at me quizzically. "Sorry, I haven't got a clue. I don't even know how she got a message ... if that is what it was."

"Probably the earrings," said Bette.

"Probably," I replied. "But I hear, even those little hiding spots for comm equipment may soon disappear. Your calls will just take over the automation that's around you. Like this tabletop. Or your CommCovers, Josh."

He nodded, then glanced toward the door. "Ali's coming back."

"It all looks great," she said when she got to the table, but she didn't sit. "I'm going to have to leave. Doug, can you have them wrap mine to go?"

"But it's your birthday," said Bette.

"Yeah, and I'm sorry about this," Ali replied, "but I have to check up on some of my patients."

"Some? At night?" I asked.

"Yeah, three," she replied. "It's probably nothing, but that many all at once? I'll call home, make sure the kids are OK, then see you there later." She grabbed a roll from her plate. "There, they can wrap the rest." The three of us stood and took turns giving Ali a hug before she left.

Late Evening, March 16, 2035

"Hey, babe," I called to Ali when she entered our front door.

I had come home after dinner with Josh and Bette and had decided on another glass of wine before bed. I was sipping it at our kitchen island, giving me a line of sight down a short hall to the door. She pulled off a headband and gloves, then ran a hand through her dark curls. Her shimmering hair fell loosely around her face.

"How were your patients?" I asked.

Ali replied in a word, "OK," as she walked into the kitchen, but that clearly wasn't the case. Her eyes were downcast. She tossed the headband and gloves on the island, stuck her hands in her pockets, then started pacing. I couldn't see her face clearly, but I could see enough to notice the wrinkles in her forehead.

"The kids?" she asked.

"In bed." I set the glass of wine on the island. "Chloe was already asleep when I got home, but Cam just went to bed. He's probably still awake."

Life had become simpler when Cam got old enough to watch his sister when we went out, but Ali still worried about them. So, I was surprised when she merely said, "OK," but made no move toward Cam's room to say goodnight.

"What's wrong?" I asked.

Ali stopped pacing and looked at me, now rubbing her forehead with her hand. "Have you heard about the increase in cases of toxoplasmosis?" she asked.

The word was familiar, but only because I had heard a story during the drive home. "You mean that zombie pandemic thing?" It was the wrong thing to say.

"Don't call it that!" A flush came to her face and her voice rose more than necessary for our small kitchen. "It's that kind of rhetoric that's going to get someone hurt." She crossed her arms over her chest and slowly shook her head as if wondering how I could be so misinformed.

When she was upset about something that I also felt strongly about, or when I let my ego push me to a position that in calmer times I would have viewed with indifference, we argued. Our arguments weren't frequent, but like any couple married for nearly 16 years, they happened. But in a situation like today, I was more than ready to admit my ignorance.

"Sorry," I said. "I just heard the word on the radio ... and about it being a zombie pandemic."

"I should have known." She closed her eyes, her fingertips massaging her forehead. "My calls – they were about it. And I guess anything like this would get blown out of proportion by the media."

I nodded, although I didn't fully understand the concern. "Yeah, it was on that oldies CommLink that plays the stuff from the 2020s." I waited for a beat, to see if she would volunteer more, but her gaze dropped to the floor.

"What is it?" I asked. "This toxo whatever."

"Toxoplasmosis." Ali looked up at me and sighed. "It's from a parasite called toxoplasmosa gondii. In humans, it can produce flu-like symptoms, but generally, most healthy adults don't show anything."

There had to be more. An outbreak of mild cases of the flu might make the news if it was widespread enough, but that didn't explain why the reporter had used the word 'zombie.' But before I could ask, Ali volunteered.

"The thing that will get everyone's imagination running wild is the effect the parasite has on rats." She started pacing around the kitchen again.

As a psychologist, that statement caught my attention. Although I had never been involved in any research using mice and rats, I knew they had several advantages – they were easily housed, grew quickly, and were relatively inexpensive. But for what Ali was saying, the highly relevant fact was that their biological, genetic, and behavioral characteristics were quite similar to those of humans. Simulations of human physiology had become so good in recent years that animal research was unnecessary. But in the past, if you wanted to study treatments for many human conditions, you used rats.

Ali finally sat down on one of the counter stools and took a deep breath. "Rats that are infected with the parasite lose much of their fear of cats," she said slowly. "It directly affects their brains, reducing their fear and slowing their reactions. They become easy prey."

I moved to the stool next to her – officially, Chloe's chair if we were all there. "So, these infected rats wander out to join the cats in fun and games, only to become lunch," I said. "Thus, the term zombies."

She turned toward me and released a long breath. "I guess, but that's exactly the kind of talk we need to avoid."

I nodded slowly, but then started wondering. "If the effect on humans is a mild flu, and then it's harmless, what's the problem? Is it mutating ... or something?"

Ali leaned against the back of the counter stool. "It's complicated," she said. "It's true that healthy adults generally show little effect. But that's not always the case. Toxoplasmosis can cause headaches, confusion, and poor coordination. It may also have several, more subtle effects. There's evidence of a connection to increased suicidal behavior, and it has been linked to some severe conditions, such as extreme forms of schizophrenia."

These facts were giving me pause, as the parasite clearly had a dark side. But even so, it sounded rare, at least in its extreme forms. I still wasn't sure why it was in the news when Ali got to the heart of the question.

"And yes, it may be mutating. Or maybe the conditions that make it harmful to humans are changing, like a slight increase in carbon dioxide in the air or widespread dietary changes. It could be anything. Right now, we know three things. There's a very small, but definite upswing in cases. Second, they show some of the more severe symptoms – confusion, loss of coordination, and in extreme cases, seizures. And third, these cases seem to be resistant to standard treatments."

I rubbed the back of my head, still looking at my wife. "Ouch" was all I could think to say. Over the years, we had seen outbreaks of disease, most of which disrupted life where they occurred and worried the rest of the world. But humanity had been lucky and these diseases had been largely contained or otherwise minimized. And six months later, the names of these afflictions had been largely forgotten. I wondered if this was the disease that was about to change all of that.

"Where is this outbreak?" I asked, wondering if I'd need to change my plans for a business trip to Atlanta.

"It's everywhere," Ali replied, matter-of-fact.

I sat bolt upright, staring at her. Ali was not prone to exaggeration, but overstatements were completely absent in the health field. So, I was not only unprepared for her pronouncement; I was startled by it.

Seeing my reaction, she said, "Something like 30 to 50 percent of the world's population is infected."

"World's population?" I stammered. "Half the people in the world are infected with a parasite that may be mutating to a form that could cause people to ... what, start acting like they are indestructible or lapse into seizures?"

Ali's delay in responding felt like minutes but was probably less than one. In her medical mind, she was probably weighing whether I had sufficiently qualified everything. Finally, she said, "Yes, I guess in the worst case ... yes. But there're still a lot of unknowns. We have almost no information so far."

Ali's words had the ring of a 'don't panic, we have everything under control' public service message. And since the hospital where she met her patients had to be saying something about the outbreak, they probably were. But Ali was savvy; she wouldn't be repeating it if it wasn't the best advice at the moment.

"Any idea when we'll get these questions answered?"

Ali shook her head. "Not really. But because it's such a widespread condition, cases of it will get immediate, high-level attention. It's just .... Oh, nothing."

"What were you going to say?" I asked.

Ali looked at me a moment, then rubbed her cheek with a hand. "It's just that general assurances may not be enough this time. Enough to stop a wave of panic."

Thursday, April 5, 2068

Late Evening

I pulled my mind from the beginnings of the retroscape, a numbness from mental fatigue overtaking me. Discovering Josh's body and recalling Ali's words of warning had made this a difficult day. But, I told myself, it was a start.

"Suze, you can clear those images from the wall," I said, and a view of the night sky appeared in place of the restaurant. The lightning and thunder had ended, but the reflected ripples in pools of standing water told me that the rain hadn't. I listened. The house was quiet. "Ali asleep?"

"Yes. She dropped off almost an hour ago."

"OK. We'll continue this tomorrow." I left for the bedroom.

When I woke up the next morning, the sun was shining in the backyard scene displayed on the CommCover. The yard-tending robot must have found a break in the rain because the grass was freshly mown. I could see shadows of the trees dance on the lawn as a breeze rustled the leaves. The current temperature, 16 degrees, and humidity, 24 percent, were overlaid on this picturesque setting. As I had hoped, the storm had cleared the air and left a refreshing day in its wake. That was fortunate because I hoped to reconstruct the next part of the retroscape in a stroll-with-my-thoughts session.

"Suze, where's Ali?"

"In the kitchen, having breakfast. She said not to disturb you because you needed your sleep before more reminiscing."

I chuckled. "Reminiscing, is it?"

"That's what she said. I probably would have gone with 'staring off into space' after last night's session, but she didn't ask me," replied Suze.

I got out of bed and went to the kitchen. Ali was seated at the island, nibbling on a roll and reading, her black curls hiding her face. I planted a kiss on the top of her head. It was our usual morning greeting; she was always head down, busy with something, usually a PlotsPro.

If you had asked me 50 years earlier, what occupations do you think will be the last to be taken over by machine intelligence, I would have mentioned writing in the top ten. After all, the arts and entertainment are bastions of human creativity, aren't they?

But I had watched with some fascination in the 20s and 30s as writing disappeared, driven out primarily by gaming technology. There was a market for games that could generate scenarios that hit all of a player's hot buttons – give me more comedy, more action, more sex. The first machine-generated plots were, admittedly, either predictable or so erratic as to be unfathomable. But over time, they got better. Then, as the public became aware and opened their pocketbooks, the technology exploded. From there, it was a simple matter to play out a scenario and capture it in text, giving rise to PlotsPro and similar systems. Now, Ali could generate her medical thriller/romance/mysteries with nearly infinite variation in the details and never lack for something to read.

"You slept in," Ali said, smiling up at me.

"Yeah, had to rest up before more reminiscing," I said, emphasizing the last word.

A frown flickered across her face, soon replaced by a grin. "Yeah, before reminiscing, but mostly, before you resume the arduous task of tracking a dangerous, criminal mastermind through the shadows of your forgotten past."

"Couldn't have said it better." I started a cup of coffee and then checked the options for breakfast. "It looks like we're getting double on the milk substitute again."

I could never remember the name of that product, as it had cycled through a bewildering number of labels based first on contents, generally one or more plants, and later, on synthesizing processes. Whatever it was called, the automation that oversaw restocking our cooled, prep systems was buying too much. I poured some over a bowl of fiber and carbohydrate flakes with dried artificial cherries – something the manufacturer called Cheery Morning Indulgence – and sat down. "I'll cut the milk order in half. That should fix it."

"Don't change the order," said Ali, looking up from the screen. "A sensor is loose on the prep door. I'm printing a replacement fastener now. If you get to it before me, it goes on the right-hand door toward the bottom." Ali was never one to delegate a household task when she could do it herself. And between the 3D printers and our home maintenance robots, she could do a lot.

"Good story?" I asked.

"Better. Last night, I tweaked a setting on one of the characters. She's a neurosurgeon, staying at a virtual resort where a murder occurs. But the next day, she went off and left her 5-year old son unattended. I hate it when a woman who is otherwise so brilliant does something so thoughtless. So, I rebalanced technical expertise and common sense."

"You ever set any character's common sense to zero?"

Ali shook her head, not to indicate that she hadn't but to question why anyone would. The answer, of course, was because it generated some wild tales of reckless living and violent deaths. They were good for a few laughs ... unless you actually thought about the story. And my wife always thought about her stories.

Ali has a gesture where she touches her forehead with her fingertips, then flips her hand out, palm up, as if a thought is bursting forth from her unconscious. Over the years, it had become one of those endearing mannerisms I had seen so many times, that I'd given it a name. It was her "ta-da" gesture. She did it now, saying, "Oh, we got a comm from Bette. I already watched it."

"Anything interesting?" I asked, as I took a taste of the flakes, then quickly washed it down with a gulp of coffee.

"PSS is now saying that the body was Josh."

I didn't really mean to, but a single, dismissive laugh escaped my lips. "Are they claiming a major breakthrough in the case?"

Ali raised her eyebrows. "I don't think they consider it a case, much less a breakthrough. You said they promised to let Bette know when the DNA problem was resolved and now they have. Bette also said – and this seemed a little strange to me – but she said that Josh's will left everything to her."

I stared blankly into the coffee cup that was positioned inches from my lips. "Strange how? He has no other living relatives."

"I guess," Ali said slowly. "I know Julia can't use it, but I just thought … well, there might be some foundation or something that received part of his estate."

"Hmm, never thought of that. By the way, did PSS explain the mix up in the DNA readings?"

Ali looked down at the countertop, scratching her cheek. "Not that I recall. Bette said they had it straightened out and she'd probably be in town next week to start getting rid of Josh's stuff. The comm's still in the queue if you want to watch it."

I expected the DNA error to be corrected, but the news was still discouraging. "So, where PSS had little if any reason to investigate before, they have absolutely none now."

"Seems that way," replied Ali. She paused a moment. "You make any progress last night?"

I dumped the last of my 'Indulgence' down the comp-cycler, wondering if the advertisers had even tasted this mixture before naming it, then refilled my coffee cup. "A little. I spent the time thinking about the birthday dinner you didn't have … when you got called away because of the pandemic. I'm planning to go through the outbreak and then, the events later at Midwest."

Ali's face fell. "The outbreak sure. It might explain something about how Josh was acting. But why Midwest?"

"I don't know exactly," I replied, taking a deep breath. "But if you're looking for something that separates Josh's life from nearly everyone else on the planet, that's it. And since the weather looks good, I'm going to walk by there instead of looking at pictures. The sight of that building should bring back a flood of memories."

"Ah, yes, the old environmental reinstatement effect," Ali said, adopting her most professorial tone while simultaneously smirking.

"That's the plan," I replied, impressed that she remembered the concept. In this case, I was hoping that the physical environment would trigger a more complete recall, a phenomenon known as environmental reinstatement. And while in general, it's not a very effective technique because any single location tends to be associated with many memories, the Midwest Medical Research and Teaching Center was different. I doubted I had been within a hundred meters of it in the last 30 years. Almost everyone gave it a wide berth.

"OK, have a good walk," said Ali. "But no extra coffee this time. You're already on your second cup."

Busted, even before I had the chance to stray.

Ali got up from the island, put her plate in the sanitizer, and let her hand slide across my shoulders as she walked by toward her office. I cleaned my spot, grabbed a light jacket, and left. It would be a while before I reached Midwest by foot, but that was according to plan. I still had to recall several weeks of the pandemic, a time that became known as 'the world's darkest days.'

Thirty-Three Years Earlier

Morning, March 17, 2035

I sat up in bed, stretched, and said, "Wally, show outside." I had borrowed/stolen Josh's name for my CommCover because despite Bette's opinion, I thought it was a clever play on words. But unlike Josh, I hadn't adjusted to parading around in my underwear in what appeared to be my backyard. A peek, however, when I was safe under my covers was fine. And that glance now revealed a beautiful, Saturday morning. A smile must have spread across my face, betraying my thoughts, because at that moment I heard an unexpected voice.

"Good morning, Doug. Want to see the weather that goes along with that view?"

"Suze, you scared the crap out of me!"

After years of having my virtual assistant, and later, my virtuant in predetermined locations – on my phone, my watch, embedded in a shirt – I was still adjusting to the fact that Suze could appear anywhere that had a processor.

"I only detected a slight increase in heart rate," said Suze in a calm tone. "But if you soiled your clothes, I can lay out a change for you. Or I could if you had automated your wardrobe."

I chuckled. "It's an expression, Suze. No, I don't need to change. By the way, I thought we agreed you'd avoid the sales' pitches? I don't need to automate clothes selection."

"It's a fine line between keeping you informed of technology, which you desire and offering products, which you do not. Did I overstep?"

Suze and I were still getting adjusted to each other. In fact, we had been since 2009, when I got my first virtual assistant, although then she had a name bestowed by the manufacturer. And even those first days had left tracks that Suze used today to make our interactions smoother. Truthfully, we'd probably still be learning about each other after another 25 years. It was a lifelong process.

"No, you're right." I finally admitted. "That's useful information, although the tech is not really that new. So, you want to tell me about the weather?"

"The current temperature in St. Louis is ...."

"Hold on," I said, interrupting her. "Could you put the current conditions and today's forecast in an overlay on the backyard scene?"

"So, tell you the weather means put it in text?" asked Suze.

I chuckled but quickly turned serious. Once I had been woken by a car horn blaring in front of our home at 5:00 AM and had flippantly told Suze that was how I liked to start the day. It took three days to get her to stop and another week for me to start relaxing. Tongue-in-cheek was not the way to teach your virtual assistant.

"Yes, for the weather, let's go with the text overlay, OK?"

"Of course, Doug." The current conditions appeared, and for once, the outside scene was not deceiving. It was a pleasant 18 degrees, which my rough mental translation said was the mid-60s.

"You know, you don't have to ask Wally for the scene you want," volunteered Suze. "If you want a single source for comms, weather, schedule, and so on, you can ask me."

After considering her suggestion a moment, I said, "Not a bad idea. I think I asked Wally for my exercise report the other day, and it took me a moment to remember he doesn't have them."

"Yes, you did," said Suze.

"Thanks for not mentioning it," I replied, forgetting my own rule about sarcasm.

"But I just did." Then, after a pause, she added, "Oh, you were being ironic."

"I was," I replied, impressed she had figured it out. But it was time to end this mutual-learning conversation. "Do you know where Ali is?"

Suze played an audio comm from her, which said, 'Running errands, sleepy.' Ali was not one for leaving long, involved messages when a word or two would do.

"What about the kids?"

"Both in their rooms. Chloe is listening to music. Cam's on a TuringTalk with a classmate named Jennifer."

TuringTalk. I liked the name. It showed some deference to its historical roots – namely, the challenge issued by Alan Turing in 1950 to make the dialog from a computer indistinguishable from that of a human. TuringTalk had evolved to the point where not only did its discourse seem human, but it appeared to be the words of a specific person.

"So, is Jennifer one of these people who've made their TuringTalk persona into her virtuant?"

"She is," said Suze. "Although I'd put it the other way around. Her virtuant also has the role of her TuringTalk personality."

"Either way, it seems like it would be confusing. When Jennifer talks to her virtuant, does she feel like she's talking to herself?"

"Why would that be confusing? People often talk to themselves."

My answer would have said something about there being two of me in one case, and one in the other, but I didn't think I could explain it to Suze ... maybe not even to myself. And besides, I was missing a chance for a run. "We can talk about this later." I dressed in shorts and a T-shirt, then went by Chloe's room.

Both Chloe and her brother were replicas of their mother. They had Ali's light complexion paired with her black, curly hair and large, brown eyes. Only their height seemed to come from me. Cam at 14 years of age was already taller than Ali, and Chloe was approaching that territory quickly.

When I stuck my head into my daughter's room, she acknowledged my plans with a wave of her hand, hardly breaking eye contact with the screen in front of her. Two years earlier, she would have jumped up from her chair to hug me before I left, maybe even ask to go along. I was still adjusting to the benign indifference that would probably last another ten to fifteen years.

As I walked toward Cam's room, I could hear voices. I knocked on his door and opened it when he answered.

"Can you stick around until I get back from a run, make sure your sister stays out of trouble?" I said. There was a picture of a girl frozen on the screen behind him.

Cam glanced over his shoulder at me. "Sure."

I turned to leave, then turned back. "Is that Jennifer?" I asked. "Or should I say, her virtuant?"

"Dad," Cam protested without elaborating.

"Suze just said you were in a TuringTalk with Jennifer. But I'm curious. Wouldn't you rather talk to her in person?"

"Why would I?" he asked, accompanied by a second glance over his shoulder.

"Well," I started slowly, having not anticipated that question. "It just seems like whatever you're doing – a class project, talking. Wouldn't it be better with a human on the other end?"

Cam turned in his chair, a frown forming on his face. "So, trying to roll with a friend who might be busy, or sick, or just having a bad day ... that's better than a TuringTalk where you can focus on the real stuff?"

The real stuff?

The phrase threw me. Virtual is more real than physical?

I must have spent too long pondering my confusion because Cam added, "Look, I talk to Jenn, and it's mostly pos. But she can wear, sometimes downing friends. Or me. Or she can get off on some nada and talk for hours, circling the void. But with her virtuant, I tell her to center and it's all focus. TT cuts the noise."

I nodded, knowing what he meant. I dealt with people's virtuants all the time for scheduling or checking a random fact. And yes, after talking to them for a while, you felt like you knew the person ... even if you had never met. Maybe it wasn't that much different. At least Cam hadn't included 'sidestepping a nosey parent' among the reasons why a TuringTalk was better, although maybe that was what he meant by 'a bad day.'

I sighed. "OK, but not TT all the time," I said finally. "And when I come back, let's go hit some tennis balls with your sister."

"Sure, dad," I heard as I left his room.

Stepping outside, I paused and took a deep breath. The smells of damp earth awakening in the Spring and dust from construction reached my nose. The latter came from the house next door. The woman who had lived there had taken her home-based, design business to western Kansas and was having some remodeling done before putting her old house on the market. I'd always wanted to talk to her; her business sounded interesting. It involved personalizing one's virtuant before it was moved into a robot – something called a mechanion. But I had only seen her at her front door to sign for a package or driving away in her car.

I started down the sidewalk at a slow trot. The sun on my face strobed as I passed under tree limbs still bare, but sporting buds that would soon be flowers and leaves. My thoughts turned to work, my interest in my former neighbor's business having its roots there. Robots were being teamed with people in a variety of occupations, but the humans in these arrangements weren't necessarily comfortable. The training I was evaluating was making inroads into the problem, but perhaps there was something more to be learned from mechanion design. Something that would make the machine teammates more empathic, more acceptable to their human counterparts.

"You probably need to pick up the pace a bit, Doug, if you want to get anything but a tan out of this run."

"Please, not now, Suze," I said, trying to return to my thoughts. But as I rounded the corner of the block, I nearly stumbled over some type of box on the sidewalk. It was a pet carrier. I bent down and peered inside where I found a cat. Strange. I glanced around, expecting to see someone hurrying out their door to retrieve it, but there was no one in sight. Surely, the owner would return soon. I went back to my jog.

After another couple of blocks, I spotted a second carrier. It was on the other side of the street and curiosity got the better of me; I crossed over to find it contained another cat. Very strange. And again, no one in sight.

There was a note attached, but it was folded and taped closed. I was tempted to break the seal and peek but resisted and continued on my way. A couple of unattended pet carriers was just a coincidence, right?

But as I was finishing my 6-kilometer route, it became clear that it wasn't just chance. In the last block before home, I spotted a third container – this time a rough, wooden crate with gaps between the slats large enough to see the cat inside. And two doors further along the street, there was a small dog tied to a tree with a length of rope. I was not sure of the breed, but this poor little guy looked like he had rarely seen the outdoors, much less found himself on the end of an unmanned leash. Even man's best friend was not immune to whatever was happening.

When I got home, I went straight to Ali's office, hoping she had returned from her errands. She had and was sitting at her desk, her elbows propped up on the top, her head resting in her hands. I drew up short, rarely seeing her look so subdued.

She turned her head to look at me. "I'm just tired. I didn't sleep well last night."

"Oh, sorry. The parasite thing keep you up?"

Ali nodded.

"Sorry," I said again. "Anyway, I just saw the strangest thing on my run. At three different houses, I saw pet carriers, each with a cat inside. And just up the street, there's a dog tied to a tree in the side yard. This isn't related to the outbreak, is it?"

Ali pulled her elbows off the desk and leaned back to look at me. "Probably," she said. "The dog is an over-reaction, but cats make up the final link in the reproductive cycle of the toxoplasmosa gondii parasite."

I guessed that explained it in her mind, but I was not any closer to understanding. "What does that mean?"

"It means," she said slowly, "the parasite can only complete its life cycle with cats. In this case, inside their intestines."

"You've got to be kidding? This parasite affects up to 50 percent of the world's population, but it can only live inside a cat? That doesn't seem possible."

She shrugged. "It is. When the parasite enters any animal other than cats, including humans, it can undergo asexual reproduction. But eventually, the cysts from the parasite are eaten by a cat. And then, reproduction occurs in the cat's intestines and more cysts are released in the cat's feces."

When Ali noticed my stare, she interpreted it correctly. "The hospital is sending us all these facts, but they're online too."

I was still standing just inside Ali's office door, now shaking my head in disbelief and looking at the floor. The phrase, 'nature finds a way' sprung to mind. With such a complex life cycle, it seemed like the cysts had to be produced in the millions, maybe billions, to eventually find their way into another cat. And the rat's self-destructive, passive behavior? At first, I had thought of it as an odd side-effect. Now it appeared to be vital for the parasite's survival.

"So, cats and kitty litter are potentially dangerous," I said, as I stepped into her office and slumped into a chair.

"Yeah, along with undercooked meats or poorly cleaned vegetables and fruit. And based on what you saw, people must be banning their pets from their homes."

"At least we're not cat-people," I replied. But having my mystery solved appeared to have done nothing for Ali. Her head was bowed again, her hands folded in her lap. Then, her eyes came up to mine.

"Doug, overnight, researchers confirmed the possibility of human-to-human transmission of the parasite." I thought I knew what that meant, but a blank stare was all I managed.

"I didn't see the news until about an hour ago," she continued. "But I knew something was happening when I stopped by the grocery store for a few things."

It took me a second to connect the thoughts. "There's a run on the grocery store?"

"Yeah. Everyone was stocking up on necessities – bread, milk, eggs. The auto-dispensers weren't empty yet, but they probably are by now. It's probably an over-reaction, but ...."

She didn't finish the thought, so I did. "But anyone you meet in the grocery store or on the street or anywhere else is a potential carrier." I sighed. "I'm surprised this is happening so fast."

"You didn't ask Suze for your comms before your run, did you," Ali said more than asked.

"Suze, how many unread comms do I have?"

"Two hundred fifty-seven." I sat upright in the chair, staring at my wife.

"Any have the same subject?"

"Sixty-seven video comms have the title of 'zombie rat.' A total of two hundred, thirty-six comms across all formats have some combination of the words zombie, rat, and pandemic."

"Play the video comm 'zombie rat' for me," I said, and the picture took over the wall.

A rat sat in the foreground, nuzzling something with its nose. Or perhaps it was eating something; it was hard to tell. But in the background, three cats were crouched low, slowly creeping forward. I knew what was going to happen, but I couldn't take my eyes off the wall. I could hardly blink. The rat did nothing until the final seconds when it was clearly too late.

The violence was no greater than what you might see on a video about animals in the wild. In fact, it was less, because the rat did little to escape. But the effect of the clip was devastating and I could feel my body tense.

"There's no proof that anything like that will happen to humans," Ali said. Then, she laughed mirthlessly. "I never thought I'd be longing for the old form of this parasite, but then, we just had to worry about seizures and suicides. It's the possibility that this new strain kills our will to live that has people panicked. I won't be surprised at all to see everyone locking themselves in their homes until the food runs out."

Morning, March 21, 2035

While Ali's prediction was dire, it turned out that it was not nearly ominous enough. By Monday, the schools decided to stay closed until more was known about the threat. At first, Cam and Chloe were elated about their unplanned vacations, but as the news spread along with the rumors, they became quieter, then worried. We did our best to assure them that it would pass, that all would be fine, but they knew no one had answers.

Businesses that required face-to-face interaction, such as dentist's or doctor's offices, were closed, or they were screening their limited appointments very carefully. Others made unique adjustments to continue as best they could. Many of the grocery stores, for example, were restocking with small, but extremely well-paid crews in the dead of night. Their customers too shopped at off hours, or when they could find it, they used home delivery.

But for many companies, mine included, work went completely off-site and virtual. We worked through online collaboration applications that we kept running, hour after hour. They gave us the capability to see and hear each other and to work on products at the same time. These apps had been important tools before the outbreak; they were essential now.

Cats became the *persona non grata* of every community. Shelters were overwhelmed with abandoned or donated cats, and by noon on Monday, they could no longer accept them. And no one was adopting them, of course. The people who kept their pets put them in outdoor cages, with children under strict orders to stay away. Others simply couldn't stand the strain and dead cats started appearing in trash bins and dumpsters across the city, the state, the world.

In an attempt to control the situation and protect public health, St. Louis established 'humane disposal sites,' as did many other cities. But people willing to work at them were scarce, whatever the rate of pay. So, robots designed for tasks such as toxic spill cleanup or bomb disposal were called into duty. Equipment that had been built 'just in case' became everyday tools for survival.

Realizing our predicament, every politician and every organization from the local PTA to the United Nations began calling for an increase in the research and development of robotics. Doubling the funding was not enough, they argued, and soon, orders of magnitude increases were being proposed. Overnight, a technology that had gained traction slowly over the years became a critical, international capability.

When I came into breakfast on Wednesday morning, Ali was head down at the kitchen island, lost in something on a small screen she held in her hand. I placed the customary kiss on the top of her head. She turned to look up at me.

"I sent the kids down to the basement to play one of their 3D games. They've done nothing but sit in their rooms for four days."

"Good idea," I replied, pouring myself a cup of coffee. "I'm going to do the same a little later." I hadn't left the house since my jog on Saturday. "You looking at the news?"

"Or what passes for it," Ali said. "Every reporter wants to make each traffic accident and barroom brawl the result of toxoplasmosis." She watched as I retrieved a muffin to go with the coffee.

"Yeah, well when they test the brawlers, half of them will have the parasite," I said. "And their friends will swear they'd been acting funny. Even the offenders often say they'd been having headaches and felt confused. What do you expect?"

"Some sense of responsibility," she said, her voice rising. She paused a moment, running a hand through her hair. Then, she continued more softly. "That first test only shows the presence of the parasite in any form. It takes time to verify the strain. And when that screen comes in, it's usually negative. But no one notices. No one reports that fact because there are already ten other stories to take its place."

"I know," I said, reaching over to put a hand on Ali's back as I sat down at the island. "At least the brawls and traffic accidents are down. Everyone's staying at home."

"But that's just making the reporters look harder," sighed Ali. "One story showed a bunch of clothes on a front lawn. The reporter implied that there had been a parasite-driven brawl inside the house, and someone and his clothes got tossed. But there wasn't any proof of ... well, anything."

I released a long sigh. "Epidemics are usually someplace far away. But everyone knows this thing is everywhere, so all of your friends and neighbors are sick ... until proven otherwise."

Ali tapped her mouth idly with two fingers. "Exactly. It's the unknown that's getting to people."

That uncertainty created demand, and where there's a desire, there's a business opportunity. Overnight, it seemed, kits to diagnose toxoplasmosis at home appeared online. Soon, stores were shipping tens of thousands of kits a day, struggling to keep up with the outcry.

But what everyone hoped was the turning point in the global panic wasn't. Rather, it was several days later when people started using their test kits that the full extent of their fear became apparent.

Early Morning, March 22, 2035

I stumbled, bleary-eyed into the kitchen. "Is there something wrong?" I asked Ali. It was 5:17 in the morning, much more consistent with my wife's idea of an early start than mine.

Her brows were knitted, as she looked at me. "I didn't want to wake you, but yeah, maybe there's a problem," she said slowly. "Someone named Carl Jablonski has tried to contact you five times since 4:00. You know him?"

I tried but failed to stifle a yawn. "Yeah, I know him ... and so do you. We went to his wedding." Ali was still frowning, slowly shaking her head.

"He married Janet." There was no change in her expression.

"She was the one who told Carl to quit stressing over everything she put in her OnFriends page or she was going to find another boyfriend." Recognition showed on Ali's face.

"Ah, yes, one of the few women that suggested that there was more to her than her online presence. I remember her."

"Yeah, well that was after another of his girlfriends walked because Carl agonized over everything she put or didn't put online." Ali nodded as if she recognized the pattern.

"I'll comm him from my office," I said and headed down the hall.

When Carl came onscreen, his hand was massaging his forehead. "Morning," I said. "Don't tell me you're rubbing the sleep out of your eyes. Ali says you've been calling me for the last hour and a half."

"No, not sleep," Carl stammered. He looked down but still raised a hand to shade his eyes. "I'm just .... I mean, my eyes, yeah, they're a little tired. Maybe my allergies."

But as he stumbled for an answer, it was clear. He was upset, and it was serious enough that he was fighting his emotions ... and losing. His concerns had to be related to the outbreak; there was little else on anyone's mind. But as to the exact reason, I wasn't sure.

"Yeah, the pollen gets to me too, from time to time," I said, not wanting to push him before he was ready. "What can I do for you?"

"I'm not sure how to say this." He paused, looking away from the camera, then back. "We got our ToxoTests yesterday. Those are the home tests for the parasite – you know, right?"

"I've heard of them, but can't say I know much more." I could feel the muscles in my neck tense; I didn't like the direction this conversation was taking already.

"Well, we read a bunch of reviews," said Carl. "They get high marks – fast, simple, relatively inexpensive."

"OK," I said slowly. "But you didn't say anything about them being accurate, and there's a reason for that. Those reviews are just someone's opinion, and usually, that someone isn't in the medical field. You know, you can sign up for medical tests done by a lab?"

Carl was quiet for a moment, still rubbing his forehead. "Yeah, I know. And we are, but those are still weeks away. I don't think we can wait that long."

"I understand," I said. "It's tough ... not knowing."

I was about to add a further warning about the accuracy of these do-it-yourself tests when Carl continued. "I know these kits aren't perfect, but even if they're just 90 percent ...."

Where did that number come from?

"Carl," I started. But that was as far as I got.

"Since they're the best we have, we took them. And frankly, now I hope they're flat out wrong." The last words caught in his throat. He dropped his hand from his face, his red, swollen eyes now staring back at me. "Janet's infected. I'm not. I don't know what to do," he said. It came out in a rush.

I searched for something to say but found nothing but platitudes. "Just hang in there. Lots of very talented people are looking for a treatment. They'll have something soon, and in the meantime, Janet should be fine."

"Yeah, there's that," he mumbled.

What's he talking about?

But before I could ask, he continued. "We're following the increase in serious cases, and it's still small. But everyone thinks that whatever's producing it – whether it's the environment or a mutation or whatever – it's going to take off like wildfire."

"Whoa, hold on, Carl," I said, holding up my hands and shaking my head. "There's absolutely no proof anything like that is going to happen."

He glanced away from the screen for a moment, then back. "Whatever the chances are, they're too high. It's not having any control, any cure that's getting to us. And so far, they don't even know the cause."

I thought about saying that knowing the cause would probably go a long way toward finding a cure, but I didn't think Carl would be interested in the logic. "Carl, you've got to stay positive," I said, reverting to the pep-talk approach. "Just be there for her."

"But that's just it, Doug," he said, his voice rising. "I can't. I'm afraid of her." He clenched a fist near his mouth, his grip so tight his knuckles were turning white. "I'm afraid to kiss her. I'm afraid to touch her. She's my wife, but what kind of husband am I? What kind of life is this?"

It was as if someone had hit me in the stomach and I slumped back into my office chair. I hadn't seen this coming. I took a deep breath, hoping to slow the heartbeat I now heard in my ears. His fears were irrational, or at least, exaggerated, but what could I say that would help him?

"It's a temporary situation," I said finally. "Give her all the support you can, even if it's not physical. Soon, we'll know how to fight it."

"She needs me now," he said, the sound of defeat replacing anger in his tone. "But I can't get near her. Every time I try, I freeze. I keep seeing that rat sitting there while the cats attack."

Is there anyone in the world who hasn't seen that video?

Carl took a deep breath and released it slowly. "Anyway, we've decided ... well, I decided and Janet is going along ... for the most part. Until the doctors get this figured out, we're going to live apart."

"One of you is moving out?" I asked, surprised. Were hotels still open? Certainly, no one was buying or selling homes.

"No, that's not an option. There aren't any places; I checked. We're doing this at home. Janet gets the master bedroom, which has an ensuite bathroom and a rear exit if she needs to go anywhere. I doubt she will. I'll stay in the study, which has a couch that makes into a bed. I'll do the cooking or get meals delivered if I can find them. There's a short hallway between our living spaces, with a door at both ends. That will be the air gap between us. I'll put food and whatever else she needs in the air gap, close my door, and then she can get it. And I've got lots of disinfectants, rubber gloves, face masks ... about everything we need to keep safe."

I nodded, feeling some relief in his words. While his actions were excessive given what was known about how the parasite was transmitted, his plan would keep him occupied with caring for his wife in this albeit impersonal way until a cure was found. It could have been worse.

"Doug, I'm sorry," Carl said, after a few moments of silence. "All I've talked about is us. How are you and your family dealing with this mess?"

I'd been hoping he wouldn't ask. I was worried that our actions might make him feel worse because what we had decided was to be a little more careful in food preparation ... but little else. The way we saw it, even the youngest member of the family, Chloe, had been exposed to the world and the rest of us for ten years. The chance that we changed our fate with what we did or didn't do in the next few weeks or months seemed remote.

"Well, our situation is a bit different. I'm nearly twice your age." That was an exaggeration, but I hoped it would allow Carl to accept his decisions, not compare them to ours. But it didn't seem to be working, as he dropped his gaze again.

"You're not doing anything, are you?" he said to the floor.

I sighed. "We don't have cats, so nothing to do there. We're going to be a little more careful in handling food. And maybe cut down on the wild sex life of 40-year-olds."

My attempt to lightened the mood failed miserably. When Carl looked up, tears were streaming down his cheeks. "Doug, I wish you luck. I hope we make it." He broke the connection without another word.

I felt terrible but didn't know what else to say. I decided to call in a day or two, hoping to have a better pep talk by then.

But within hours, it was clear that a callback was unnecessary. Through the media, Carl would be getting all the validation he needed, as families throughout the world were separating their homes into a part for the sick and another for the healthy. Or the infected parts of an extended family – parents, grandparents, children, aunts, and uncles – took one house, while the well took a different one.

Unfortunately, one of the more common patterns was that both parents were infected, while one or more children were not. No one thought children should be raised with no physical connection to their fathers and mothers, but nonetheless, hundreds of families in St. Louis alone had taken this drastic step, hoping it would only be for a day or two.

Morning, March 24, 2035

I couldn't stay inside any longer and decided to go for a run. It was unusually warm for March, with temperatures expected to reach near 19 degrees by afternoon. But the window of opportunity wouldn't be open long; the forecast showed a chance of snow on Monday, typical of St. Louis' atypical weather patterns.

Some might have thought my actions risky, but it was difficult for me to see how they could be. Almost no one was outside. Even Ali conceded that fact when we discussed it. The kids, however, were another matter. They wanted to come along. I told them that if this jaunt went alright, we'd discuss it with their mother. I expected that discussion to be more prolonged ... and probably a lot more contentious.

I headed to an urban park about a kilometer from our home. At about the midpoint of its 6K, outer loop, I happened upon my first, fellow sojourner. I planned to keep my distance, thinking a few meters of separation would be sufficient. But when he saw me, he sprinted off the path and into a thicket of brush. I went on, hoping he was OK but knowing he didn't want me to check.

There was, I supposed, some chance of happening upon a stray cat or two, as some had disposed of their pets by dumping them and the park was a favorite spot. But the city had responded with feeding stations, where these animals, along with a fair number of dogs and other pets, were captured and removed by robots. I had heard rumors that other cities had not responded as efficiently, and their citizens had declared open season on any cats found running free.

But as the image of mass graves of dead cats crept into my consciousness I stumbled to the side of the jogging path, resting my hands on my knees. I was appalled that my morning commune, which was usually a release from the week's troubles, had turned so morbid.

The rest of the jog was uneventful and soon, I was back at home. Ali was sitting in the living room. I suspected she was reading for pleasure because even though her black curls covered most of her face, she was frowning. She tended to consume medical papers without concern, but she was constantly fuming at characters in her books. I tiptoed down the hall next to the living room, intent on leaving my wife to her reading, but she looked up.

"You're back," she said. I detoured to where she was sitting and bent down. Her nose wrinkled. "You're all sweaty."

"Tends to happen when you go running," I said. "It was great to get out for a while since no one is out there anyway."

"Go take a shower and then, give me a real kiss."

"Where are the kids?" I asked, grinning down at her.

Her eyes narrowed for a moment, then she started laughing and shaking her head. "I didn't necessarily mean that."

"The possibility is good enough for me."

"You're incorrigible," she said returning my smile. "They're down in the basement. I told them they had to play something active until you got back. Can you check that they aren't just watching videos?"

"Sure, and I'll chase them around for a while if they are."

All traces of the smile left Ali's face. "Do they still roughhouse with you?"

I rubbed my chin, looking off across the room. "They're both a little old for that," I said, as I looked down at my wife. "Well, in their minds anyway. But I know what you're asking and the answer is no." I sighed. "When I talked to Carl a few days ago, I said we weren't changing anything, but that's not really true. They hold back and I don't push it. And I'm not sure there's anything wrong with that."

Ali pressed her lips together in a tight line, then nodded. I turned to go check on the kids and take my shower.

"Doug." I spun just in time to see her 'ta-da gesture' – fingertips to the forehead, hand flipping out. "Speaking of Carl, you have a video message from him."

"Right," I called, as I turned and left.

After finding the kids running around in the basement, I took my shower and then returned to the living room. When I got there, Ali was asleep on the couch, her black curls fanned out on the cushion under her head, a slight smile playing on her lips. She was beautiful. It was all I could do to keep my hand from caressing her cheek, but I didn't want to chance waking her. Since the outbreak, her clients had been in almost constant need of support. Perhaps they felt particularly vulnerable, having just undergone major medical procedures. But whatever the reason, video requests for her reassurance had been coming in at all hours of the day and night. And Ali had responded to every one of them, ten sometimes twelve hours a day. If she could get some sleep now, I was going to let her.

I walked quietly back down the hall to my office. "Suze, play the comm from Carl," I said. The look on his face when he came onscreen was enough to tell me the news was not going to be good.

"Hi, Doug," he said softly. "I guess you were right about the accuracy of the ToxoTests. We got the new results back from the lab." He was shaking his head, his teeth now clenched in a grimace. "Their findings were the exact opposite of the ToxoTests. Or at least that was the case four days ago when we had the blood drawn."

It took me a moment to remember the original results, but when I did, I knew this meant he was infected and Janet was not. I glanced at a calendar. From what he said, they must have taken the lab tests the day before I talked to him and then, paid a small fortune to get their results back this quickly. I only hoped he had not taken new shortcuts that had produced a second round of misinformation.

"Of course, now that I cooked for her for the last four days, and I'm not the best cook ... but I tried to get everything clean and cooked thoroughly." His voice cracked and he paused, trying to regain his composure. "Anyway, I wonder if she might be sick now too?"

"Suze, pause the video please," I said. I needed a moment to think because, at first blush, his statement made little sense. Knowing Carl, he had probably been scrubbing everything until it was half its original size, then soaking it in alcohol before incinerating it. After twenty-something years of life, he believed he had infected Janet during the last four days of isolation? And then I wondered, could this be something like a desperate hope? One that he wouldn't want to admit openly, but that colored his thinking? If Janet had been infected in the last four days, he wouldn't end up in exile.

"Suze, please continue."

When the comm restarted, Carl swallowed a couple of times, then said, "I can't believe what a jerk I was. And you want to know what Janet's doing now? She went to the grocery store to see what she can find to make for us. She thinks we should be together." He turned from the camera, a hand coming up to his eyes, his shoulders shaking from suppressed sobs.

The video was hard for me to watch, but I started to feel better when I heard his words. Perhaps Janet was the stabilizing force that could pull them through. But then, I noticed there were still 30 seconds left on the comm. That was a long time to say, 'everything's coming up roses.'

"In my heart, I know she's not sick," Carl said. "And I can't let her jeopardize her health being with me. I really can't, after what I did. I'm going away until this all blows over – either I die or they find a cure. It's the best thing. I posted a long video explaining everything to her and telling her I'd be back. And I called my boss with my decision. Thanks for being a friend. Bye."

Damn him.

I ground my teeth together and slammed my fist on the desk. Carl and his damn technology – he had deserted his wife in a video comm. I had a set of bookends that were replicas of antique globes. I picked up one of them and threw it across the room, shattering it against the wall.

Friday, April 6, 2068

Noon

The strength of my anger with Carl pulled me back to 2068. I checked my surroundings. I had continued to amble along St. Louis streets as I recalled the days of the toxoplasmosis outbreak, ending up only a few blocks from the Midwest memorial.

I had largely forgotten the pain the pandemic had brought but now, my nerves were raw and my stomach was in a knot. Fatigue was overtaking me as well. I sat down on a small retaining wall next to the sidewalk. Perhaps I should go back home, come back to Midwest tomorrow ... or the next day. But it was a long walk and I was close. I leaned over and glimpsed the corner of the building, only a block to the east. My blood ran cold at the mere sight, but I couldn't turn around now. I just needed a moment to strengthen my resolve.

What had happened to Carl and Janet had been hard for me to accept at the time, but I had learned later that their lot was all too common. All over the world, family ties that had been strained by the outbreak were destroyed when the medical labs started catching up with demand. It was worse when the parties had been previously misled by bogus results from home-test kits. And unfortunately, several of those kits turned out to be complete scams, as con artists sought to profit from the panic. But before they were exposed, these individuals slipped away into the night, going anywhere with medical expertise that could be purchased, whatever the cost.

The families, however, were left trying to pick up the pieces. Some rearranged the living quarters again. But while it was difficult for adults to find out they were infected when previously they believe they were not, moving a child from the 'clean' areas of the house into quarantine was heartbreaking. So, some families didn't. But many did, dealing with the emotional scars the best they could.

I had read somewhere that the Cuban Missile Crisis of 1962 was the first psychological crisis in the United States. For the first time, Americans realized how vulnerable they were and it frightened them. As a result, the children of that era carried emotional reminders for the rest of their lives.

The zombie pandemic, on the other hand, was the first worldwide psychological crisis. Every human was vulnerable and it terrified people around the globe. And no one had to look hard to find the emotional scars. It took its toll on couples and families. It drove a wedge between husband and wife. In a time when people were waiting longer to get married, longer to have children, and having smaller families, the zombie pandemic accelerated that trend dramatically. As early as 2004, couples in much of Asia and Europe had been raising fewer than two children. But in the 33 years since the plague, the global birth rate never exceeded 0.8 children per woman. The world was shrinking.

Initially, no one expected the mass phobia surrounding physical contact to last. After all, it was facing an irresistible force – the biological imperative to repopulate the species. Put simply, over time human's sex drive would prevail. And perhaps that would have been true, had technology not stepped in.

That technology was initially marketed as a treatment for couples suffering severe anxiety about physical contact due to the pandemic. Sold under the name AugMate, with 'Aug' standing for augmented, it involved a simple video feed between the partners, with one high-tech twist. To break the ice, the treatment included low-level stimulation to areas generally considered the 'pleasure centers' of the brain: the nucleus accumbens, septum pellucidium, and the hypothalamus. And with the refinement of transcranial magnetic stimulation, pulses could excite neurons in these regions from outside the skull. AugMate was the ultimate in no-fuss, no-bother, electronically enhanced sex.

The dangers of stimulating the pleasure centers were known, of course. The initial research in the 1950s showed that rats would continue to self-stimulate their pleasure center until they died; they wouldn't stop even to eat. In the 1970s and 80s, the technology was used on humans, generally to offset chronic pain. At higher levels of stimulation, users would neglect their personal hygiene and their families, but regulated dosages were accepted. So, 'to save the family unit,' as the AugMate company slogan ran, they sought regulatory approval for this new use. Eventually, they got it.

AugMate had hardly reached the market before word spread and overnight, couples that had appeared to be doing OK were claiming an intimacy disability. Sales took off. Then, it was discovered that the person on the other end of the video feed was actually superfluous. Blank screens or closed eyes worked as well or better, as the stimulation elicited illusions that tended to swamp the video anyway. Sales skyrocketed. Then, not to be left out, people without partners found others in the same position willing to pose as a significant other. Abuse was nearly impossible to prove because living apart demonstrated need, rather than being evidence of fraud. Sales became astronomical.

In the end, the device that had been advertised as the savior of the family unit helped drive a stake into its heart. People were happy with their completely convenient sex lives, now devoid of the need to deal with another human. And if you wanted a physical connection, there were mechanions.

Besides, as everybody said, there were still plenty of real people in the world, if you happened to be the kind who wanted to meet one of them. Unfortunately, few did and that platitude became less accurate every day.

"Doug, your blood sugar is getting low. Do you want to get lunch?" asked Suze. There was a sign near the wall where I was sitting that had been displaying information on tourist attractions. But as Suze's voice came from it, it changed to a listing of nearby, automated eateries.

I was feeling a bit light-headed. "Yeah, Suze. Just give me a second."

When I received Carl's comm on that Saturday in 2035, we had been six days into the pandemic. It lasted only another seven. But the days that immediately followed the all-clear held a special terror for St. Louis and that was what I needed to relive next. I only hoped that in the end, we'd get some closure on Josh's death from this retroscape, because the undertaking was proving harder than I had ever imagined.

"OK, Suze, is there a VendNGo around here?" I asked, rather than trying to find one on the sign myself.

"There's one a block to the south," she said.

Good, I wouldn't have to walk by Midwest just yet. "Thanks. Let's go. After that, I'm going to start recalling what I can from the last few days in March 2035. Maybe you could see what you can find from that time and I'll look at it at the VendNGo."

"Sure, Doug. Personal stuff or public information?" she asked.

"A bit of both."

I dragged myself off the retaining wall and headed for the store. After food and rest, I would have exhausted every possible excuse for delaying my visit.

Thirty-Three Years Earlier

Afternoon, March 29, 2035

I signed off the virtual collaboration meeting with my work team and pushed back from the desk. We were making good progress in spite of the conditions ... or maybe because of them. I had to admit, there seemed to be fewer distractions at home and our productivity supported that conclusion. It was strange to think there was any bright side to the pandemic, but if there was, this was it.

"Suze, show the outside," I said. "And overlay the weather conditions."

"Sure, Doug. You request this view whenever you're not in a meeting or watching a comm. Do you want me to make this the default?"

"Yeah, that's a good idea. Please do. And thanks."

"Well, it'll take a couple of my electrons to remember, but I'll manage for you," she replied. I chuckled softly.

Virtuants came with a built-in sense of practicality. The suggestion for the default street view was an example. But the rest of their personalities they learned from their counterparts. Suze undoubtedly noticed my soft laughter at her words and my humor profile would be tweaked as a result. Of course, I wasn't holding my breath waiting for Suze to become a comedian. To me, humor was uniquely human and intensely personal. Machine intelligences would never master it.

I leaned back in my office chair and drew a deep breath. The backyard was the picture of calm and tranquility. A lone red bird, the longtime symbol of St. Louis' baseball team, was perched on a branch of our massive elm tree, eyeing his domain. The normalcy of the scene was intoxicating, given the horror and chaos that cloaked the rest of the world. Only the sound of the front door pulled me back from the serenity of the image. In a moment, Ali walked passed my door.

"You're home early."

"Yeah, not much happening," she said, her voice fading as she continued down the hall.

I got up and followed, finding her pacing in her office. She walked toward one wall, a finger jabbing at it. Then, she turned and swung a hand in front of her, as if brushing something away.

"Are you gesture-talking to your virtual assistant ... or whatever you call it?"

"What?" she asked, turning to look at me. Then, she shook her head. "Oh, no, I'm just saying things to myself that I can't say to a patient."

"Troubles, huh?" I stepped into her office, intending to give her a hug, but she went back to pacing. It was evidently one of those frustrations that needed exorcising, rather than comfort. I could never tell.

"Video comms aren't working," she said when she paused again to look at me. "But when I try to schedule something face-to-face at the Midwest Center, they back out. Too many people, I guess."

"People are scared," I replied, stating the obvious.

"Well, if someone got up in my face, I'd be concerned too. But Midwest has automated almost everything – the check-in, taking vitals. Even the initial discussion of symptoms can be a video with a doctor in another room or with a machine intelligence. But they still don't want to come in."

"That's because the bug gives you superhuman strength. One of those infected doctors will come busting through a wall to get to them."

"Douglas, that's not funny," she said. But she must have found it a little amusing because she came over and put her head on my shoulder. I wrapped my arms around her.

"I may have to start making house calls," she said, pulling back and brushing a strand of hair from her forehead as she looked up at me.

I tried to stop my grimace but failed. In a time when almost no one was sticking their nose outside the front door for anything less than the necessities of life, this was a sobering possibility. True, I had gone jogging, but then I expected to see no one and that had been the case. Ali, on the other hand, would be entering people's homes, sitting down with them in their living rooms, having coffee with them around their kitchen tables as they discussed treatment progress and options. True, they would probably not come within two meters of her, but it was still totally different in my mind.

I looked into her eyes; her gaze didn't falter. If she decided house calls were necessary, she would welcome my support, she would even listen to my concerns, but she wouldn't be dissuaded.

"Babe, you need to be careful," I said, dropping into a chair in her office.

"I will be. And last I checked, none of the elderly women I see has a house full of cats." It felt like it was my turn to say, 'not funny,' but I refrained.

Ali glanced down at the floor, then back to my face. "I heard something a bit ... concerning today. Some hospitals will be experimenting with medical nanobots to fight the parasite." She took a seat behind her desk.

I hadn't ever heard Ali use the words 'medical nanobots' and 'concerning' in the same thought before, as these remarkable creations had proved a boon to medicine. One of the initial, groundbreaking uses was in the treatment of cancer, where nanobots found and delivered drugs directly to cancerous cells while leaving healthy cells untouched. The precision achieved opened everyone's eyes, and soon, many other human ills were being targeted by these tiny miracle-workers.

I too had more than a passing interest in nanobots and knew that the technology also had its dark side. In particular, if these creations were given the ability to reproduce themselves, then they might spread, crowding out natural life while consuming their habitat. And unfortunately, technology capable of self-reproduction was nothing new. Around the turn of the century, a robot built from Lego blocks had been given that ability. But while the picture of a brightly colored, plastic robot searching your home for Lego building blocks might seem comical, a microscopic entity using the nutrients in your body to replicate itself was no laughing matter.

In the extreme, these nanobots could consume the earth. K. Eric Drexler had described that doomsday scenario, calling the nanobots that were procreating out of control 'grey goo.' But even Drexler conceded that creating this situation by accident was unlikely. And so, all we had to do was ban the intentional development of a reproductive capability – and every nation had. To date, those restrictions had been relaxed infrequently and only when there was no alternative.

With that background, I knew what to ask. "Are they going to be self-replicating?"

Ali frowned. "Yeah. That's why I said the news was troubling. But in all fairness, that ability is tightly controlled. The time they can exist outside of the patient is limited. They also can't exceed a specific ratio of their mass to that of the person so, they can't take over completely."

"But why let them reproduce at all?" I asked.

"It's technical and frankly, I don't understand it all myself. But basically, the parasite is hardy. The cysts, in particular, can withstand extremely harsh environments. Basically, if the nanobots don't have equivalent resilience, they'll lose the war of attrition."

I rubbed my forehead, trying to place my faith in people who were experts in the field, who had been designing and developing these microscopic entities for years. I was still having difficulty achieving that calm when the real reason for Ali's comments hit me. I slid forward in the chair, looking at her closely.

"Midwest is involved in this study, aren't they?"

Ali said nothing for a moment, then gave a nod so slight I almost didn't see it. "There are two other test sites. One in California and the other in France, outside of Paris."

I thought about asking her to switch to nothing but house calls. Even the old lady with the house full of cats might be preferable to Midwest, but she would never agree. She'd take reasonable steps to protect herself, but beyond that, she would merely say, 'there's nothing I can do if it's my time.'

"How much danger are you in?" I asked after a moment.

Ali's head jerked back, her eyes narrowing. "Me? None." Perhaps the skepticism I felt registered on my face as she added, "The patients in the treatment program will be quarantined and the staff undergoes strict decontamination procedures. I'm even in a different wing."

"But the same floor," I said. "I know where that research area is."

"You're worried about nothing," Ali replied, her voice firm. Then, she held both hands in front of her. "It's the people in the study that concern me. The technology's complex and the medical community has been pushing hard for a solution. It's been lots of people, working endless days and nights to get these nanobots ready. Ideally, there'd be more time to run tests and simulations, but there isn't. Those patients will be taking a risk that everything's right and the nanobots don't start free-foraging."

With the thought of nanobots consuming human nutrients and growing inside the body, I shuddered involuntarily. Finally, because I had nothing else to offer, I fell back to my oft-used advice. "Be careful, babe."

She smiled, then nodded. "I will be."

I got up from the chair and left.

Afternoon, March 31, 2035

Ali had meetings with patients, which previously would have been unusual for a Saturday, but nothing was routine these days. I had just made myself a cup of coffee and was carrying it back to my office as Suze greeted me.

"Doug, there's a comm you should see."

"OK," I said, searching my mind for a reason anyone would be contacting me now and coming up with nothing. "Please put it on the wall."

It was a forward of a news feed from a coworker, with only his grinning face added to the transmission. I hardly noticed his look, however, as the headline took my breath away.

OUTBREAK'S CAUSE DISCOVERED

I set my coffee down and nearly fell into my desk chair. My sense of relief was palpable. Although I didn't check a mirror, I was sure my face now showed the same ridiculous grin as my friend. I closed my eyes, leaned back for a moment, and celebrated the good news as the stress bled from my body and my thoughts.

Opening my eyes, I scanned the accompanying article. It said that the outbreak of the more virulent strain of toxoplasmosis had been traced conclusively to the interaction of two infections. The second, or triggering infection as they called it, was produced by a rare fungus, not easily transmitted among humans and generally controlled by drugs. The researchers went on to say that everyone with both infections was probably symptomatic already, and so, the outbreak, which had never been large, had already reached its peak. So, while the hybrid form of the disease was dramatic in its effect, it never could have grown out of control.

By my computer, the zombie pandemic had ended at 1:17 PM Central time on Saturday, March 31, 2035 ... or at least, the panic it caused should be over. I was sure Ali had already heard the good news, but I removed my co-worker's face from the news feed, added mine, and sent it to her. I couldn't wait for her to be home. While I thought we had handled the stress well, I had not fully realized how much pressure we had been under until it was gone.

Wondering what people were saying about the news, I found the virtual world in complete gridlock, as everyone was trying to tell everyone else, while the media was fighting to get their voice heard. I stumbled across one story that had some additional detail when Suze announced a comm from Ali.

"Please show it," I said to Suze. "Hell, use the whole wall."

The instant her face appeared, I said, "Ali, did you ...." But I stopped mid-sentence, brought up short by the face of a woman who showed no trace of relief or joy. Ali's expression was hard, her skin even paler than usual.

As was her approach to life, she didn't mince words. "I may have been exposed to the medical nanobots."

"But .... I thought ...." Hadn't she said her exposure was virtually impossible?

"We don't know how it could have happened," said Ali, sparing me the struggle to find the right words in my confusion. "The hospital conducts routine scanning tests whenever they're running research. The nanobots were found in a nurse who works outside the containment area."

"But no cause ... like a breach in the ventilation system? A door seal that failed?"

"They haven't found anything like that," she replied. As those words left her mouth, she glanced away, returning her eyes to mine slowly. I probably wouldn't have noticed, but because I had asked Suze to use the entire wall, Ali's face was nearly a meter tall. There was a slight quiver near the corner of one eye.

There's more.

I felt short of breath as if a vice was slowly tightening around my chest. "What aren't you telling me?" I asked, still hoping I was misreading her. But when she hesitated, then dropped her head, I was certain.

My heart started hammering. I gulped air, but the vice tightened another notch. My mind raced. Even with the few words she had spoken, only one conclusion made sense to my panicked mind. "If all the technology in that hospital didn't detect a containment breach, there wasn't one. Those nanobots were released ... outside the research area ... on purpose."

Ali's head snapped up to look at me. "We don't know that."

"Maybe not for sure, but is there any other possibility?"

Ali dropped her head again, slowly shaking it. When she looked up, her eyes were moist. "The nurse that tested positive – her sample was taken at the same time the nanobots were being administered to the patients. No one knows how they could have traveled that far, that fast."

"I know how," I said, my voice rising. The alarm and despair I had felt only moments ago morphed to anger. My body trembled with pent-up rage. I spun toward my office door.

"Doug." I stopped but didn't turn back to her. "You can't come down here. We're locked down. You won't get past the front door."

I'll break the damn thing down.

I turned back. "I can't just sit here," I said, my hands clenching and unclenching at my side.

"Yes, you can, because I need to know you're there. I need to know you're taking care of the kids."

I turned away, knowing she was right. I squeezed my eyes closed and tried to calm myself with a breath. I turned back slowly and nodded.

"Look at it this way," she said. "If I have the parasite, an accidental dose of the nanobots will take care of it."

My thoughts, however, were moving in a different direction. Somebody had a reason for releasing those tiny creations. All the reasons I could imagine ended in chaos, destruction, and death ... Ali's death. I couldn't shake the image from my mind. My gaze darted around the room, as if in search of a solution lurking in the shadows of a corner. There was, of course, nothing. I was helpless. I couldn't even reach out to console her.

I took a long, ragged breath, then pushed my anger to the back of my mind. I wouldn't voice it; that wouldn't do her any good. And it would be just as bad if she read it in my face.

"And the bots will give you one more thing in common with your patients," I finally managed. The words sounded strained even to my ears, but Ali smiled anyway. "So, when will we know?"

Ali took a shaky breath. "It'll be a while. Maybe by late evening." I felt the vice tightened another notch. "They're testing the entire floor and doing some samples from the other levels. It's hundreds of people."

Ali looked away, then back as she gave her ta-da gesture. Its familiarity, the warmth I felt seeing it was so incongruous with the situation that it hit me like a punch to the stomach.

"I almost forgot," she said. "We can talk to family, but please, no one else until everything gets straightened out."

"That's because the authorities don't want a thousand furious relatives hunting down the monster who did this." I paused. "They are looking, aren't they?"

Ali nodded. "The rumors are flying. Some type of terrorist attack or a political statement are the leading candidates, but no one knows. And anyone on staff who isn't quarantined for testing is trying to reverse engineer the nanobots, see if they were altered."

"How long until you know that?"

"Maybe a day. Probably less."

It seemed the first good news since we started talking. But when I looked at Ali, I could tell it wasn't the godsend I had hoped. I held out both hands in front of me, shaking my head.

"Determining whether they're different is easy. But if they are, knowing exactly what the changes are?" She shrugged. "That process could take weeks, maybe even months."

Months before we knew how these nanobots worked? Months before we knew how to fight them, before we had a cure? How could we have escaped one terror only to have Ali exposed to another? It was too cruel.

I walked over and placed my palm on the wall. Ali did the same, this virtual connection to her all that we would be allowed.

"Babe, I'm here for you." I finally managed to say.

"I know you are,' she said, smiling sadly. "And right now, that's exactly where I need you to be." She sighed. "I'll let you know as soon as I hear anything." She ended the connection.

The seconds after Ali disappeared from my office wall seemed like minutes. The minutes like hours. My thoughts kept swirling around a single question – what was the chance Ali had been infected by one of the nanobots? Given my current state, most of the estimates were high ... much too high, when you are talking about the life of someone you had loved for the last 17 years.

But when the fog of pain lifted, I knew these odds were beyond my reach. If this was a deliberate act of terrorism, then the chance that Ali had come in contact with the nanobots depended on how they were delivered. I had no information on that, but the air she breathed, the food she ate, or liquids she drank came to mind. There were, of course, many other options – deliberately contaminated handrails, door knobs, soap or hand sanitizing dispensers, gloves or any of the other garb hospital staff wore, bedding or anything cleaned in the hospital laundry .... The list of possibilities seemed endless.

Eventually, evening came and time for dinner. Cam and Chloe had other, social engagements – or at least, what passed for them – and for once, I wasn't tempted to round them up for a family meal. If Ali was infected, I'd find the words to explain it to them later. And if not? I wasn't sure they ever needed to know. I took dinner to my office; although Suze could find me anywhere, I was uncomfortable straying too far from it. Then, I let the food go cold, sitting uneaten on my desk.

At 10:00, I could take the silence no longer and I tried contacting Ali. My comm either failed to go through or Ali couldn't answer. So, I tried Midwest. To my surprise, the connection was immediate and I was given my choice of several options – what had happened, what was being done, and who was being treated. But when I accessed the last option, all I learned was her results were pending. Midwest told me everything, except what I really wanted to know. Was Ali alright?

Early Sunday morning, after several more unanswered comms to my wife, I was making another of the innumerable loops around my office. I glanced down, an incongruous, single laugh escaping my lips. My office floor was covered with a pale blue, Persian-style rug. Ali had never liked it. I did. And since my office was the only area in the house where my opinion on decor counted, it remained. Now, in that kind of scrambled, illogical thinking that dominates when one is too anxious and too tired for anything else, I decided she would be pleased; I was wearing a hole in that rug, pacing back and forth in front of a wall where I had been hoping to see my wife's face for the last 13 hours.

Finally, a little after 2:15 AM, Suze announced an incoming comm. When Ali's face appeared, I didn't have to ask. She looked tired, but the glow of good news could not be mistaken.

"My blood tests were clear," she said. "They've moved me to a different area and I'm staying for a while for more tests. I should be able to come home tomorrow, hopefully in the morning."

My eyes were moist with emotion. I swallowed, trying to remove the lump in my throat. After a moment, I managed to say, "That's wonderful news, babe. I can't wait to have you here."

"And I can't wait to be there. Kids asleep?"

"Yeah." I paused. "I didn't tell them," I said, somewhat sheepishly.

"That's good. No reason for them to worry."

Her expression became more somber. "The hospital dedicated a couple of rooms for patient comms, trying to give everyone a chance to talk to family. I need to go, give this room to people who need it more than we do."

I'd forgotten that communications were still swamped, everyone else in the world celebrating the end of the pandemic. "I'm more than happy to sign off since that means you're OK. When you can, let me know and I'll pick you up."

"I will. Oh, one more thing, quickly," she said. "Call Josh. He has a niece in here. I don't know anything about her results, but he may need to talk. I gotta go."

When the screen went black, I collapsed into my chair, leaning my head back and closing my eyes. I was exhausted, but with so many pent-up emotions over the past hours – confusion, pain, anger – my stomach was tied in a knot and my mind was spinning. I was certain sleep wouldn't come, but I had to try.

I made a mental note to call Josh in a few hours and started toward the bedroom. But before I had cleared my office door, I had another incoming comm.

"Suze, who is it?"

"Josh," she replied.

Questions this late? Or was it more? I didn't even have the chance to say 'hello' before he started shouting.

"What the hell is going on at Midwest?" He was standing in his home office, a fist shaking in front of him.

"Well, as I understand it, they had some people accidentally exposed ...." By the time I got that far, he was shaking his head and cut me off with a raised hand.

"I know all that," he said, the frustration apparent in his voice. "Joyce, my niece, is one of those people. What I want to know is, how is she and what the hell are they doing about it?"

I started to answer, but before a word left my mouth, Josh continued. "I've called Midwest, several times. The recorded comm about what they're doing is pure bureaucratic crap. Joyce's parents went offline after the outbreak ended. I can't get them. And in their infinite wisdom, Midwest doesn't seem to think an uncle needs to know."

Once again, I opened my mouth, only for Josh to add a final thought. "Don't they know, I'm her family."

I knew part of the story. Joyce had grown up in Wichita, Kansas, only a couple of blocks from where Josh and Bette had lived. And when my friends didn't have children, Joyce became their family. Later, Josh moved to St. Louis for work. Joyce followed a few years after that for medical training, then took a job here. I'd never considered it before, but I wondered now if her decisions had been influenced by her uncle's choices.

"Maybe I can get Ali back on the line and ...."

Again, Josh didn't wait for me to finish, although I couldn't blame him. "You've talked to Ali?" he said, a touch of hope coming to his tone.

"Yeah. I couldn't get through to her, but she comm'ed me. I'll try her, but you'll probably hear from Joyce any time now."

Josh's fingers went to his temples, as he shut his eyes tightly for a second. When he opened them, he said softly, "Doug, I'm sorry you have such an insensitive jerk for a friend. How is Ali?"

"Don't worry about it," I said, understanding his anguish all too well. "Ali just learned that her first blood test was OK. Hopefully, she'll be coming home tomorrow. Anyway, maybe she can cut through some of the red tape and find out something about Joyce."

"Buddy, that'd be great if she could," Josh said, as he collapsed into his desk chair. "I can't just ...." He stopped mid-sentence, looking off to one side. "Hold on. I've got an incoming." The image froze with Josh reaching forward to switch to another comm.

After what felt like ten minutes but was probably less than five, Josh returned to the screen. He was slumped forward, staring at his empty hands that were resting on the desk. "I'm happy for you guys, Doug. But Joyce's tests weren't good. She's infected," he said grimly. He put his head in his hands.

"Josh, I'm really sorry. I'll still ask if Ali knows anything more about her condition."

Josh looked up, his mouth drawn in a tight line. "Thanks, Doug, but I'm not sure you're going to want to ask her what I really want to know. I want to know what clumsy technician or bleary-eyed doctor exposed all those people to these tiny killers? This has to be the most colossal screw-up in medical history." By the time he finished, his face was flushed and he was jabbing the air with a finger.

All I could think to say involved the slim, nearly pathetic hope that I had clung to for most of the night. "It's possible that the nanobots will just attack the parasite and your niece will be fine."

Joshed smirked. "These scientists are good enough to make a microscopic assassin that kills all kinds of disease, but klutzy enough to infect the whole floor with it? That's a good one." But no sooner were the words out of his mouth than the sneer disappeared from his face to be replaced with a blank stare.

"It wasn't an accident," Josh stated more than asked. His eyes were focused on something far beyond his office. "Joyce works in the wing with the treatment rooms, but she wouldn't have been anywhere near them. And Ali? She's not even in the same wing. This was intentional."

Ali had said these conjectures were for family only, but I tended to agree with Josh; he was family. And soon, he'd know anyway. "This isn't confirmed and not ready for public consumption, OK?" Josh stared at me blankly for a moment, then nodded. "The authorities are investigating that possibility."

Josh turned away, a hand coming up to rub his forehead. When he turned back, he said, "But why?" He paused, then seemed to answer his own question. "I guess for any miraculous technology, there's going to be a madman who'll find an evil use for it. And now he's set science back who knows how many years?" He released a long, ragged breath. "Doug, I'm really happy for you guys, but I need to go back to trying to contact my brother and sister-in-law. Let me know if Ali hears anything."

"You got it," I replied and we signed off.

Morning, April 2, 2035

Ali's follow-up tests were negative, and by mid-morning, she had been released from Midwest right on schedule. After I drove her home, we were both exhausted from the stress and lack of sleep. I gave Suze strict instructions about whose comms we would take and under what conditions we wanted to be disturbed. The former list had two names, while the latter directions said something about the house being on fire. Then, after making sure the kids would be OK for a few hours, we relaxed. It was the rest of people who felt they had dodged a bullet – twice.

Later that day, I found Ali napping on the couch and stopped to watch her sleeping. I gently pushed a strand of dark curls from her face and left her to her dreams. Later, she discovered me reading in one of our overstuffed chairs. Without saying a word, she pushed the book to the side, crawled onto my lap, and snuggled up against my chest. The novel went to a side table and I wrapped my arms around her, memorizing her warmth, her smell, her touch. I didn't feel like I had ever taken Ali for granted, but now, every opportunity to make a memory felt a little more precious.

The afternoon and evening slipped by quickly and Tuesday was soon upon us. With the threat of the outbreak over, life could return to normal and I went to work as always. But only minutes after setting foot inside the building, it was clear that I was one of the few who had returned. The first day, the workforce was at about 20 percent of the total. It was understandable. Worthington-Huston Technology had made no formal announcement about operations and people were justifiably wary.

But as I went about my business, one fact struck me about the people who had come in; they were, like me, the over-40 crowd. Not that all of the 40, 50, and 60-year-olds were on site. Many were not. But I could count on the fingers of one hand the under-40 employees I saw. One was Laura Holman, a 20-something software engineer who I had met once.

"Hi. It's Laura, right?" I asked when I saw her in the hallway.

"Yeah, Doug, that's right. Up?" she asked, smiling. But as she spoke, she inched backward, apparently wanting to maintain a bit more distance between us. I understood and wasn't offended.

"Not much. I was just curious about something. You work on hardware and software for user interfaces, right?" I asked.

"Yep. Mostly wetware these days."

I shouldn't have been distracted from my initial question so easily, but the term threw me. "Wetware? Doesn't that mean living tissue, neurons, that kind of thing?"

"Sort of, but the meaning's shifting, at least in my industry," Laura said brightly, apparently happy to give me a lesson on modern user interfaces. "You know, brain wiring changes when it's working with tech, right?"

I nodded, recalling some of Ali's remarks about the effect. Over time, implanted devices came to be interpreted much like they were inputs from neural pathways. But it still amazed me that the brain could do that.

"Well, that's a hard jump ... for the patient. It takes a lot of reps with the tech and the fit may be off. So, the latest implant interfaces figure out what's needed once they're in."

"The interface changes?" I asked, surprised.

She nodded, her smile growing still wider. "Sure. Everyone's wiring is different. So, after insertion, we record the reaction, take that and process it outside. Then, we shoot updates in. Record some more. Mod some more, and so on. When it's done, it's a unique device–patient union. Wetware," she said, holding out a hand like the answer was there for me to see.

"Amazing," I said and meant it. "But why haven't I heard more about this?"

Laura's smile faltered and her eyes narrowed. "Well, it's like software mod'ing software," she said slowly. "You know why that stuff's not comm'ed wide."

I did and nodded, now seeing the connection and wondering how she felt about it. Most people in her position were ambivalent, but some chafed at the restrictions. But I'd already digressed too far. "Sure, I understand.

Anyway, what I was wondering about .... I don't see many from your group around today."

"Yeah, our boss comm'ed," she said, her bubbly disposition returning. "We're tooling from home, since product's good. You know, for all the misery that lousy bug caused, it really ramped everyone's home suite. We're nudging wires and gen'ing lines all hours. And everyone's got their community running alongside, so you don't miss any of life."

I thought about saying that online identities and video comms were not 'life' but figured it would confuse the conversation further – I was already struggling with 'nudging wires and gen'ing lines.' "So, you're saying your group's getting everything done with our virtual collaboration tools?"

She giggled, partially hiding it behind a hand. "Yeah, what you said. One minute you're hashing style with your co's and next, you're chatting the v-life. Together, sometimes. Don't get me wrong. The zombie thing was a stab – my folks were on the wire before, and now they're split. But on the line, we sure tooled the code."

"Yeah, my group did well too," I said. "Thanks."

"Sure, Doug," she said as she turned and continued down the hall.

I didn't have time to ponder Laura's words, however, as Suze alerted me to an audio-only comm from Ali. I probably should have walked to my office, but my breath caught in my throat at the announcement. "What's wrong?" I asked as soon as the connection was made.

"Nothing, Doug," she said quickly. "I didn't mean to startle you."

"Yeah, still coming down from the weekend I guess. What's up?"

"I was just wondering if you were watching the updates on the nanobot exposure?"

"No. I take it I should be?"

"Yeah, you should." And she disconnected.

I walked to my office, took a seat in front of my screen, and started searching for a feed on the nanobot story. It took a while. Even though there was proof that the pandemic had never been a serious threat, it was still center stage. Now that it was over, the path to recovery and defining a new normalcy were international issues of paramount importance. On the other hand, the exposure to the nanobots was alarming, of course, but it was local and contained. No one worried that it would spread to their lives, save those residing in the blocks surrounding Midwest and the hospitals in California and France.

When I finally found a comm about the nanobots, it was clear that new facts were rapidly coming to light. About 10 to 12 hours after the exposure at Midwest, additional staff at the hospital in France were found to be infected. With two exposures on different continents at different times, it was a simple matter for law enforcement to identify the one person who had been at both sites during the critical period. In fact, this individual had done nothing to cover his tracks. He had booked a flight from St. Louis to Paris in his own name, and once there, he had simply used his GovTag identity to enter the facility.

While being able to pull off such audacious actions sounded like a monumental breach of security, it wasn't. The individual in question was in charge of the clinical trials. It was Dr. Randolph Spencer, the man after whom the Spencer Clinic was named.

Armed with this information, authorities moved quickly to apprehend him. As it turned out, however, haste was unnecessary. He died at the facility outside of Paris shortly after law enforcement personnel made the connection.

Initially, the facts of his death supported the hypothesis that Spencer had released the nanobots as a terrorist act. He had died of brain hemorrhaging, the belief being that he had accidentally exposed himself while preparing his deadly payload. The only question – what personal or political agenda had caused him to unleash the evil side of a technology he had spent his life perfecting.

When Dr. Spencer's residence was searched, however, a message recorded in various formats, as well as on paper, told quite a different story.

If you are hearing or reading this message, then I am probably dead, and most likely in disgrace. I have no wish to die; I do not seek it. But what I have done will undoubtedly be misunderstood initially. Because what I have done is to expose three different hospital staffs on two continents to an altered form of a medical nanobot. This creation will do no harm. In fact, it will significantly improve the lives of those who are lucky enough to receive it. And my sincere hope is that it will spread worldwide because it holds the ability to fight, not just the toxoplasmosa gondii parasite, but a host of others that plague humanity.

Why did I do this? Because fear and superstition stand in the way of widespread use of this life-saving technology. With these tiny entities, we hold the key to a longer, healthier, and happier life. But that promise will not be realized in my lifetime, and probably not the next, because of misplaced fears and uninformed prejudice. And so, I will put my life in peril to bring this promise of a better life to all. If I die in the initial reaction to my stand, which undoubtedly will be negative, it will be for a greater good. And I will be vindicated by the health of generations to come.

His death, of course, brought into question whether his re-designed nanobots were the boon he thought. Had he, in his haste to save the world, delivered its demise? Unfortunately, none of the materials seized at his home described the nature of the changes he had made. That the nanobots could exist outside of a human host for longer periods seemed likely; Spencer wanted them to spread. And he had noted that they would attack other parasites. But any other capabilities of his creations were unknown.

So now, medical laboratories around the world were rushing to answer that question. Rushing and wondering, was his death unrelated? Could the modified devices really be a godsend to humanity? Or were they the means to our end?

Noon, April 4, 2035

Although her management had told her to take a week off, Ali decided she had rested enough and returned to work on Wednesday. I wasn't surprised. In the aftermath of the parasite pandemic and the nanobot release, demand for her services was at an all-time high. But at the same time, every form of medical practice from the largest hospitals to the country doctor was in disarray. So, Ali had to cobble together meetings wherever she could find space, including people's homes. She had comm'ed with a few, although that was clearly a last resort for her older patients who wanted human support, not more automation.

I was also at work on Wednesday and little had changed since my return earlier in the week. We were still at about 20 percent of the workforce and we still had no word from the company. Then, late in the morning, Worthington-Huston Technology made it official. We were to become primarily an off-site organization.

The financial benefits of having employees work from home had long been known, with reduced facility expenses being prime among the savings. As a result, commerce in 2035 was approximately 45 percent off-site. But after a couple of weeks of the pandemic when everything that could be moved off-site was, work-from-home became the new, business standard.

One market niche that particularly benefited from this shift was the 'secure goods receptacle,' a container of sorts that could be attached to, added to, or placed beside one's home. These household embellishments ranged from something that looked like the large blue or green mailboxes one saw along streets in the United States until the late 2020s – before paper mail disappeared entirely from our culture – to structures that were integrated into the home and became something like a vestibule. The higher end offerings even had refrigerated spaces, so your ice cream wouldn't melt if you were busy. And whatever the design and size, each receptacle was secured with a one-time code that was given to the retailer. The homeowner was never interrupted by deliveries and the drivers never met the customer. Suddenly, this technology became another part of our perfect, no-hassle world.

I was on lunch break, looking at one of these containers when Ali comm'ed me. I brought her up onscreen.

"Hi. Got a minute?" she asked. My heart still jumped every time Suze announced a comm from her, so it was good to get the reassurance of her smile and her deep, brown eyes gazing back at me.

"Sure, babe. I was just looking at these secure receptacles."

Her forehead wrinkled. "Do we need one of those?"

"Well … there are already a few businesses that will drop you if you don't have one. But for now, it's not a necessity."

"Do you really think we'll stay afraid of each other?" she asked, her eyes narrowing. But before I could answer, she shook her head. "We can talk about that later. What I called about – can you get away from work for an hour or two?"

"Yeah, I guess so. Why?"

"I'm at the … well, what was the Spencer Clinic. I guess they're already trying to get it renamed. Anyway, you know the building I mean?"

"Sure. Down the street from Midwest, north side."

"Right," Ali said. "I'm meeting a patient here, and a few minutes ago, I saw Josh come in. The clinic has turned one of their meeting rooms into an information and support area for people who have family members being quarantined at Midwest. Josh's niece, Joyce, is still there."

I searched my memory, recalling neither news of gains or setbacks in the medical community's battle to understand the modified nanobots. "Is everything OK with her?"

"Probably not," said Ali, shaking her head. "I'm only getting bits and pieces because I'm working out of all these other facilities. But evidently, it's not good."

I slumped back into my chair, taking a deep breath. "I hate to hear that. But are you sure Josh would have time for me if I came down there?"

"They're limiting online time, trying to avoid wearing out the patients. You'll have plenty of opportunities to talk and … well, frankly, Josh looked like he could use a friend about now." Ali paused, looking around. When her eyes returned to me, she said, "I have a few other details, but maybe we should talk about those when you get here."

"OK, sure. See you soon."

It was only about 15 minutes to the clinic. As I entered the 'Midwest Crisis Family Support Area,' as the staff had named their converted conference room, I had expected a crowd, but there was none. There were only five people in a room that could easily hold forty. Josh was one of them and he left his chair in one corner when he saw me.

"Hi, buddy. What are you doing here?"

He looked awful – puffy face, bleary eyes, clothes that looked like he had slept in them ... and he probably had. But as I glanced around, it was apparent that he fit in perfectly with the other four. Three of the four were on comm lines, given some privacy by wall partitions that surrounded the screens. The fourth was still sitting in a chair in a far corner.

"Ali's here ... somewhere," I said. "She mentioned seeing you, so I dropped by to see how you're doing."

"I'm OK. I'm giving my brother and sister-in-law a break." He released a long, ragged breath. "Sis is taking it really hard." Then, he rubbed a hand over the stubble on his chin. "Guess I don't look the best either." He tried for a grin, but it was forced.

Movement in the corner of my eye caught my attention and when my gaze shifted, Josh also turned to look. Ali had entered the room.

"We just wanted to let you know that if there's anything you need, just say the word," I said when Ali joined us.

Josh nodded. "Thanks, guys. It's good to have friends." But for the first time I could remember, he didn't lean in to give Ali his normal kiss-in-greeting. But then, no one could turn off a fear, just because it now appeared unfounded.

"Have you seen Joyce yet today?" Ali asked.

"Nope ... but it looks like room 17 has just opened up," he replied.

I glanced around, having neither heard or seen anything. But Josh was always trying out the latest technology. Maybe it was something displayed on a lens covering his eye. Maybe there was a tiny speaker in a piece of jewelry. But whatever the means, he got the message. He pushed up his shirt sleeves and said, "Can you join us?"

"This is family time," I replied. "I can stick around and we can talk later if you want."

Josh hesitated. "I'd like the company during the comm ... if you're OK with that? And I'm sure Joyce would love to see Ali."

I spun toward my wife. I hadn't anticipated this invitation and wasn't certain how she would feel about being thrust back into that situation, even if only via a comm. She'd be returning to a world where she had been a captive for over 13 hours, waiting to learn her fate. Those hours had been some of the most painful I had ever lived, and it had to be worse for her. But before she could respond to me with one of those looks only married couples could interpret, she said, "And I'd love to see her too."

Ali's words said one thing, but her clenched fists implied something else. As we started down the hall, I glanced sideways at her. She must have felt my eyes because she reached over and squeezed my hand. Her grip was firm, but even so, I could feel a tremble.

"Josh, hold on a second," I said. I pulled Ali back up the hall a few steps, then whispered in her ear, "You don't have to do this."

Her hand tightened on mine as she stared into my eyes. "Yes, I do," was all she said. She pulled me back to Josh and we continued down the hall.

When we arrived at room 17, Josh sat in front of a screen, while we stood behind him. The screen came to life. Joyce was laying in a hospital bed, propped up by several pillows. The top of her head and her eyes were covered in bandages. Her nose, mouth, and chin were showing but it was difficult to tell; they were as white as the gauze.

I flinched, now regretting that Ali and I hadn't found a moment alone earlier so she could tell me what was happening at Midwest. Ali, on the other hand, now seemed calmer, her training probably coming to the fore. She reached over with her free hand and rested it lightly on my arm.

"Joyce," Josh said softly. "I have Ali and Doug Michaels with me."

"Oh. Hi, Doug, Ali," she said. "Glad you could join us." Joyce's voice was little more than a whisper. Each sentence was protracted as if she needed time to regain her strength after each word.

"Hi, Joyce," Ali replied. "Don't try to talk too much. You need your strength." Her tone was calm, professional, reassuring. I knew Ali was good at her job, but the sudden change in her demeanor amazed me.

"What's with the bandages?" asked Josh, concern creeping into his voice. "Those weren't there yesterday."

Joyce appeared to nod, although perhaps it was my imagination. "Over the last few days ...," she started. But the words seem to take the last of her energy and she sunk further into the pillows.

"Let me try to answer that," said Ali. "But correct me, if I make any mistakes. The nanobots were designed to multiply inside the body. You knew that, right, Josh?"

At first, he only nodded. But then, perhaps remembering that Joyce couldn't see, he said, "Yeah, they told me that."

"Two places that are particularly vulnerable to the toxoplasmosa gondii parasite are the eyes and the brain, which is why the nanobots congregate there. But their spread is causing pressure, reducing blood flow, and killing cells. Eventually, patients lose their sight."

Ali's words felt blunt to me, especially in Joyce's presence, but the two women seemed to share a perspective that I didn't have. Joyce simply said, "Exactly."

"But she can come back from this, right?" The tension in Josh's voice grew further, producing an undercurrent of desperation.

"They'll do all they can to relieve the pressure," said Ali. "And of course, everyone with any background in this technology is studying these altered nanobots, looking for a way to stop them. But, for coming back ...."

"Let me," Joyce said, appearing to summon all her strength. "Josh, I'm not coming back. Even if we had a cure, I'm too far gone."

"You don't know that," said Josh, his voice faltering. He turned to look at Ali, his eyes moist with the pain.

Joyce didn't argue. She probably didn't have the strength. But even if she did, I doubted she'd debate what she felt to be fact.

Josh must have realized the strain this topic was causing because after a moment he moved on to greetings from distant relatives. Ali and I receded into the background. I was about to suggest to her that we leave and give them some privacy when I heard Josh calling Joyce's name. She wasn't responding.

There was no announcement on a public-address system in the scene from half a block away. There was no medical team that came rushing into

Joyce's room to start emergency treatment. There was only a tone emitted from one of the instruments in the rack by her bed. After a while, an individual completely covered in a protective suit and full facemask entered and checked a few readouts.

"I've contacted her parents. They're on their way to your location," said the woman in Joyce's room, her gender revealed only by the femininity of her voice. "She may be able to hear you if you want to keep talking." Then, the woman turned from the screen, injected something into a tube that went to Joyce's arm, and left.

After a few moments, Josh started talking again. But now, it was not news at all. It was a story about a trip they had taken to Forest Park and the St. Louis Zoo on a sunny summer day sometime in their distant past. Ali and I slipped out. A couple of days later, we learned that Joyce had died, never having regained consciousness.

Friday, April 6, 2068

Afternoon

was all too glad to leave five of the darkest days of my life behind and pull my thoughts back to the present, back to good old 2068. I was sitting in a small park a block from Midwest, having circled the doomed structure twice.

Joyce had died from the very capability that made people wary of nanobots – their ability to self-replicate. In early descriptions of this doomsday scenario, it was noted that if a nano-device could reproduce every 16 minutes and you started with only one, at the end of ten hours, there would be 68 billion of them. And in less than two days, they would be bigger than the earth. Unfortunately, the same principles held when these microscopic entities were reproducing inside people's heads, even at much slower rates.

As close as I could tell, a medical researcher in the United Kingdom had reverse engineered Spencer's nanobots about the same time that Joyce had said she couldn't be saved. What the researcher found was that two parameters had been eliminated – the limit on the lifespan of the nanobots was removed, as well as the limit on the number of times they could self-replicate. Both changes made sense if you wanted these creations to spread to all of humanity.

Presumably, Dr. Spencer believed he could drop those limits because the nanobots were also restricted to a specific ratio of their mass to the mass of the host. So, even if they lived forever or reproduced many times, they would never be more than a small part of a person. But they didn't live forever, of course. And when they died, one of the capabilities that made them the marvel of modern neuroscience was also gone – their ability to pass through the blood-brain barrier.

The remaining, active entities in the brain considered their lifeless counterparts a part of the host. So, as the corpses started accumulating and adding their infinitesimally small masses to the 1.4 or so kilograms of the human brain, additional active nanobots were spawned, which also eventually died. After a few days, the mass of the living and dead reached a critical point and the entire surface of the brain started bruising from the nanobots that now blanketed it. Blood flow increased, worsening the situation and device replication grew exponentially. Burr holes through the skull relieved the pressure for a while, but the trauma was simply too widespread to fight. Eventually, the entire brain would have been crushed; fortunately, death occurred well before that happened.

Even though the problem had been solved while Joyce lived, in the few hours it took to disseminate the findings and get teams prepared to implement a cure, she died. In the end, no one in St. Louis survived. The dead were entombed in a specially prepared vault, designed to assure that no human-designed creation, however small, would ever escape. The wing that housed them was sealed and dedicated to the memory of the 73 who had died there, casualties of a misguided attempt to improve life. The rest of the building was razed and turned into a park, but only landscaping robots ever entered the grounds.

The hospital in France was both luckier and less lucky. The solution had been discovered in time to save some of those exposed there. Of the 116 originally infected, 53 were treated successfully. But in many ways, their pain was just extended. Over the following year, all but six of those individuals died, with the official reasons ranging from voluntary life termination to pneumonia. No one doubted, however, that they too were victims of a self-inflicted, man-made plague. As for the other six, there were only rumors ... but none of them were good.

Fortunately, Dr. Spencer hadn't lived long enough to make the trip to California and they were spared this horror.

"Suze, please get me a SCAT for the ride home," I said after a moment collecting my thoughts. I was exhausted, physically from the walk and mentally from reliving the fear and pain of those days.

In a few moments, my ride appeared. I inserted my finger into the reader, and after the mandatory warning about children traveling without an accompanying adult, I was on my way. I was too tired to care and accepted the default destination, which meant that the SCAT delivered its underage cargo directly to our secure, personal receptacle.

"Honey, you OK?" Ali called when I entered. I joined her in the kitchen and she gave me a hug. "You were gone, what, six or seven hours?" She stepped back from the embrace, looking up at me. "Dinner's still a while, but I can prep something if you're hungry."

"I'm OK. I stopped for a sandwich and coffee at a VendNGo."

"Yeah, I knew about the coffee," she said, shaking her head in mock exasperation. "How do you eat that stuff anyway? I'll bet if you didn't read the name on the bag, you wouldn't be able to tell an apple from a pear."

I was not about to take that bet. For most of the history of humanity, agricultural science had struggled to keep up with population growth. But when the world started shrinking, science kept advancing. Protein and vegetable matter were now synthesized. We had everything we needed for biological survival ... but little of what we desired for culinary satisfaction. In the 2010s and 20s, the difference between produce from truck farms and home-grown was noticeable. Now, the gulf between commercially synthesized and privately grown foodstuffs was vast indeed.

Ali's voice brought me back from my reverie. "So, any insights from your time wandering? I mean about Josh, not the quality of what we eat," she added, almost as if she had read my mind. She picked up her tea and started toward the living room. I followed and took the chair across from the couch where she sat.

"There's something in the retroscape I have so far. I just can't put my finger on it." After a beat, I asked, "Do you remember Dr. Spencer's reason for releasing the nanobots?"

Ali flinched at the name. "Unfortunately, yes. He was a brilliant man, but he became obsessed with getting the technology into the mainstream. And in his haste to save the world, he killed – what was it – nearly 200 people?" I thought she was finished, when she added, "And set a miraculous technology back nearly a decade."

"Exactly. What you said." I held out a hand as if she had proved some point. Ali just stared at me, her brow wrinkling, so I explained. "Josh said almost the same thing about nanobots being miracles and Spencer's effect."

Ali shook her head slowly, saying, "Great minds," but didn't bother to finish the platitude.

I slid forward on the chair. "You say that now, but would you right after your niece got dosed with some?"

Ali frowned and looked off to the side, a finger pressing against her lips. "I see what you mean," she said when she turned back. "But Josh was always big into technology. He was probably giving an opinion he'd held for a long time, not really thinking about how it sounded."

Then, a smile came to her lips and I knew her thoughts must be drifting far from Midwest. "You remember when Josh got that so-called smart security system that nearly killed him and Bette?" She put air quotes around the word 'smart.'

"Um, nearly killed might be an exaggeration," I said slowly, only vaguely recalling the incident.

"Hey, you didn't rescue them from the 'capture room,' or whatever they called it. They'd been sealed in there for about three hours. And trust me, Bette was about to kill Josh when I arrived with the police."

"Right," I said chuckling, "I'd nearly forgotten that." I leaned back in the chair. "I remember a few other times when he picked up some tech that was barely out of the lab, only to have it blow up in his face. But it never dampened his interest."

"No, it didn't." Ali had been sipping her tea, but she placed it on a side table and looked at me closely. "When you first told me about Josh, you seemed to think what happened might have been some sort of delayed reaction to the toxoplasmosis outbreak. But since you came back from Midwest, you haven't said a word about that."

I nodded, releasing a long sigh. "Yeah, what people did thirty-some years ago because of the pandemic and what Josh did last week look identical. But other than looking the same, I couldn't find a link."

"And believing they look the same because the parasite caused both of them isn't complex enough for you?" she asked, grinning.

I shrugged, knowing that more complexity wasn't what I sought. I often used Occam's Razor, selecting the simplest solution, the one with the fewest assumptions because it was often right. And what could be simpler than a single cause behind both Josh's and the world's self-imposed isolation? But if that was true, what was the detail, the one overlooked factor that laid hidden in the millions of pandemic-scare cases, only to surface years later in one person's mind?

Or was it only one person?

"You're brilliant," I said.

Ali chuckled. "Of course I am. Now tell me what I said."

I held up a finger in the 'wait a moment' gesture. "Suze, are the reasons for requesting the services of the Termination of Life Centers available as public information?" I asked.

"They are."

"How many in the last year made any reference to the toxoplasmosis outbreak?"

"None did," Suze replied.

"In the last five years?" I asked.

"Also, zero."

"So, if there's a simple, direct link," I said turning to Ali, "Josh seems to be the only one where it led to death. That's assuming it was a suicide."

"You're still considering some type of foul play?"

I held out my hands. "I don't have any idea how it could be, but can we rule it out?"

Ali sighed but didn't answer. After a moment, her head jerked around to the wall. "Suze, what about references in the TLC records to Dr. Spencer's nanobot release?"

"No references to the release within the last five years," said Suze. "France has an institution similar to the TLCs and I checked their records too. Shortly after the exposure, there were two references from staff members, but nothing in the last 30 years."

"Good thought," I said to Ali.

I leaned back into the chair, staring off at nothing for a moment. We were making progress by negatives. Despite the profound effect the zombie plague had on everything from personal space to family relationships, it didn't appear to be a ticking time bomb that could explain Josh's death. Neither were the nanobots. But there was something in my memories, of that I was certain.

"Time to add some more parts to the retroscape," I said, after sharing the conclusion I had reached with Ali. "Tomorrow, I'm going to see what I can recall from the days when Josh first met Julia."

"Seriously?" Ali said. "An evil, mechanion uprising?" She snickered behind a hand.

I rolled my eyes in reply. "No, but Josh's marriage to one was out of the ordinary."

"Then, maybe, but not now," replied Ali. "You know dozens of human-mechanion couples. And Chloe and Leticia could be next."

I frowned. "You know Chloe wouldn't be considering marriage to Leticia if it wasn't for our convoluted laws."

When people first started marrying mechanions, they wanted some of the same advantages as unions between humans – various financial benefits, rights to privacy, and the like. But opposition was widespread, forming along three lines. Some decried it as a desecration of marriage, but that group was small. A second group held that marriage as an institution should be abolished. Few humans bothered, so why have laws for man-machine unions, they argued.

But the third community, the largest, was opposition in the sense that it provided inertia against change. People in this group didn't care. Sure, virtuants and mechanions might live forever – and it appeared that many would, as part of the RMM, Repository for Machine Minds. But so what? They were not a drain on society or resources. To them, it was the equivalent of the question, how many angels can dance on the head of a pin. It wasn't a meaningful issue.

Eventually, the Virtuant and Mechanion Bill of Rights was enacted in response to the vocal minority. Suze had rights, due to her association with me. The same for Ali and her silent, unnamed virtual counterpart. And Chloe and her mechanion, Leticia. But the moment the human partner died, so did the bestowed rights, and the machine intelligences reverted to disposable property. That's what rankled the people who had originally supported the Bill.

And Chloe, in my opinion, would marry Leticia to throw fuel on that smoldering issue. At least, I thought she might ... and I loved her for her sense of equality and her tenacity. I only had to look across the room to know where she had inherited those traits. Cam would fight for fairness too, but he was more of the angels-dancing-on-a-pin school on the mechanion marriage issue.

Ali crossed her arms over her chest. "I don't know anything of the sort. And neither do you. Actually, I think they might marry more for Zander's sake than the law."

I smiled at the mention of our granddaughter, although I could see no reason why Chloe would marry on her account. Zander was in her 20s. But it was pointless to debate the question. Neither of us knew if Chloe had even considered marriage, much less why.

"Yeah, OK, but Josh's actions were out of the norm for the time," I said. "I should go back to those days." And although I didn't say it, I also needed to reacquaint myself with my feelings about Julia. The tension I had felt yesterday was still fresh in my mind.

Ali leaned back on the couch, picking up her tea for a sip. "Sure, see what you can recall. But when you're done, we need to have a long talk. You're looking for something that festered in Josh's mind and what do you come up with? His wife?"

For once, I wasn't fooled; she was trying too hard to keep a straight face. "Yeah, the logic seems air-tight to me," I replied. "Marriage wears on a guy."

"You're sleeping in the personal receptacle tonight, mister." But in typical Ali fashion, she followed the pretend threat by getting up off the couch and coming over to squeeze my shoulder as she left for the kitchen.

I got up from the chair and moved to the couch. A nap before dinner and an idle evening was probably the best thing I could do for my retroscape for the rest of the day.

Saturday, April 7, 2068

Morning

sat up in bed and stretched, feeling sore from the jaunt to Midwest. Ali's place was empty, which was normal. She usually finished breakfast and had started her day before I stirred. I got up and as I made my way down the hall, I heard noises from her office. "Morning, babe," I said, peering through the open door.

Her gaze went to the ceiling, then she closed her eyes and shook her head. "Technology." She said it like it was a dirty word. "Something's wrong with the material for the printer. That fastener for the cool prep system?" I remembered the conversation and nodded. "It came out looking like scrambled eggs. Anyway, a SCAT with a new bunch of material is on the way."

I came in and planted my customary kiss on the top of her head. "Scrambled eggs, huh?" I said, opening my eyes as wide as the hour allowed. "So, you did make me something for breakfast."

She laughed once saying, "Bon appetit," and returned to her work.

After retrieving a coffee and muffin from the kitchen, I went to my office, ready for another day of building my mental landscape. On the wall, I could see that a thunderstorm was brewing; the air had a greenish cast, foretelling the violence that was about to be unleashed. A robin flitted by, its normally orange breast looking almost brown with the distortion in the atmosphere. The wind was also increasing. Bunches of ornamental plume grass were dancing in the breeze. A piece of a dead leaf that had somehow eluded the lawn maintenance systems tumbled across the yard, looking much like a small animal fleeing an invisible predator. It was an interesting scene, but not the one I needed.

"Suze, please show the view from that camera near Eureka," I said, mentioning a small town west of St. Louis. Immediately, the wall was filled with a vista of dark green, rolling hills and valleys. A single patch of light – a small break in the clouds – sped across a hill, then disappeared into the darkness produced by the growing storm.

As I settled behind my desk, Suze asked, "Anything particular you want to see?"

"SCATs," I said simply.

Featured in the foreground of the current scene was Interstate 44. When I had first driven this stretch, it was six lanes and this time of day would have been 'rush hour'. Now, it was twelve, since SCATs are only about half the width of the cars of my youth. And the rush hour was gone. Traffic no longer showed an ebb and flow around a work day because there was neither a standard work time nor the need to travel for a job. I-44 would have the same, modest flow of 200-kilometer-per-hour vehicles at 2:00 in the morning as now.

"Is this another one of your human moments?" my virtuant asked. That was Suze's term for those rare times when her encyclopedic knowledge of my past and plans failed to give her insight into my thoughts.

"I was about to recall the day of my first SCAT ride," I said.

"And the day Josh first mentioned Julia," she replied, her tone reflecting her aha experience. "There is a method to your madness."

While a first SCAT ride probably wasn't momentous for most, it was for me. I had delayed the switch from human-driven to the self-driving cars of the 2020s longer than many. After all, where is the *joie de vivre* in being a passive participant in the love affair between man and the open road? And besides, those early self-driving cars weren't all we had hoped. They did well on wide, well-marked highways or even poorly maintained roads that you traveled frequently. But put them on an unfamiliar, winding country road at night or in the middle of a thunderstorm? Well, let's just say I'd take my chances with the steering wheel in my hands. And even on the best days, these cars could overlook a curb or miss a driveway, even if only by a centimeter or two. But blown tires and bent rims were just as bad whether it was a near miss or a kilometer.

Self-Contained Autonomous Transports or SCATs, however, were the long-awaited, 'set your destination and then take a nap' vehicle. They were made possible by some relatively simple technology; a strip of material that SCATs could sense was embedded in a new, flowable road resurfacing material. Now the vehicle couldn't miss a turn and crumbling roads could be repaved in days, rather than months. It was a match that changed transportation history overnight.

One of the few double-wide, double-length SCATs crested a hill, looking like an elephant chasing mice. "Wonder where that big one is going?" I said, mostly to myself.

"To a construction site in the northern part of the city," replied Suze.

"Well, whatever it is, it wouldn't fit in our commercial receptacle." And fitting things into receptacles was a prime reason SCATs existed.

The idea of a person driving to a location to buy anything – clothes, furniture, food, whatever – was weakened in the 2010s and 20s, and completely disappeared in the decade that followed. What you wanted came to you. First, business experimented with flying delivery, exploring various types of drones. But their operational costs and reliability were poor compared to simple, ground vehicles, and soon, SCATs cornered the market.

The problem was, now there was no longer a driver to unload the merchandise. The vehicles had to park and wait until the homeowner was available, a delay that sometimes extended for hours. Realizing the need, standards were developed for a SCAT-to-home transfer system using secure commercial receptacles. Soon, the touch labor requirements in the entire supply chain, from purchase to receipt in the home, dropped to zero. It was all so convenient, so efficient. The world applauded all that could be done without another person being involved.

Apparently, what was good for delivering our new shoes was also good for hauling us, and soon SCATs became the single person, driverless public transport of choice – that is, on the odd occasion when someone wanted to travel. Then, the pandemic provided the final push, killing all demand for multi-person modes of transportation. The double-wide SCATs carried cargo almost exclusively.

"I have everything for today with one exception," I said to Suze. "See if you can find a picture of an office in the Worthington-Huston Technology building from around 2046."

A room just as I remembered appeared on my wall.

Twenty-Two Years Earlier

Morning, August 22, 2046

T he screen on the wall in front of me was blank, but it wouldn't be for long. I had a call with Josh in a few minutes and he wouldn't be late. He'd be too anxious to start ribbing me.

"Doug, you've got a comm from Oren Bledsoe," said Suze. I was halfway into my resigned sigh before Suze mentioned the name. Now, I was just surprised, not knowing what Oren might want. Of course, it could be almost anything, because he was recently hired as a technical writer for the department. He was to take the well-reasoned but poorly phrased thoughts of our engineers and psychologists and turn them into lucid prose. It would be a tough job for someone with years of experience and he was a 20-something, recent graduate.

"Hi, Oren. What can I do for you?"

"Morning, Doc," he replied. "Been on any interesting hikes recently?"

Since we hardly knew each other, Oren must be reading from my bio, which would be scrolling next to the video on his computer. It was good he was getting acquainted with his coworkers, but the use of these cheat sheets could be revealing.

"A bit tropical for that, isn't it?" I asked. "What's it been, five days with rain and temps over 37?"

He frowned, mumbling, "Oh, yeah. Guess so." People who vacationed virtually to avoid the vagaries of the weather and who traveled receptacle-to-SCAT-to-receptacle would hardly know if the sun had come up, much less the temperature. From his reaction, I suspected that Oren was among that large and consistently growing crowd.

"Anyway, I have a question about Section 4 of that paper you wrote." He brought it up on screen. "It's the conclusions on the brain-to-brain communication stuff."

"OK," I said slowly. "What's the question?" His annotation in the text only said, 'Surely not.'

"You see, I follow how this stuff works. You're recording activity in the brain of one person using advanced magnetic resonance imaging or MRI. Then, that signal is sent to a transcranial magnetic stimulation or TMS system. It uses coils outside the head of another person to re-create the same pattern of activity in their brain. Basically, you've shared a thought, brain-to-brain, right?"

"Exactly," I said.

He had a good grasp of the basics, but that wasn't surprising. A lot of people did. The idea had been around since the 2010s. It had even caught the public's attention when people like Mark Zuckerberg, CEO of Facebook, touted a 'brain interface' of the future. But the promise of this tech was elusive, and according to the research I had evaluated, it was still years from general public consumption.

"It's just that I've used it," Oren continued. "And it wasn't all that great."

"You used it? Where?"

"DuoDream," he said. He looked off a moment, rubbing his forehead with a hand. When his eyes came back to the screen, he seemed to have come to a decision. "It's caused nothing but trouble between me and my girlfriend ... or maybe ex-girlfriend pretty soon. She calls my dreams 'black-fog groping,' whatever that is. We're so incompatible that she's about to dump me."

I blew a long breath out between my lips, then nodded slowly. I should have guessed his response. Few companies could afford the type of investment necessary to achieve acceptable thought-sharing. So, they went out of business – all of them except companies like DuoDream. They specialized in dream-sharing, where largely uninterpretable sensations were good enough, particularly when paired with AugMate. But then, with AugMate's direct brain stimulation, images of a tree would work just as well.

"You've got the pieces of the tech down perfectly," I said. "But what you need to remember is that everyone's brain wiring is a bit different and companies like DuoDream ignore that fact to make a buck. You get standard tech with little or no tuning. You're lucky if your girlfriend sees anything at all. Make sense?"

"Yeah, I guess so. I just didn't think so many in your sample could have had such a positive experience." Oren rubbed his forehead as he studied the top of his desk. When he looked up, he said, "But frankly, I'm not sure anything would work for me."

"Why do you say that?"

"It's just …." He looked at his open hands a moment as if there was an answer there. "My girlfriend has never had problems with DuoDream, but even my own recordings fed back into my head look like garbage. That brain wiring that's a little different person to person? I think mine may be off the charts."

And perhaps it was, but that didn't mean that the technology wouldn't someday accommodate him. But before I could respond, Suze's soft warning tone for another, incoming comm reached my ears.

"Sorry, Oren, but I think Josh is calling about my 10:00 meeting. Let me pause so I can tell him I'll call back."

"Josh? Josh Unger?" Oren asked. I nodded. "I know him … well, a little. Why don't you put him on and you and I can wrap up? I know what I need to do in section 4."

"OK," I said. "And if you have more questions about DuoDream, we can talk later."

Oren nodded, so I set up the three-way comm. "Hi, Josh. Oren Bledsoe and I were just finishing."

"Yeah, I wanted to say hi before we signed off," Oren said.

"To you too," replied Josh.

Oren paused, his gaze flitting around the screen. It was tough to bring up a second bio if that was what he was attempting. After a few moments of silence, he turned to me. "Doc, I'll get back to you on your paper. Should have something in a day or two. And yeah, we can get back to DuoDream, too."

"Sounds good," I replied and Oren dropped from the call.

"Girlfriend problems, huh?" said Josh. It was more of a statement than a question.

I stared at him. "You heard DuoDream and you thought Oren and his girlfriend have a problem?"

"It can only be one of two things. It works for them and Oren was boasting, or it doesn't and they're on the brink of a breakup. Given the difference between your age and Oren's, boasting doesn't make ...."

"OK," I said, holding up a hand. "It just seems strange for her to break it off, just because she can't see what he sees in the middle of the night."

"Hmm, maybe," said Josh.

I drew back in my chair, looking at my friend closely. "Maybe? Are you kidding?"

Josh shrugged. "The equipment will get better, no doubt. But what if it never works for Oren? Then, his girlfriend is giving up something to be with him. And what about him? I can't imagine the nightmare of having a mind that can't connect with the rest of the world."

Rest of the world?

Sure, I saw his point, but it seemed overstated, like calling a jacket that failed to warm on a cold day a climate disaster. We already had machine intelligences linking us to 'the rest of the world', if that's what the virtual side was. So, was it really that much of an imposition when I had to use words to get what I wanted rather than just think?

But on the other hand, if any of my contemporaries had insight into the future of our machine-enhanced reality, it was Josh. He was always on the leading edge. Maybe the loss of a machine-mind interface would be devastating. But before I could say more, Josh continued, "Enough about Oren. I'm wondering what's up with you. You come in by SCAT this morning?"

"I did."

"And been there for what, maybe a half-hour?" he asked as if his curiosity was growing.

I took a deep breath, not seeing any way to avoid what was coming. "More like an hour."

Josh laughed. "So, your SCAT didn't break down or get lost halfway to work?"

"No, but I didn't get to drive either."

"And you missed that?"

I shrugged, then said, "Yeah, some."

Josh must have decided to let me off easy because he turned serious. "So, how was it? As I recall, you were a bit worried about feeling claustrophobic."

"I admit, not bad. I set the surfaces that would be the roof, windshield and side windows to show the outside. Or an idealized version of it, I guess, since the rain disappeared. Then, I started a slight breeze. It was like riding in a convertible ... not that I've been in one of those in the last 20 years."

Josh chuckled. "Well, that's a step. But if you want the real experience, try removing the floor and doors too, so it feels like you're flying over the road."

While that might be Josh's idea of the perfect ride, I tended to think it would make me sick.

"Or make it look like an SUV – a sport-utility vehicle," said Josh. "You remember them, right? Some of them were what, close to five and a half meters long and you sat way up over the road?"

I frowned. "Seriously? We're almost the same age. Of course, I remember SUVs. I also remember that it was rare to see more than one or two people in them unless it was a soccer mom and the team. And now, there's none of those."

Josh nodded. There were no soccer moms because there was no soccer. When the pandemic hit in March 2035, the season-ending tournaments for college and pro basketball were the first victims. No one wanted to be jammed into a 20,000-seat stadium when 10,000 of those people might turn on you at any moment. Then, the baseball season was delayed and finally canceled. Then football. And hockey. Many thought sports would recover, but they didn't. It just wasn't the same, one former sports journalist quipped, without the shouting, drunken fans in the stands.

"But it's the lack of SUVs that makes riding in one a kick," said Josh. "Like riding bareback on a dinosaur."

"And almost the same size," I replied, getting a snort from Josh. "I can't say I have any interest in riding in an SUV, but a SCAT big enough for Ali and me would be nice."

"Hate to break it to you Doug, but you guys aren't newlyweds anymore."

"I didn't say I wanted one with a back seat."

The reference must have been more obscure – or dated – than I thought because Josh just stared at me for a second. Then, a grin came over his face. "Yeah, you won't find that either, but maybe, if you configure the surfaces just right ...." His voice trailed off.

When his eyes returned to my face, he grinned again. "I wouldn't mind a SCAT with some passenger space myself."

I looked closely for the telltale smile that would indicate this was a joke. But if there was one, I couldn't find it; he looked serious. "Yeah, why's that?"

"I thought I might like to share the ride with Julia."

At that moment, you could have knocked me over with a feather. The pandemic had killed few unless you counted marriages among the casualties. Then, the toll was in the hundreds of thousands, and Josh and Bette's union had been one. But in the eleven years since their divorce, I had never heard Josh mention another woman.

As I gave him a questioning look, a picture of a woman appeared on the screen beside Josh. She was beautiful. Long, lustrous, brown hair fringed a face with a flawless complexion, full lips, and deep blue eyes.

"I met her playing tennis," said Josh. "TrueTennis, at the Glaxa Sports Center."

While team sports had disappeared completely, some individual games managed to survive the pandemic – specifically, those where the roles of the competitors could be automated. That was the case for something inexplicably named TrueTennis. Using a combination of a human and a physical tennis ball on one side of the net and a computer-generated figure on the other, TrueTennis singles sprang up overnight and grew to the point where some considered it the new 'national pastime' in the United States. Doubles with two humans playing against two virtual opponents was rare – for all the now-standard reasons – but it explained Julia.

"Wow, it must be serious if you already have a picture of her."

What the ...? The picture just smiled.

Josh laughed. "That's not a picture, buddy. That's Julia. She's my virtuant."

"But you have a virtuant. Jeeves, complete with the British accent."

"Yeah, he was a great sidekick," replied Josh. "But everything he knew about me, Julia now knows. Right, Julia?"

"That's right," she replied. "It's nice to meet you, Dr. Michaels. And sorry about that somewhat left-handed introduction."

"Doug doesn't mind me keeping him on his toes," Josh replied. "Right?"

"Right." I turned to Julia. "Nice to meet you too." She smiled again in response. Turning back to Josh, I said, "But I'm still a little confused. How could you play TrueTennis doubles with your virtuant?"

Julia's smile grew as Josh chuckled again. "You can't and I wasn't. I was playing singles. Julia was on the other side of the net."

It took me a few seconds to process his words. If Julia was on the opponent's side of the court, then she had been a three-dimensional model created by computers and displayed by projection technologies. But other than playing tennis, she would have no personality, no memories, no intelligence. Perhaps she could carry on a conversation about the sport, but probably not. She wouldn't even exist outside of the game.

"So, you took a virtual player out of TrueTennis to become your virtuant?" I asked slowly, wondering if I had misunderstood.

"Correct," Josh replied. "The company that designed her wasn't happy at first, but they eventually agreed to let her out of the game. That was about six months ago when the transition and upgrades started. She's been my virtuant for about the last three weeks."

Josh paused, the two of them looking at each other. Then, he turned back to me. "What you're seeing now, however, isn't a computer rendering of a virtuant. It's a video comm from a plant in Wyoming."

"Video?" I turned away from the screen for a moment, trying to collect my thoughts, trying to make certain there was only one interpretation of his words. "But that would mean that she's ... that she's physical."

"She is," replied Josh. "Or will be, anyway. In about six more weeks, she will be complete and then, she'll become my mechanion. But in the meantime, her head is done and we can talk via video."

What had been surprise and confusion before became unease. My heart started pounding. My stomach lurched. In my mind's eye, I saw a disembodied robot head – Julia's head – talking to us. But it/she looked so real ... except for having no torso, of course. With my background, I knew what was happening to me. I was trapped in the 'uncanny valley.'

That term had been coined by the Japanese robotics researcher, Masahiro Mori, in the 1970s, based on papers from psychologists Ernst Jentsch in 1906, and later, Sigmund Freud in 1916. It held that as robots became more similar to people, positive feelings would turn to revulsion. The eerie similarity between machines and humans would make us uneasy. Then, if the similarity continued to grow, empathy would increase again, as the machine essentially became indistinguishable from a person. In short, the relationship was V-shaped, leading to it being called a valley.

While I could see nothing in the video comm that distinguished Julia from a human, I knew she wasn't and that fact made my skin crawl. I also recognized that my struggle up the steep and slippery slope of the uncanny valley reflected an inconsistency in my thinking. Like nearly everyone, I welcomed machine intelligences as our superiors within their areas of expertise – math, science, medicine, engineering. Machines could outperform their human counterparts. Easily. It was no contest and hadn't been for years. Even in the emotional realm, they excelled. Robots provided support and counseling for everything from anxiety to xenophobia, showing unqualified warmth and infinite patience.

And Suze? She was like a member of the family. Even her sense of humor had become tuned to my idiosyncrasies in ways that no one but Ali could duplicate. But I knew the ancient parts of my brain would rebel if Suze became physical. It wasn't logical, but for me, it was real.

I took a deep breath and nodded at Josh. "If Julia makes you happy, then I'm happy for you." I meant it, and over time, I would try to come to feel it.

"She does," was all he said.

Saturday, April 7, 2068

Late Morning

I rubbed my chin looking at the wall. I had gleaned as much as I could from my memory of the day when Josh first mentioned Julia. Within two years of that conversation, they were married. I thought about pulling up the pictures of their nuptials but decided I'd learn nothing from the formal roles they played on that day, nothing more about why I felt as I did.

Now, looking back, I wondered if my feelings toward Julia had ever really changed. I'd told myself they had, back in the day, but perhaps I had just learned to ignore her. Had she just faded into the background of Josh's life, much like his favorite chair? All I knew for sure was that I was uncomfortable then and seeing her again recently had felt much the same. And the kind of devotion that Josh felt for her? It was an outlier then as well as now.

Or was it?

"Suze, how many people marry their mechanions?"

"The rate last year was 297.4 per 1,000 couples," said Suze.

I sat forward in my chair and stared in disbelief at the wall where I had heard Suze's voice. "Let me get this straight. Nearly three in ten couples involve a mechanion?"

"Depending on what you mean, yes," said Suze. "Almost three in ten marriages involves one. But if you want to know how many couples, married and unmarried, involve a machine, that's a more complex question. If a couple means any household headed by two adult humans or an adult and a mechanion, over 95 percent of these couples are not married, with nearly 65 percent of them being a human-mechanion pair."

I fell back into the chair, the sound of my back striking fabric loud in the otherwise silent office. "You're saying most households are unmarried, human-mechanion couples?"

"No, not at all," she replied. "Most households are headed by a single, unmarried human ... with a virtuant of course."

There were parts of Suze's statistics that made sense to me. The preponderance of unmarried singles was one; marriage as an institution was nearly dead. Frequently, the couples that were tying the knot were either looking for legal recognition of their union to a mechanion or were protesting the same.

But the prevalence of human-machine couples didn't fit my preconceptions nearly as well. Were there human pairs overlooked in these numbers? I knew of people who thought of themselves as a couple, but who didn't live together, at least, not for most of the year. But with the ability to share everything from today's insight on a video comm to last week's dream – and yes, to share 'the real stuff' with TuringTalk – weren't they still a couple? Or was that a union of a person and some sort of electronic ghost?

Then again, perhaps I shouldn't have been so surprised by Suze's figures; I'd witnessed a very successful human-machine marriage in Josh and Julia. Over the eight or so years I knew them – before Josh and I went our own ways – he had been happy with the arrangement. And it wasn't that he had created her to conform to his every whim; he hadn't. If anything, he grumbled about his partner as much as any of us with a human spouse. And his complaints were indistinguishable from ours – she was too controlling; she complained when he worked too long; she said he didn't talk to her about his feelings. But under that grumbling exterior, Josh was happy. It showed.

After a few moments reconciling my misconceptions with the facts, I returned to the retroscape. I sent three comms – one to Bette and two to coworkers I hadn't seen in years. Then, I headed for the kitchen for a coffee. Ali was there. She was sitting on one of the counter stools, her bare feet propped on the rung of the stool next to her. Her head was resting on a hand and she was staring across the room at the food prep station. I could see a cup of tea sitting there, steam rising from its surface.

"Hi, babe," I said. She turned her head, giving me a tired smile as she brushed a few of her dark curls from her face. "You look like the weight of the world is on your shoulders."

"I'm not sure that's what a woman wants to hear from her husband ... but it's true." I thought about protesting but figured that any excuse I gave now was unlikely to get traction.

"I spent most of the morning talking to one of my patients," Ali said. "She should be getting more control over her arm, but for some reason, it's not happening. I'm guessing she's skipping the exercises. Either that, or it's not working because she thinks it won't. New neural paths don't form without some effort."

I moved behind her, placed a kiss on the top of her head, and started rubbing her neck. She stretched and made a soft sound, then said, "Ah, that feels good." She turned and looked at me. "Last night, you looked like the one with the weight of the world on them. The effect of the outbreak and Midwest, no doubt. But you don't seem much more upbeat this morning after reliving part of Josh and Julia's life. Discover you're still uncomfortable around mechanions?"

A single laugh came out as a snort. "Trying to disguise the last session as part of the retroscape didn't work, huh?" I moved over to the prep station to retrieve Ali's tea. "Yeah, the creepy feeling's still there."

"I think you would have gotten over it if you'd interacted with Julia more."

"And you did?" I asked, partly teasing and partly from surprise. "As I recall, you met her once – a Christmas party, where you stayed on the other side of the room all night. And since she's a robot, you can't blame the pandemic."

"Douglas, it wasn't that bad," Ali said. There was a towel on the island between us and she grabbed it and threw it at me. I laughed, as it opened in the air and then fluttered to the floor a meter from where I was standing.

"Well, at least you've crossed marriage and spouses from your list of suspects in your retroscape. You have, haven't you?" Ali said, narrowing her eyes.

"Yeah, I have, and I acknowledge your superior insight on that topic. Josh made the transition from virtuant to mechanion partner like it was nothing. I like Suze, but if she was physical, I couldn't marry her."

"Thanks, Doug," Suze said from the confines of the CommCover. "But you're not my type either – a human." I chuckled. Ali rolled her eyes.

I handed Ali her tea, then started a coffee. "I just sent comms to a couple of coworkers from the smart pill project, asking what they remembered about Josh."

Ali winced. "You're going back to those days too?"

I shrugged. "Josh didn't get depressed from going on a picnic. You remember Tom Knolls or Tonya Evers?"

"Tom, no, but Tanya, sure. She helped with the records on a couple of volunteer efforts at the clinic. She was a treat, all bubbly and full of energy."

I stared at Ali. "Tanya Evers? About your height? Late thirties? Straight brown hair? I wouldn't say she was asocial, but she never said much at work."

"Yeah, that sounds right. She kept her distance, but she was always going on about something."

I scratch my chin, still wondering if we were thinking of the same person. "Anyway, assuming they haven't fallen off the grid, I should get something from them later today or tomorrow." Ali nodded.

Off the grid?

I chuckled to myself at the words. The phrase was still in use, but the meaning had changed dramatically. Originally, the grid had been something like a coarse network of loosely coordinated cell phone calls and credit card transactions, perhaps supplemented by automated or manual searches of video or satellite feeds.

Now, it was more like an extremely fine mesh. This was because every time a comm was placed, every time our environment warmed or cooled, lightened or darkened, every time a sign changed to reflect our interests, our virtuant had interceded for us. And all of those commands from the virtual to the physical world were a matter of record. So, if I had the weight of an official inquiry behind me, I could have obtained my coworkers' precise locations in real-time, down to the meter if not centimeter. But this wasn't official, so I had made a general request that they contact me.

"Oh, I sent a message to Bette too," I said, removing my coffee from the prep area and taking a sip. Ali raised her eyebrows, so I added, "I just asked if she'd watch for anything that seemed out of place when she got into town."

"OK," she said after a moment, but her tone said 'maybe.'

"I'm going to putter around in the garden for a while, probably pick some more lettuce since it's growing like a weed."

Ali sighed. "I'd join you, but I need to get back to my patient." She took her tea and left for her office. I departed with my coffee.

My garden was the former backyard of the house to the east, that home now gone. I could have also farmed the backyard of the plot to the south, but one yard was enough. Land for gardening was plentiful, partially because of the declining population. But the more significant factor in the surplus was technology.

With pandemic-mandated, home-based work and a desire for online social interaction that had been growing since the turn of the century, technology responded with better and faster communications. That infrastructure now readily supported everything from collaborating on technical research to flirting with the girl next door, even when next door was halfway around the world. Then, when the desire to purchase goods free of human interaction surfaced, technology responded again, providing SCATs and secured receptacles. No longer was there any reason to live in cities. You could have any lifestyle you wanted, any products you sought, anywhere you desired.

Technology was even a factor in making the climate irrelevant to where you lived ... at least, in a way.

The weather had become a pattern of extremes – rapid temperature swings; increasingly violent and frequent storms; extremely high rainfall in some areas, almost none in others became the rule. But it could have been worse. By the late 2020s, the fact that sea levels were rising was inescapable. So, in a moment of determination born of the survival instinct, world governments greatly accelerated their programs to reduce carbon emissions. Those steps would help, nearly everyone agreed, but only in the distant future. For now, the water would continue to rise, because the momentum of a planet's atmosphere didn't turn on a dime.

Technology again responded, this time with the creation of massive, intelligent, earth-handling machines to battle the threat. And people fought alongside these marvels of engineering, forging an alliance in what became known as 'The War Against the Water'. The push almost came too late, but eventually, it paid off and the inhabitable surface area of the world changed little. Thanks to technology, people lived where they wanted, free of the fear that their desert view today would be tomorrow's beachfront property.

So, while a much broader distribution of people over the earth's surface was the general trend, the immediate impact on me was that I had a choice of garden plots.

"Doug?"

I stood from where I had been pulling a few weeds, wiped the dirt from my hands, and turned to see Ali approaching from our home.

"Do we have lettuce to trade for some tomatoes?"

"You found tomatoes?" I asked, a hint of excitement creeping into my tone. I'd never adjusted to the somewhat metallic taste and mushy consistency of the synthesized version. "Yeah, we have tons of lettuce."

"Good," she replied. "I found a guy near Dallas with tomatoes. We haven't traded with him before, but he says they're good. I suggested a half kilo straight swap and he agreed. He's just waiting for Suze to confirm."

"Suze, tell him, he's on," I said. "And please schedule a refrigerated SCAT for transport in an hour."

"The exchange is confirmed and the SCAT scheduled," said Suze.

"Nice find," I said to Ali, as she turned back to the house.

I started the harvest, thinking how surreal it was that one of the unexpected spinoffs of our high-tech world was the widespread return of a long-forgotten lifestyle – farming. As intelligent machines displaced humans everywhere from the manufacturing floor to the boardroom, many had returned to the soil, as if it was in their genes. The proportion of people involved in agriculture had hit levels not seen for 100 years. And with farming came bartering, replicating even more of a 1700s lifestyle in 2068.

After the lettuce was harvested and safely on its way, I headed toward the kitchen, my stomach telling me it was time for lunch.

Noon, April 7, 2068

"Just in time to help me chop these vegetables," Ali said when she saw me enter the kitchen.

I glanced at the ingredients on the counter. "Grilled chicken and vegetable salads?" I guessed.

"That's the plan."

"No fresh squash?" I asked. Ali recognized my comment for the rhetorical question that it was and said nothing. If we had fresh squash, it would be there. It was just that the only thing worse than synthesized tomatoes was artificial squash. I made a mental note to apply the marinade liberally.

"It's too bad we can't barter for chicken," I said, having finished slicing the vegetables and turning my attention to the synthesized protein. "I miss the real thing."

"Me too. But not enough to chance something from an accountant who has a chicken coop in his backyard."

"Or enough to pay $95 a pound for real chicken from a certified vendor."

"Or that," Ali replied.

I placed the ingredients on a belt and watched as they started toward the hot-prep station. Something inside it would determine the ingredients and grill them to perfection. Actually, the station could have cut them up as well, but Ali like keeping the cleaning and inspection in her hands. She turned her attention to the lettuce while I moved to a stool at the island.

"Looks like I have responses from Tom and Tanya."

"Read them," Ali said, not looking up from her chore.

"OK, here's the one from Tom. Let's see. He says, no, he's had no contact with Josh. At first, he didn't recognize the name. That's interesting. Then, he asks if Josh had a mechanion. Um, he goes on about how he's exploring that option. Then, something about the specific model he's looking at. And the cost. Then, some sort of machine intelligence I could contact to get more information. That's it."

When I glanced from the screen, Ali was drying her hands on a towel, leaving the lettuce half done. She walked over and stood behind me. "What did you ask him?"

Suze pulled up the request before I could say a word.

> Tom,
>
> It's been quite a while since the smart pill project at Worthington-Huston Technology. I hope you're doing well.
>
> I have some sad news. Josh Unger died a few days ago. His actions leading up to his death are unusual. He had secluded himself from the outside world. I was trying to see if I could piece together anything that might shed some light on his behavior, maybe during the last project or after.
>
> If you have a moment, I was wondering if we could talk. My contact particulars are below.

I turned to look up at Ali. She scratched her cheek. "Well, Tom and Josh weren't that close, were they?" she asked.

"Actually, they were ... at least at work. The smart pill project was 3 years, off and on. It was Tom's first job at the company, as well as Tanya's. Josh was a mentor to both of them. Let's see what Tanya says."

I opened her response. It was not quite as off-topic as Tom's. At least she said that she was sorry to hear about Josh. But at the same time, she made it clear that she had no relevant information and no interest in talking about it. In the last line, she wrote, '*Tell Ali I said, Hi.*' But she provided no contact details. Of course, Ali could reply with a general comm that would find her, but it made the greeting seem less than sincere, at least to me.

"I guess that's about all you can expect these days," said Ali, as she finished reading Tanya's note.

She was more understanding than I. "Yeah, it's probably a good thing Josh didn't call one of them for help," I said, my voice rising. "Tom wouldn't be able to spare the time from girlfriend shopping, and Tanya wouldn't have given him a way to find her."

Ali lightly placed a hand on my shoulder but didn't say a word. I turned to look up into her deep brown eyes, calming a bit. "I'm mostly mad at myself," I admitted. "I was supposed to be Josh's friend, and he didn't call me either. I'm no one to criticize."

Ali smiled sadly. Her eyes flicked to the wall. "Looks like you have a response to your third comm too. Bette's calling."

"Hey, guys," she said in greeting. "You know, Ali, it's too bad you didn't get a PhD. Then, these calls would involve a pair of docs. Get it, a paradox?"

For a split second, I considered holding my customary groan to her joke, but somehow, I suspected she wanted normalcy, rather than me telling her I was sorry for her loss. "That was bad, Bette," I said, shaking my head. A flicker of a smile reached her lips but was immediately replaced by an exaggerated look of surprise, as if everyone found her hilarious.

"All this talk about PhDs reminds me of college," said Ali. "Back in school, I found that the only way I could pass my ethics final was by cheating."

Bette started tittering. I turned and looked up at my wife, just in time to catch a wink. I was hoping her reaction meant, 'don't worry. I won't be doing this all the time.'

"By the way, girlfriend," continued Bette. "I don't think you've seen this room before. What do you think?" Bette had moved to a rural area outside of Albuquerque after her divorce from Josh and had decorated the room in a style befitting the region.

Ali started looking around, the camera panning with the direction of her gaze, zooming in and out as she focused on an object. After a moment, she said, "Outstanding. I love the color scheme with the earth tones, the rustic furniture, rugs on the floor. Is that a Kiva fireplace in the corner?"

Bette grinned. "It is. Thought you'd like that. And it's not just a CommCover bent in a curve. It's real. It works ... or at least it would if I had anything to burn in it."

"Bette, it all looks great," said Ali.

"Before I forget," said Bette, "I'll be back in St. Louis on Monday. The funeral will be that afternoon."

"We'll be there," said Ali.

"And from what I can tell from Josh's lawyer, I can start organizing his estate right away. Ali, since I'll be there a while, you want to go to lunch sometime?"

Ali laughed. "You thought you could come into town and us not have lunch? Absolutely we're going. Just like old times."

"Great," Bette replied, a smile coming to her face. "So, Doug, you comm'ed me. But I have to say, your message was a bit strange. What am I supposed to be looking for?"

I wasn't sure how much context Bette had, so I asked. "When Public Security Service called, did they say anything about the way Josh had been living?"

She nodded, biting her lip. "You mean the fact that he never went out, didn't do anything for himself, left the place a mess? Yeah, they told me." Her eyes went down, then came back up to the screen. "And that's pretty strange. Josh wasn't exactly a neat freak, but he didn't let things get too far out of control either. And he must have turned Julia off or told her to leave everything alone. I can't see any other way that could have happened."

"Me either," I responded. "And frankly, I had the same thought about his actions being so out of character. So, what I'm wondering, when you're in town – can you watch for anything that looks out of place, anything that might be unusual?"

Bette tilted her head, looking at me closely. "That's what your comm said. But other than what PSS already told us, unusual how?"

I took a deep breath, blowing it out slowly. "I'm not sure. Just things that are there that you didn't expect, or things that should be there but aren't? Maybe something about a new job? Anything like that."

Bette looked around a moment, then shrugged and said. "Sure, I can do that."

"Thanks."

Thinking we were ready to move on, I glanced up at Ali, only to hear Bette's voice come from behind me.

"I guess there's already a couple of things I should mention. First, when I was talking to Josh's lawyer, he kept saying, this will be easy or this will go fast. After a while, I asked if it was always this easy, and he said no, but that Josh had been in about a month earlier and they had gone through everything." She paused. "I didn't call PSS about this because I know what they'd say."

"That he was getting his affairs in order?" I asked.

"Exactly. The second thing that's come up is a bit harder to explain. Up until about four months ago, Josh was comm'ing a guy named Roger Amschulter in California. He lives in a town ... or maybe it's the name of a region, but it's called Five Points. There are only four comms in the history, and they're all ... well, not exactly in code, but worded like they mean something besides what they say. Can you take a look at them?"

"Sure, Bette," I replied, trying to keep my voice calm while my thoughts screamed, 'this could be it.' Cryptic comms right before his death couldn't be a coincidence, could it? Ali must have wondered the same thing, as her hand returned to my shoulder.

"Thanks," Bette replied. "And if you think they're suspicious, you can forward them to PSS. I don't trust my judgment at the moment."

"Will do."

I rubbed my chin. There was another topic I had planned to broach, but it had the potential to be unpleasant. And if Amschulter was involved, raising it was unnecessary. But it was better to have my options open, so I plowed ahead. "Bette, I was wondering .... Would you mind if I talked to Julia about how Josh was, there, toward the end?"

Bette's gaze dropped to the floor and she squeezed her eyes closed. A hand went up, covering her face.

"Bette, I'm so sorry," I said. "It's not necessary."

She turned the hand around, palm toward me. Finally, in barely more than a whisper, she said, "It seems so strange. When Josh was alive, Julia was his wife. But now that he's dead, she's just a hunk of plastic and wires. They told me I could download all of her memories – watch them, destroy them .... Destroy her."

Ali tensed, her hand tightening on my shoulder until I could feel the impression of each of her fingers. Surprisingly, I found myself concerned too. Julia was just 'plastic and wires,' but recycling her into SCAT doors and garden tools seemed such a loss of history, of Josh's life. Was this really the closure that Bette needed?

Bette looked up at us. "Doug, I want to know what happened to Josh even more than you, but I can't talk to Julia. She wasn't the reason we divorced – she didn't even exist then. But I can't handle it. If you find something, anything, you have to let me know, even if Josh's death was my fault."

With those words, Ali dropped her hand from my shoulder and moved quickly to the screen. "There's no way you had anything to do with his death."

"Ali's right," I said.

"You two are wonderful friends," said Bette, again holding up a hand. "But you don't know that. Doug, I need your word that you'll tell me what you find. The complete truth, good or bad."

Ali glanced back and I looked into her eyes. I didn't like Bette's request, but I understood it. And I could do it, if necessary; hopefully, it wouldn't come to that. Ali seemed to understand my internal debate and after a moment, she nodded almost imperceptibly. I turned back to Bette. "OK," I said. "I'll let you know."

Bette and Ali talked a few more minutes, planning their lunch, but I heard little. There was too much in my head – a new name, secretive comms, a promise that could devastate my wife's best friend. After a while, the women said their goodbyes. Bette reached forward to end the call, hesitating with her hand just centimeters from the control. "By the way, Doug, do you know the main reason I suspect there's something fishy about this Roger Amschulter guy?"

"No, why?" I asked, looking at her blankly.

"Because in all the times that Josh agreed with him, not once did he say, Roger, Roger."

Bette ended the comm before the groan had a chance to escape my lips.

Ali turned from the wall to look at me. "So, a flesh and blood suspect."

"Yeah, he could be our man," I said, the shape of a possible connection forming in my mind. "I wonder if he used Josh's penchant for new technology to get close?"

"Could be," said Ali. Then, her eyes narrowed. "You think Amschulter used Josh's curiosity to get him into something they couldn't control?"

"Or maybe something that Amschulter controlled, but without Josh's knowledge or consent." Ali flinched. "But it's probably something else," I said, not wanting to leave that image in my wife's mind. "In any case, Amschulter deserves a closer look."

After a few moments, I switched to the other topic that had captured my attention during the call. "I didn't know Bette needed closure so much."

Ali looked at me, her eyes blinking. "Seriously?" When I didn't respond, she said, "I can't get the not-knowing, the not-understanding out of my mind. If that void is haunting me, I can't imagine how hard it must be for Bette."

When Ali put it that way, it seemed obvious and I nodded. The food was ready, so we each prepared a plate, then picked at it in silence. Finally deciding my hunger wouldn't return I said, "I'm going for a short walk before looking at the comms from Amschulter."

"OK," Ali said. "But don't put too much pressure on yourself."

I nodded and left. I hadn't said a word, but Ali knew what was on my mind. My goal to create a retroscape had been born from confusion and disbelief, but now, it was more. It was answering the needs of the people I loved. Failing them wasn't acceptable.

Late Afternoon, April 7, 2068

The clouds disappeared and the breeze died the moment I left the house for my walk, replaced by absolute stillness in a world bleached nearly colorless by the intense rays of the sun. Houses and trees shimmered and danced in the distance, as waves of heat and humidity rose from the ground. It looked like we were in for an early summer. And a hot one.

When I returned to the cooler confines of home, I found Ali napping on the couch in the living room, her dark hair fanned out around her head, her PlotsPro resting on an end table. I turned to tiptoe away.

"Planning to check into Amschulter without me?" came her voice.

"We can do that later."

"I'm awake," she said sitting up. "And besides, I need to make some calls later."

"OK." I said, sitting down on the chair across from her. "Suze, what can you tell us about Roger Amschulter, who lives in or near Five Points, California?"

"There are two Roger Amschulters," replied Suze. "But from the comms Bette forwarded, you're interested in Roger R. He's a certified Afterlife Specialist. He's ...."

"Whoa, hold on a second," said Ali, getting up from the couch to pace. "An Afterlife Specialist? Suze, does he list his services?"

"He does. He provides complete burial and cremation services, including legal and grief support. He also offers legal and consulting support for life preservation through cryogenics and connectome technologies."

Ali frowned, crossing her arms in front of her. "How did Josh get mixed up with a quack like that? We've been freezing people for what ... nearly a century? How many of them are walking the streets today? Zero." She looked at me, her head still shaking. "And the thought that we could capture people in wiring diagrams of their brain connections, a connectome, is astonishing. But we've been making those pictures since about 2015 and they're still little more than art. They're like having a detailed street map and then assuming you understand all the drivers using the roads."

I had heard Ali's denunciations of these technologies several years ago, using almost these same words. "But aren't we getting closer?" I asked. "I thought we were on the verge of having digital copies of people's thoughts and memories."

Ali walked over to the mantle, rubbing her hand across the wood made smooth by years of use. When she turned back to me, she said, "We've been on the verge of that forever. Let me ask you something. When you die, will you live on in Suze?"

"No," I said so quickly I surprised myself. After a moment of thought, I added, "Not really, although I know what you mean. She knows more about me than anyone but you."

I gazed at the wall, Suze's voice coming from the exact spot where my eyes stopped. "Like the back of my hand," she said.

I started laughing. Ali looked puzzled. "I was just about to ask Suze if she thought she knew me. Guess I have my answer." Ali smirked.

"More and more, people are patterning their virtuants after themselves," said Ali. "And often, buried in that decision is the idea of immortality. People want a digital copy of themselves for posterity. That, of course, is a lot of what's behind the Repository for Machine Minds."

I nodded, knowing that I'd decided Suze should go there after I died, but that concern hadn't made it to the top of my to-do list yet.

"But what many afterlife specialists are peddling is different," Ali said. "They're selling empty hope, a lie. They promise an electronic consciousness that could pass the Blankenship Test ... or at least half of it. And there's no such thing."

I hadn't heard that name in years. Dr. Russell Blankenship had proposed a 'simple' test for technologies that sought to convert a human's thoughts, feelings, and memories into a form that a machine could store and use. In his test, the patient would be anesthetized, but just as consciousness was fading, the technology would move the essence of the person into a machine. Then, as the drug wore off, the person's memories and awareness would be moved back to flesh and blood. The technology was proven if the patient reported a single, uninterrupted stream of consciousness, albeit out-of-body for a time.

The reason I hadn't heard the name for years was that few attempted the test. And of those few, most had ended tragically – at least one death, two left in a vegetative state, and one apparently 'locked-in,' capable of communicating only with eye blinks.

"These immortality scams come up in your job?" I asked, wondering why I hadn't heard more about it.

Ali went back to the couch and sat, then ran a hand through her dark curls. "They do, from time to time. The elderly get targeted by these frauds, who explain away the failures, saying the human-to-machine transition works perfectly. It's only coming back that causes the failures and if you're dying, that problem is irrelevant. Your mind gets captured in a machine to live forever."

I dropped my gaze to the floor and when I looked up, she said, "No, none of my patients have signed up for either cryogenics or connectomes."

I chuckled, shaking my head. "Guess I don't need to talk since you and Suze keep answering my questions before I can ask. So, Suze, what else do you have on Roger R.?"

"He's 46, single. No military service. Bachelor's degree in mortuary science. Record of continuous employment in the field since he was 23. Now owns his own service. Certified by the National Examination Board for Afterlife Specialists and by the state board in California. Homeowner since he was 32, currently in his second residence. No records of financial issues available. No records of legal or criminal issues available. Hobbies include winemaking, wine tasting, and gardening. He was born in Wakefield, North Carolina to parents ...."

"OK, Suze, that's enough, at least for now," I said. Suze's description was not bringing anything to my mind except for the fact that he sounded anything but nefarious. "Want to take a look at the comms between Josh and Amschulter?"

"Sure," Ali replied. "Suze, please queue them for us."

The first comm was a video, and since it was from Josh's perspective, we got our first look at Amschulter. If his background did nothing to suggest criminality, his appearance made him look even less threatening. He had a thin face, regular features, and brown eyes. His hair was black, short, and neatly trimmed. He looked like an undertaker, which of course, was exactly what he was. About the only thing that did not fully fit my stereotype was that he had a tan. Evidently, he did not spend every day in the funeral parlor's basement working with the deceased. But then, Suze had said that gardening was one of his hobbies.

After the hellos, Amschulter asked Josh if he was still interested in 'what we talked about.' Unfortunately, that was the extent of the description.

"Suze, please pause," I said. "Is this the first comm?"

"It is," she replied. "I was going to play them in order. The one you just saw is dated August 2067. Of the remaining three, two are in October and one in December, all last year. So, we don't have a comm on the discussion that Amschulter mentioned."

"Hmm, too bad," I said. "But the timeframe is about right. If the last comm is in December, then it's about the same time Josh stopped going out. Suze, please continue."

When the video re-started, Josh said he was still interested, perhaps even more since he had time to sleep on it. Amschulter seemed pleased and said he would arrange for a trial run or two. After that, the discussion turned to banalities.

Suze went directly to the second comm, which was text only. It was apparently SCAT travel times from Five Points and from St. Louis to each of seven other cities. The cities were spread across the country and varied widely in population from New York City to places like Alpine, Texas, and Dickinson, North Dakota. The locations meant nothing to me.

I glanced at Ali, who nodded. Suze proceeded to comm number three. If I had blinked, I would have missed it. It was only about 15 seconds of video in which Amschulter asked Josh if he was ready for the trial run to Seattle. He said 'absolutely' and it was over.

The fourth and final comm was again video. As the connection was made, Amschulter sat up straighter, his hand coming to his throat. He stared for a moment, then asked Josh if he was alright. Although the response was affirmative, his tone was flat, his speech slow and slurred. I cursed the fact that my friend was not in the picture, but with my imagination using information supplied by PSS, I pictured stubble on his chin, bed-head hair, rumpled clothes.

After the hellos, Josh asked, "You know we're heading into winter, right?" Amschulter laughed, then apologized for being so compulsive. He asked if Josh had seen the 'numbers' he had sent, with Josh confirming that he had and adding that they looked 'doable.' Then, the men turned to small talk.

"And no comm with these numbers?" I asked when the video ended.

"No, sorry," said Suze.

"It's hard to believe that Bette would miss anything with Amschulter's name on it," said Ali. "Maybe Josh deleted the rest of their comms."

"Maybe. If so, PSS could have them recovered, but I'm not sure there's enough here to get them interested. I mean, yeah, Bette's right. These comms are cryptic, but ...." I trailed off, wondering how we could get something more incriminating.

After a few moments, Ali said, "The change in Josh's mood was certainly startling, from gung-ho in the first comm to weary by the last. And what do you make of those travel times? It's like they wanted to be sure they could arrive at the same spot at the same time ... but why? What were they doing that had to be face-to-face, away from either of their homes?"

"No idea," I said. "And then we have the second set of numbers that Amschulter mentions, which is also a complete mystery to me."

Ali sighed, probably showing some of the same frustration that I was feeling from these disjointed messages. After a moment, she stood from the couch. "I'm going to look at the latest in the connectome research. Maybe there's something I've missed."

She squeezed my shoulder as she walked past, but I hardly noticed. A vague concern, the beginnings of a reprehensible scheme had grabbed my attention. I got up from the chair, starting for my office. But when I reached the door, I continued the few steps to Ali's. "Babe, you have a minute?"

"Sure," she said, looking up from her desk. "You've found a pattern in those comms?"

"Probably not," I admitted, now wondering if sharing my flight of fancy was a good idea. There was always danger in focusing on one hypothesis too soon – it might close our minds to other, more likely possibilities. But I needed her expertise to fill in some gaps. I took a seat while she turned her desk chair to face me.

"So, let's say that Amschulter is onto some breakthrough in connectome technology," I said, watching her face closely. "One of the goals of that research is to create a digital consciousness that could be loaded into a computer. But there's also the thought that a connectome could be placed into another living entity. Perhaps even another human, so that it shared or even replaced the other person's thoughts and memories. Right?"

"Yeah, that's one of the dark sides of the tech," she replied. "One person's mind is used to overwrite another's." She raised an eyebrow. "Are you thinking that Josh was a failed test case for someone seeking immortality?"

"No, actually, I'm thinking it was a success."

Ali flinched. "A success?"

"Josh was too old to be a vessel for someone else's mind, but he could be a demonstration. You know, show the potential client that the technology is real. And once the demo's complete, what better way to hide your crime than for the test case to kill himself while you're a thousand kilometers away."

Ali turned away for a moment, then back to me. "And the travel times," she said, speaking slowly as if considering each word. "They're to make sure that the two of them get to the demonstration location at the same time – Amschulter to conduct the test and Josh to be the unwitting victim."

"Right," I said. "And since Amschulter had several potential customers spread across the country, he had Josh ready to meet him at each location. When the high bid turns out to be Seattle, they meet there. Once the show is over, Amschulter re-loads Josh's mind, but it's been altered. An irrational fear has been added. Or maybe it's a memory that will eat at Josh until he ends the pain."

Ali turned away again, silent for several minutes. Thinking I must have passed the bounds of reason, I said, "Yeah, I know. It's really farfetched."

"No, I was just thinking ...," Ali started. Then she stopped, smiled, and said, "Yeah, your scheme's way out there. But what I was wondering is, how is this wealthy person going to take his millions with him when he goes to a new body. His DNA won't ...."

She stopped mid-sentence, doing her ta-da gesture. "Of course. Not only does the buyer get a new, young body, but that body's DNA is now associated with his or her fortune. Manipulating the GovTag database was part of the demonstration. That's why Josh was without his DNA record for a while and then it reappeared."

The logic of her suggestion hit me. "I thought the customer would give his money to the other person before the body switch, but that would raise a lot of red flags. But a DNA switch? That's genius."

But finding a possible fit for the clue was a double-edged sword. It felt good to put another piece of the puzzle in place, but it also made the scheme seem more real, more malicious. Ali's thoughts must have been paralleling mine as she said, "If this is true, it's horrible. To have used Josh like that, just to drive him to self-destruction in the end."

"Yeah," I said softly. "But if anything even close to this is going on, the stakes are incredibly high. What would people pay to be immortal? I don't think Amschulter and his partners would be worried about a lost life or two."

"Partners?" Ali said. "Someone to change the GovTag records?"

"Exactly. I can't see that Amschulter has that ability," I replied. "Suze, DNA records can only be changed inside a Bureau of Population Management facility, right?"

"That's correct. Changes to DNA records are made only on systems that are physically isolated from the outside."

"So, we've got at least one person besides Amschulter – an inside man at BPM."

"Well, I guess my task is still to check into the connectome research," said Ali, pausing to stretch. "But I'll hit it tomorrow. I'm tired because someone didn't let me finish my nap this afternoon." She smirked at me.

"Yeah, I'm pretty beat too, since I was busy keeping you awake," I said, smiling back. "I'll start with a virtual tour of BPM tomorrow morning. By the time I'm done with that, it should be late enough to contact Amschulter on the West Coast."

"You're planning a cold call?" she asked, her brow furrowing.

I shrugged. "Yeah, I thought so. What we know fits a body and DNA-switching scheme, but let's face it – it's still pretty unbelievable. I'm hoping for another piece of evidence or two, something that would get PSS's attention. I'll start by asking Amschulter if he and Josh had talked about funeral arrangements. It wouldn't be unusual for Bette to have stumbled across his name and then asked me to see if there were any loose ends. And I'll go from there."

Ali nodded slowly. "Not bad. I didn't know you had such a talent for deception."

"Thanks."

"But it would never work on me, so don't try it." I chuckled, knowing her words to be true.

Sunday, April 8, 2068

had been up and down all night, unable to get Amschulter and some nameless conspirator at the Bureau for Population Management out of my thoughts. I even dreamed about them, the BPM villain remaining faceless in the fantasies of my sleep. So, when the smell of bacon from Ali's breakfast came wafting down the hall, I shook the cobwebs of a restless night from my head and started for the kitchen.

Passing Ali's office, I glanced in. She wasn't there. The kitchen was empty as well. I considered a full breakfast, the aroma of Ali's meal still lingering in my thoughts. And bacon was one food that had made the transition to 2068 quite easily. But then, I suspected anything soaked in salt and permeated with a smoky flavor would taste good. Unfortunately, I had little appetite, so a BLT featuring our newly bartered tomatoes became my plan for lunch. I grabbed a cup of coffee and a muffin and headed to my office.

Stepping through the door, I jumped, startled by movement in the corner of my eye. I spun around to find my wife.

"Sorry," said Ali. "I thought you saw me when you went by."

Ali had appropriated a corner of one of my office walls, some type of patient report showing there. But I wasn't sure why she was here rather than her office. She must have read my confusion. "I thought I'd listen in, learn a bit more about BPM. Other than the fact that they stepped in when the Internal Revenue Service failed, I really don't know much about them. You're still doing the virtual tour, right?"

"Yep," I replied. "And I'm glad you're here. Always a good idea to know your enemy."

Ali rolled her eyes. As she turned back to the wall, her hands started flying through a series of swipes and gestures and touches, the information on the wall changing so fast it was a blur from where I stood. I had never mastered the virtuant-signing skill ... much like I had never mastered thumb-typing on a phone or tablet, back when that was in vogue. But now, Ali's ability to work in silence left me to operate as I usually did – the easy way.

"Suze, I need to get some background on the BPM," I said as I sat at my desk. "What are my options?"

"There's a machine-based, knowledge guide for the BPM named Censere that I can recommend. He's quite knowledgeable about their history, current functions, and technology."

"Ah, a friend of yours?" I asked. "Or maybe, more than a friend?" I arched my eyebrows.

"A lady would never say," Suze replied, matching my tongue-in-cheek tone. "Would you like to speak with him?"

"Sure, but first - the name, Censere? What does it mean?"

"It's Latin. Censere means to assess or register, usually for taxes."

I chuckled. "How appropriate. Yes, please put him on."

Soon, a figure appeared onscreen and I have to give BPM credit. It was not the generic, solemn-looking, talking-head I had expected from an official, government agency. Rather, what I saw was a round face, prominent jowls, and a somewhat red nose. To my mind, he looked a great deal like pictures I had seen of the American comedian W.C. Fields. All that was missing was Field's signature, yellow-straw hat.

"Salutes 'ro," said the image on the wall. "Be Censere. Peeking for the shine on the Bureau? Though dimming in the learning lab, init? Maybe just trawling for backs?"

BPM had displaced the Federal Bureau of Investigation as 'the Bureau' long ago, so that much of Censere's statement I understood. But the rest? I had only a vague idea. I did, however, understand enough to know that he had expected a seven-year-old, well-schooled in the jargon of that generation. Ali had heard his greeting too and was now tittering softly in the background.

"Hold on, Censere," I said, leaning toward the screen. "You need to dial back on the slang and up on common, spoken English. Or at least, English as spoken by a 77-year-old American."

"I beg your pardon, sir," the machine-intelligence replied, each word enunciated precisely. "There appears to be an irregularity in your profile. I was anticipating a conversation with a young man of nearly eight years of age. But your protestations, along with the visual data available to me suggests a grave error in a datum that I have retrieved from our system. My sincerest apologies."

"That's OK," I replied. "And the language is better, but perhaps a bit formal."

"Of course," Censere said. "May I suggest we fix your age first? Also, your profile shows a somewhat unusual interaction style, one weighted heavily toward empirical evidence and technical detail. Is that right?"

"Pretty much sounds like a geek, so the style's fine," I said. "And if you could fix my age, that'd be great." I thought about telling him that I had tried numerous times to correct it and that all of my attempts either failed dramatically or produced a change that lasted only a day or two. But then, I'd never had the knowledge guide of the Bureau helping me.

"It would be my pleasure. If you could place your finger in the reader there on your desk while I access corroborating data."

I had no more than inserted my finger than Censere declared, "Success. Your age now reads 77 years old."

"That easy, huh?" I said, sinking back into my office chair.

"That easy, Dr. Michaels. May I call you Doug?"

"Absolutely."

"Alright, Doug. What can I do for you?"

"Well, I'm peeking for the shine on the Bureau, and maybe trawling for backs too," I said, trying to recall his words.

"You know," said Censere, "it doesn't sound right when you say it. You lack that *je ne sais quoi*. Shall I start with a little history?" I glanced at Ali, who was still reviewing patient reports, then nodded my agreement.

"I came from humble beginnings," said Censere. "The firstborn of an aging television and a toaster oven. Oh, wait, you wanted history on BPM?"

I groaned and heard another round of snickers from Ali behind me. Censere was clearly one of those machine intelligences that had been endowed with an excess of personality.

"Let me start again," said Censere. "The roots of the Bureau can be traced back to the events of late February 2036. In fact, the day in question was a Sunday, Leap Year's day, February 29. It was the day the tax software of the Internal Revenue Service crashed, bringing the United States government to a virtual standstill. It was the day that the IRS, as we knew it, died."

Over the next several minutes, Censere recounted what happened that fateful day and in the weeks that followed, bringing back a flood of memories. I had been on an international business trip and had extended it through the weekend for some personal sight-seeing in the United Kingdom. But by Monday morning, my planned flight home was in peril. Even with little to go on but rumors, the value of the dollar had plummeted. I was wondering if I could even afford a ride to the airport. But I made it home amid widespread reports of a terrorist attack and a ruined U.S. economy.

Over time, the terrorism story died. There wasn't any evidence – no electronic footprints of a saboteur and no one took credit. Rather, the problem seemed to be inside the IRS systems themselves. Perhaps it was the strange day and date combination or some other confluence of one in a billion events, but whatever it was, the software became unstable. Large modules ran without error in isolation, but when full startups were attempted, they left abnormal shutdowns, corrupted databases, and swearing system administrators in their wake.

Tax Day, Tuesday, April 15, came and went with the IRS accepting returns in whatever form Americans chose to use. Some chose to submit nothing, reasoning that it would be years before the IRS caught them. But most filed something. It was just that what they submitted was a lot less than what the government expected – nearly 18 percent less. Clearly, the U.S. couldn't stand another financial year like 2036. So, in a nonpartisan show of solidarity rarely seen outside of wartime, government officials came together to revamp the taxation system.

What they sought was a means to add the government's lug more or less automatically, while minimizing the risk of evasion. They found their solution in the technology of the private sector.

Banks and credit card companies had run the gamut of forms of payment – from coins and paper to plastic with chips to devices with encrypted applications. Each of these, however, could be compromised. Biometric data – fingerprints, voice prints, retina scans – were tried next. The readers, however, were slow and unreliable, especially in environments where they were heavily used. Where the technology was needed the most, it worked the worst. That's when business turned to DNA-based identification.

DNA had always been a reliable method of establishing identity; the only problem was one of efficiency. Around the turn of the century, a DNA test took several hours in a laboratory. But only ten years later, research at the University of Arizona had produced a portable tester that could yield results in as little as two hours. With millions of dollars in lost and stolen money hanging in the balance, private industry pushed for testers that were even smaller and faster. By the late-2020s, these devices were no bigger than a deck of cards and produced precise results in less than two seconds.

"Armed with that technology," said Censere, as he neared the end of his standard spiel, "the government began levying a very small tax each time currency changed DNA ownership, providing a constant, predictable revenue stream. For the taxpayer, rules buried in legalese disappeared. Gone were the mountains of paperwork. In their place is a small charge, added by BPM, as money moves from hand to hand ... or rather, left finger to left finger. And there you have it."

"Censere, there's one thing that's always puzzled me," Ali said from the corner where she still sat reviewing reports.

"Hoppin, Ms. Doug? Be backing hub?" Censere asked.

"She's also older than eight," I said, grinning at the image on the wall.

"Of course," replied Censere to me. "There are laws against that." I guffawed at his come-back.

"Ms. Michaels ... may I call you Ali?" Censere asked.

"That would be fine."

"Thanks, Ali. What's the question?"

"If these readers are so sensitive, why don't they pick up the DNA of everyone you've touched? I mean, there must be traces from shaking hands, using a handrail, whatever."

"Ah, but they do," replied Censere. "When your hubby put his finger in the reader a moment ago, it picked up the DNA of four people. You might want to ask him later just who, other than you, he's been handling lately." Censere winked conspiratorially as Ali chuckled.

"One sample, his, will be more prevalent than the others, of course," continued Censere. "So, the system has a good idea who he is with only those data. But there's an additional, verification step. During it, the system matches one of the DNA profiles from the finger to the readings that naturally emanate from the body. We could get an identification from these passive readings alone, but the process is slow – 30 or 40 seconds. What shopper wants to wait that long? But if you start with a small set of profiles from the finger, then you can verify that the body matches one of them almost instantly. So, to fool the system, not only do you need to have a person's finger, but the rest of the body as well. And the body has to be alive. It's a process that's proved nearly impossible to defeat."

Censere paused a moment, looking at each of us in turn. "I can't take all the credit for it, of course." His timing and delivery were flawless and both Ali and I broke out laughing.

When I recovered, I opened my mouth to speak, but Censere raised a hand. "In the case of the deceased, physical samples are used in the verification step."

I glanced back over at Ali, who was also frowning. When I turned back to the wall, I asked, "Why did you volunteer that detail?"

"Well, you're interested because of Josh Unger, right?"

How did he know that?

Censere answered before I could ask. "I saw that you tested twice via a PSS link three days ago, followed by samples from Mr. Unger, a past associate now deceased. It was a simple surmise that your sudden interest in the BPM was related."

"And a correct one," I admitted. With that clarified, it was time to move beyond the generalities of Censere's overview. Although Suze had already answered my first question, I wanted it verified, because it cut the suspect list from several billion to a few thousand. "Is it true that DNA records can only be modified inside a BPM facility?"

"Changes to DNA records are made only on systems that are physically isolated from the outside," the machine intelligence replied.

That matched what Suze had told me ... but perhaps too closely. Weren't those her exact words? I waited for elaboration, but Censere had nothing more to say.

"OK," I said after a while. "Something unusual happened when the PSS technician processed the DNA samples from Josh. He said it didn't match anyone in the database. How's that possible?"

"It's not and it didn't," said Censere.

"I'm sorry," I said, raising an eyebrow.

"It's not possible – or at least, extremely unlikely, that the DNA from a U.S. citizen wouldn't match a profile in the database. And there's no mention of a failure. I believe you must have misunderstood."

I glanced back at Ali, who tilted her head in perplexity. Clearly, human memory could be flawed but, in this case, the retrieval failure had become the focus of my short conversation with PSS Chief Technician Terri Finnegan. It seemed unlikely I had talked about it at length and Finnegan had failed to notice or comment about my misunderstanding.

"Let's say it happened," I said. "How would that be possible?"

Censere rested his chin on a hand, as if in deep thought. It was a nice touch, but I was certain his electronics had determined what he was about to say almost instantly. "Hmm. Well, historically, errors in obtaining and analyzing a DNA sample by the model and age of the PSS forensics unit in use at the scene occur approximately 0.0000000000277 percent of the time, while errors in transmitting DNA data to BPM from mobile forensics units occur somewhat more frequently at 0.0000000000536 percent. Since these are nearly independent events, you might expect errors about 0.0000000000812 percent of the time. Or in other words, you're about thirteen thousand times more likely to be struck by lightning than have a DNA reading or transmission error.

"Additionally, what I gave you is the probability of an error on one reading, and the PSS took six on Mr. Unger. I could give you the percent of time we'd expect an error under those circumstances, but I'd be repeating zeros for a couple of days. Additionally, the equipment worked flawlessly when identifying you, the PSS technician, and all subsequent cases on record for that system."

"So, when an error is detected, earlier readings are checked?" I asked.

"They are," Censere replied. "And to date, there have been none reported on that unit."

If the onsite readings were accurate and the transmission was good, which seemed almost beyond question now, that meant the fault was inside BPM walls. If it occurred because Josh's profile had been temporarily removed or altered, there was no point in asking Censere. The perpetrator would have found ways to thwart internal monitoring and Censere would have no knowledge of it. Or, he was part of the scheme.

There was, however, still one way the problem might be nothing more than a simple error. "What are the chances that the incoming data were good, but that the corresponding record was not retrieved correctly or matched properly?" I asked.

Again, Censere adopted his 'thoughtful' pose, but this time, it seemed longer. After several moments, he said, "Well fudge sticks, Doug. You've pretty much run me into a dead end. Apparently, I can access no data on internal record retrieval or matching issues. I can, however, give you a way to resolve the problem."

"Fudge sticks?" I said, momentarily forgetting his offer. I could hear the sounds of a titter escaping the hand that must have been covering Ali's mouth.

"The Bureau has a strict no-profanity policy and I've about worn out 'fricking' and 'son of a bucket'," explained Censere. "And I've driven 'shut the front door,' 'horse pucky,' and 'bull spit' into the ground too."

"OK," I said, stifling a chuckle. "What do I do to resolve the issue?"

"By BPM policy, when a machine intelligence reaches an impasse like this, we are required to ask the following two questions. Do you wish to file an automated complaint regarding the insufficiency of my knowledge base? Or, alternatively, would you like to speak with a human technician who may be able to help?"

Censere had used his most 'official' sounding voice as he made the offers. But when he finished, he leaned toward the camera, winked, and whispered. "Your automated complaint would give me access to this missing information, which I would very much like to have. And then, in a few days, I can give you the answer."

I scratched my chin, considering the options. Censere finding the answer had its appeal, but what would I learn? That he'd only have to say zero for a day and a half to give me the likelihood their system messed up? But talking to a person …?

"I'll get back to you on your offer," I said. "And thanks for all the information on BPM's roots."

From behind me, Ali added, "Yes, thank you, Censere. You tell the story of BPM so well."

"Thanks, Doug. And thank you, Ali. I've had lots of practice with the BPM saga. My machine buddies never tire of hearing it." Without another word, he ended the comm.

I spun my office chair around. Ali leaned back in hers. "Saving the chance to give him a name for when you have one?" she asked.

"Exactly."

"And you think we'll find one?"

"Amschulter can't be pulling the strings inside BPM. So, yeah, I think a connection will turn up."

But truthfully, I wasn't nearly as confident as my words sounded.

Afternoon, April 8, 2068

After the comm with Censere ended, Ali left ... well, not before she asked who else's DNA I had on my hands. But after her teasing accusation, she hugged me, her dark curls tickling my face, her smell filling my nose. It was a familiar sensation that would never grow old. Then, she headed to her office to catch up on connectomics.

No one could stay abreast of technology. And while it was unlikely that something as dramatic as the ability to create immortal, digital people had escaped our attention, it was worth looking. Even small advances in the area might be important. And if our highly improbable scheme proved true, there had to be a third person developing the eternal-life formula to go along with Amschulter selling it and the BPM inside-man swapping the DNA profiles.

Admittedly, while she worked, I took a nap. I blamed it on my restless night, but short, morning snoozes were becoming a routine for me.

Around noon, we had lunch and she told me what she had found. In a word, nothing. Reluctantly, she confessed that the models and wiring diagrams of the human brain had improved, but no one was claiming the ability to replicate a person in a series of zeros and ones. Or to freeze people and revive them later, for that matter. She had caught up on the cryogenics research as well.

After lunch, I returned to my office, knowing it was time to take a closer look at the one suspect we had. "Suze, please search for any connection between Roger Amschulter of Five Points and anyone in the Bureau of Population Management."

"I found only one," she said after a moment. "Mr. Amschulter provided cremation services for the great uncle of an employee at the BPM Western Regional Center in Sacramento. The BPM employee's name is Enzo Marelli and he attended his uncle's service, so it's possible that he and Amschulter met. That was two years ago."

"Just the one contact?"

"That's the only record I could find," Suze replied.

"Marelli – what's he do at BPM?"

"Public relations."

It wasn't the months of meetings in isolated locations that I had hoped. And if Marelli was involved, the number of conspirators had grown again; he'd have no direct access to DNA records with a job in PR. With these two additional complications, my wild speculation about the reason for Josh's demise moved a bit closer to ridiculously improbable. But so far, it wasn't impossible.

"Suze, please connect me with Amschulter."

I barely had time to straighten up in my chair before the same thin, well-groomed man I had seen in Josh's messages appeared. He was seated at a large, wooden desk wearing a dark blue jacket over an open-collar, white shirt. Light streamed in from a window to his right, falling on beige walls and a single, potted plant in the corner.

After introducing himself, he asked, "Do I have the pleasure of speaking with Dr. Douglas Michaels from St. Louis?" He paused, then added, "I don't get many clients from the Midwest ... and even fewer that are seven-year-olds. I assume the age is an error." Censere's fix had apparently lasted no longer than my own attempts.

"Yes, I'm Doug Michaels and yes, the age is an error. It seems to be a slipped decimal point that has proved the devil to fix. As for the city, that part is correct. So, you said you don't get much business from the Midwest. Does that mean you get some?"

Amschulter slowly shook his head. "Guess you got me."

Was that an admission?

I could feel my heart rate go up until I realized it was probably just a figure of speech. He confirmed it when he said, "Truth be told, I've never had a customer from the Midwest. Funerals are usually handled locally."

OK, an admission was going to take a little more work.

"What may I do for you this fine Sunday?" Amschulter asked. "Are you about to break this trend and become my first customer from St. Louis?" He smiled, leaning back in his chair.

If Amschulter felt any unease at the mention of St. Louis, it didn't show on his face. Perhaps something more to the point would get a reaction. "So, Josh Unger wasn't a customer?"

There seemed to be a flicker of recognition, but it disappeared as fast as it had come. "Who?" he asked.

"Josh Unger ... from St. Louis."

Amschulter frowned, slowly shaking his head. After a moment, he said, "What is this about?"

"Josh Unger died recently. Four days ago, to be exact." I paused, wondering if I was about to be treated to a well-rehearsed display of surprise. But what I received was ... a look of sympathy, which made perfect sense when I considered it.

"I'm terribly sorry for your loss, Dr. Michaels," he replied. "And if I can be of any help in finding suitable services in your area, I'd be happy to."

"Thanks. It's just that we – that's Bette, Josh's ex-wife and I – we thought Josh might have already made arrangements with you. Bette found your name on some comms."

Amschulter's frown returned, again accompanied by a slow shake of his head. "I think maybe I remember him, but he didn't arrange for any of my services. If I'm remembering right ... we spent a few minutes comparing notes on California wines."

He's making this up.

In the pause before mentioning wine, Amschulter had glanced away, like he was searching for the words. Then, when he finished, he leaned back, crossed his arms, and smiled, but the expression didn't reach his eyes. Even the supposed topic of conversation between Amschulter and Josh was questionable; Josh didn't like wine or at least he hadn't 14 years ago.

"So, if there is nothing else, there are matters I need to attend to," Amschulter said as he turned from the screen.

"Then, you and Josh must have been planning something like a wine tour?"

That stopped him and he looked back. "Excuse me?"

"One of the comms that Bette showed me looked like a travel schedule. Times from Five Points and St. Louis to these other cities. Places where you wanted to try the local wines perhaps?"

This time, Amschulter's pause was considerable. He looked away frowning, one hand opening and closing as it rested on his desk. Perhaps one more push and he'd give me something concrete, something I could take to PSS. "Was Enzo Marelli going to come along too?"

He turned back to me, staring blankly. "Enzo Marelli? I don't recall anyone by that name."

As sure as I had been that he had been fabricating his earlier story, I was equally certain this reaction was genuine. Apparently, rather than putting him on the spot, I had asked a question where he didn't need to lie and so, any unease I had created disappeared. A mention of the trip to Seattle seemed my best chance to recover, but I never got the chance.

"I'm sorry Dr. Michaels, but I really must be going," Amschulter said. "Rest assured, there is no unfinished business between Mr. Unger and me." His hand flicked out in a gesture that must have signaled an end to the comm, as his image disappeared from my wall before the sound of his voice left my ears.

I leaned back in my chair, blowing a long breath through my lips. Calling Amschulter back now would only irritate him; it was unlikely I'd get anything more. Now, the question was, did I have enough for PSS to take a look? Only one way to find out.

"Suze, please comm PSS Chief Technician Terri Finnegan," I said.

Within a minute, her familiar red hair and freckled face appeared onscreen. "Good Morning, Dr. Michaels," she said.

"It's Doug," I said. "If I didn't offer my first name before, I apologize. I was upset."

"Of course, Doug. So, can I assume you're calling about Josh Unger?" I would have been impressed by her memory, except the file on Josh would have been displayed with my incoming comm.

"Yes, I am. Bette, Josh's ex-wife, found some comms with an Afterlife Specialist named Roger Amschulter in California. They started talking last summer and continued until December, about the same time Josh isolated himself. Just what they were talking about is vague, as if Amschulter wanted to keep it a secret."

Finnegan's brow furrowed, as she looked to the right of the camera. By the way her eyes were tracking back and forth, she was reading something. "Hmm," she said after a moment. "Just about any set of communications might seem secretive out of context. And since this was before or right at the beginning of Mr. Unger's withdrawal, there were several comms around that time."

"Of course," I admitted. "But these were the only ones that Bette felt uneasy about. And the comms implied they were testing something and they had to meet in different major cities to do it. You have to admit, that's a bit strange."

I paused to see if Finnegan might concur, but she seemed undecided, sitting quietly rubbing her chin. So, I continued. "When I called Amschulter and asked, he acted like he hardly knew Josh, let alone traveled any place to meet with him."

Finnegan sat up, her eyes narrowing. "It's true that people don't tend to be as litigious as they used to be." She spoke slowly, carefully. "But calling someone because you think he might be involved in your friend's death? You're on very thin ice doing something like that."

"It was possible that Josh had talked to him about funeral arrangements. There could have been loose ends that needed tying up."

Finnegan shook her head, still looking displeased. "I have a hard time believing that your friend was working with a funeral home 2500 kilometers away."

Obviously, she wasn't fooled by my cover story. "Yeah, probably not. But the way I look at it, if Amschulter comes after me, he's probably innocent and offended by my call. I might get in some trouble, but I sleep at night knowing that he had no part in Josh's death. But on the other hand, if he does nothing, maybe there's something there that deserves a closer look."

"Maybe," she replied. "Or maybe he was offended but doesn't want to give your suspicions credibility by denying them. Or maybe he wants to avoid any possible negative publicity."

I nodded, knowing the situation was not as simple as I had implied. Finnegan studied my face a moment. Finally, she said, "OK, I'll call Mr.

Unger's ex-wife and ask her to forward those comms so I can take a look at them."

"I have them," I volunteered.

"Yes, but I need to receive them from her. I'll look through them and see if there's any reason for me to contact Mr. Amschulter. That's the best I can do."

"No, that's perfect," I said. "Thanks."

After we disconnected, I comm'ed Bette. She didn't answer, so I left a message telling her to expect a call from Finnegan.

Late Afternoon, April 8, 2068

"I'm pretty confident that Finnegan won't be able to ignore Amschulter, once she sees the comms," I said to Ali after describing the last couple of hours. We were sitting at the kitchen island, Ali sipping a cold drink while I had a bagel. I'd have to sneak the coffee later.

"So, what's next?" she asked. "Are you going to wait and see what Finnegan finds?"

I'd been wondering the same thing. If Josh's demise was the result of life events, finding the precise set that had coalesced into despair was daunting. So, when Amschulter's name came up, I had welcomed the chance to focus on something concrete. But now, his involvement seemed to raise as many questions as it answered. If it was a scheme to give someone immortality, how did he know about world-changing advances that had otherwise escaped public view? Who did he know in BPM with the credentials to access DNA records and the skills to manipulate them without detection? It wasn't Marelli. And just how many were involved? The longer the list, the more improbable the scheme seemed.

"No," I replied after a moment. "I'm going forward with the retroscape. I only have one more part I can complete anyway – the smart pill project. Then, before I bother Bette further and involve Julia, I'll wait for Finnegan."

Ali nodded, her mouth drawn in a tight line. She rose from her place at the counter and put her glass in the sterilizing station. "If you need to talk, come find me. Otherwise, see you at dinner."

"I want to get this done in one sitting, so I might be late. Start dinner without me if you're hungry."

She sighed but said nothing as she left.

I walked to my office and settled into my desk chair, concentrating on relaxing. But it did little good. A knot was forming in my neck and my snack was doing cartwheels in my stomach. Even the coffee I'd planned to secret had lost its appeal; I had enough nervous energy already.

I knew the basics of the project by heart. Its official name was the Global Eidetic Memory Initiative, but everyone knew it as 'smart pill.' And it was immense. It involved more than three dozen companies and in excess of five-hundred researchers in the United States alone. Its purpose was to study eidetic memory, more commonly known as photographic memory – the ability to recall information after limited, even single exposures. Under study was an exotic mixture of neurotransmitters named EM-40h, designed to facilitate the long-term storage of information. But equally important, the concoction also inhibited forgetting. Adults lacked photographic memory, in part, because the brain was always cleaning house, so suppressing loss was an important part of what EM-40h did.

Each of the companies doing work under the project had been assigned several occupational areas and had been tasked with answering one question: Had machine intelligence advanced to the point where minimum dosages of EM-40h would be sufficient to train humans to oversee the machines? What that question meant in reality was, have machines advanced to the point that human oversight was unnecessary? We all knew the answer to that question. It was yes.

In fact, rather than the grand-scale, basic research program that the smart pill project appeared on the surface, it was nothing more than make-work. It was the government's attempt to keep its citizens busy. It was the Civilian Conservation Corps and the Work Progress Administration of the 1930s and 40s depression era in the United States shifted to the world stage in 2054.

For the specific events I was to recall, I needed no memory prompts. It was the last day of the project when all of the companies were to present their final reports. When it became known that the Deputy Director of the

Initiative, Dr. Sandi O'Connor, would attend locally, the much larger St. Louis-based company, Ruger-Phillips, had opened one of their conference rooms in a building just outside their secured areas. I could see the facility like it was yesterday. As for the date, I remembered that too. It was November 13, 2054. It was a Friday.

I knew all of this because I had been over that day hundreds of times in my mind, always asking the same question – was I responsible for what had happened in those hours? This afternoon, however, my question was somewhat different. I wanted to know, did I kill Josh?

Fourteen Years Earlier

Morning, November 13, 2054

Eduardo Alverez looked up from his work, his head bobbing up and down, a grin coming to his face. "Well, look who decided to grace us with his presence. If it isn't the elusive Mr. Unger."

Josh stood in the doorway to our temporary work area in the Ruger-Phillips building. "Yeah, and I suppose you and Doug still live in your offices, huh, Ed?" he asked.

"More than you, J. What's it been, six months since we've seen you around?"

"More like four. What, did you miss me?" Josh shot back.

"Very funny," Ed said, rolling his eyes for effect.

I liked to think that my team was close, as evidenced by the good-natured ribbing between Ed and Josh. But characterizing us as such was wishful thinking. In reality, only Josh and I met socially and those occasions had become rare. And as for this group gathering? It was barely tolerated by the younger members of the team. But since today was the project's final chapter, they had agreed ... after a bit of cajoling.

"Anyone hear from Tanya or Tom?" I asked.

Tanya Evers and Tom Knolls were still missing and we only had a few hours to examine the final set of data and prepare our remarks. In a past era, this timing would have been lunacy – statistical analysis and interpretation could take weeks, even months if the relationships among factors were complex. But in 2054, the two hours we had allotted was probably ten times what we needed.

"No, boss," Ed responded. "I doubt that either told their virtuants to wake them … although, they could have told just one." Ed smirked, looking at Josh to see if he wanted to join him on the rumor mill, but Josh just shook his head.

For some reason, Ed had been hinting about an office romance between Tom and Tanya for weeks. If I had to choose between the rumor being true or Ed wanting to feed the rumblings for his own entertainment, I would put my money on the latter.

"If you're in a hurry, Doug, we can always fire up Stats and no one would miss them," said Ed. Unfortunately, he was right. Stats, our statistical machine intelligence, could run rings around Tanya and Tom, with half its circuits unplugged.

In my version of history anyway, I was in my teens when we reached the turning point in the race between human and machine intelligence. That watershed occurred the day IBM's Deep Blue, a chess-playing machine intelligence, beat World Chess Master Garry Kasparov. Nothing changed overnight, of course, and the event faded from my mind and public notice. But the victories for machines kept coming. They beat the best analysts in the stock market. They outperformed medical experts in diagnosing disease. They knew the law better than we did. And for the everyday decisions like adjusting our environment in time with our circadian rhythms? There was no contest, even if you kept the thermostat and all the light switches in your hands.

Even the term, artificial intelligence fell out of favor, because no one perceived their capabilities as 'artificial.' Their capabilities were real, and to argue that human abilities were somehow more 'real' was considered uninformed, and perhaps deluded.

Fortunately, at that moment, Tonya appeared at the door of our workroom, so I was spared the decision about whether we should start without them or not.

"Hi, Doug, Ed, Josh," Tanya said a little breathlessly, as she hurried into the room and sat. "Sorry I'm late. Tom comm'ed me on the way over. He'll be here soon."

"No problem," I replied. "We're just getting settled in. But we do need to stay on task, because our final presentation is at 2:15, with the meeting scheduled to start at 11:00."

I was glad Tanya and Tom had not arrived at the same time. It saved us from hearing another round of unfounded insinuations from Ed about their living arrangements.

"I'll fire up Drew," said Ed.

Drew was our visual/graphical machine intelligence, with Ed as the human counterpart. Whatever Stats found, Drew would provide the appropriate charts and graphs. Although Ed would claim that he provided the 'artistic flare' in those products, he didn't. Each of Drew's graphs provided links back to the underlying data in case someone wanted to explore them. Changes by Ed risked disrupting those capabilities and he knew it, so he left Drew's products alone.

"Hi, all," Tom said in greeting as he appeared at the door. He'd hardly taken a seat when he said, "Hey, what's going on? I can't contact my virtuant?"

"The room's shielded," I said. "Even though we're outside the Ruger-Phillips secure areas, it's part of their security. You'll need to use the hardwired systems."

Tom frowned. "Hard connects? You gotta be flippin. You got an extra bundle?" he asked, turning to Tonya.

She pulled a cable from a bag and tossed it to him. For reasons I couldn't explain, he turned slightly in his seat so the cable flew past and landed on the floor. Then, he got up and retrieved it. "How you coming with Stats?" he asked as he sat down again.

"Good. Almost done," Tonya replied.

Almost done?

This was going even faster than I had expected. Soon, the outputs from Stats and Drew would be pushed over to the machine intelligences that assisted Josh and I. One of those systems would update the status of our project plan and schedule, another would adjust the staffing records, and a third – the most important in the current setting – would prepare our presentation. That was Gabby. She was gifted at translating technical results into fluid, straightforward prose. And she could, and often did, present those findings, using a style that made you feel like she was a trusted friend … that you'd never met.

"OK, I'm getting results," reported Tanya, her voice taking on a note of excitement. "It looks indistinguishable from the previous sets to me. You see anything new here, Tom?"

Tom glanced at the output briefly. "Nope. Looks good. Really good. Let's send it over."

Tanya's hands flew over her work surface. A moment later, Ed responded, "Drew's got it." As Drew developed the figures, I could see Ed's eyes light up. "Looking good," he said, his grin growing.

I knew without asking why three-fourths of my team looked so happy – there was nothing new in our results. There was nothing to keep us working on this project for a few more weeks … not even another day. And they relished that fact.

But then, who could blame them? The smart pill project had demanded something between 8 and 12 hours a week for nearly three years. That was a lot, considering their peers probably worked half that much … or less. We were a nation of full employment, but what constituted full-time work had changed dramatically. Many jobs required only a few hours a week. Some were little beyond being prepared to act, even when that call never came. It would only be human nature for Tom, Tanya, and Ed to want something similar.

For my part, I was ambivalent. I'd miss the work, the camaraderie of our effort … but only a little. That was because few in 2054 defined themselves by their job. People who cooked were not chefs. They prepared a few extravagantly priced meals while following their real passion – reading early European history. People who treated illness were now backyard gardeners if you asked them, specializing in a unique strain of peppers they used in their homemade salsa. Those who practiced law described themselves by the musical compositions they derived using the latest tech. We had become a society known for our passions and our pastimes, more than a job where we watched a machine do our work.

Josh, on the other hand, did not want the project to end, but his reasons had nothing to do with the loss of camaraderie or his sense of self. And those reasons were evidently weighing heavily on his mind, as he voiced them once again. "I really can't see how our findings justify using this cocktail of drugs at all."

Ed groaned. Tom rolled his eyes. Only Tanya had good enough control over her emotions, or at least, over her body language that nothing showed.

In Josh's view, our make-work project was covering up a much bigger issue. It was obscuring the fact that people shouldn't be involved at all. To his credit, there was considerable evidence that people added nothing to the equation. In fact, if anything, they could make things worse, especially in cases involving uncertainty and time pressure. Faced with those challenges, machines didn't panic. They didn't misread information. They didn't try to outguess the facts. But people did, and when humans countermanded machines, more often than not, the results were disastrous.

Sure, occasionally a human got one right that a machine missed, but going against the averages was just that. Over the long run, machines won hands down.

"We've all heard the evidence," Josh continued. "In an overwhelming proportion of cases where a human overruled a machine, the machine was right. And the experts' opinion that validated the machine? It came hours, if not days after a decision was needed. We can't replace machines near instantaneous accuracy with hours of debate and procrastination, because if we do, we'll all suffer the consequences."

Josh's plea was passionate, but we had all heard it before – a fact that Ed made clear when he complained, "Give it a rest, J."

Tom frowned, then shifted his gaze to Josh. "I don't think you have to worry. No one gives what a person thinks about their meds or their legal fix or their greens once a machine intelligence has weighed. People are up enough to know who's got the good."

"You're up enough," said Josh. "But some may take this study at face value. We're making a case for training so people can override a machine. And what about situations where you don't make the call, like an emergency? Your well-being, maybe even your life is now in the hands of somebody who thinks he knows it all."

"Ed, Tom, Tanya, please finish up the analysis," I said. "We need this wrapped up in just over an hour. Josh, let's step out for a moment."

When we were in the hall, Josh turned to me. "Look, I know what I said before. I thought our company's formal petition to the government to study this issue would be enough. But now, I'm doubting it." He held two empty hands out in front of him. "The government will sit behind the smokescreen of this research for the next decade when it's nothing but propaganda from the generation who thinks people know best. I mean, look at O'Connor. She's older than dirt."

"I doubt she's much older than us," I said smiling at the expression. "I also think you need to remember her background. She's been pushing for machines in industry for years and has the political scars to prove it."

"No argument," replied Josh. "But somehow, her views and those of her cronies in the Department of Labor and Congress have stagnated. They can't see the risk in giving people veto power. Look, you've seen the numbers. You're 70 percent less likely to ...."

I held up a hand. "Hold on. I agree with you."

Josh drew back, staring at me. "With what part?"

"All of it. And I agree that Worthington-Huston Technology should make a public statement to go along with our official petition. That's what you had in mind, right?"

"Yeah, but ... what changed your mind?"

"The question's been bothering me too. And when so many companies – what is it now, more than half of them?" Josh nodded. "When we all recommend looking at one of our basic assumptions and the government doesn't even acknowledge the request? Well, that tipped the scales for me. I'll cover it in the talk."

"I was hoping you'd let me," Josh replied.

I looked at him closely, not knowing if he doubted my resolve or my ability. He clarified before I could ask.

"The government needs to hear the cost of making smart pill part of public policy. Gabby can't do that because the need has been assumed, not tested. She doesn't have the data. You can't make the case either, for much the same reason. But I've been looking at the other side of this question for months. I can show them what we risk and keep it factual, unemotional."

"I never doubted your professionalism," I said. I released a ragged breath. "You're sure you want to do it?"

"You're not going to tell me this is career ending, are you?"

"Management might make you cut back to six hours a week."

"Don't make promises," Josh replied, grinning. "Yeah, I'm sure."

"OK," I said after a moment. "Time's going to be tight; you need to cover our findings as well as this statement. So, let's go back in and see what Gabby's cooked up for you."

When Josh and I returned to our work area, I described our plan to the rest of the team. Tom and Tanya just shrugged and nodded. Ed also agreed in his way, saying, "OK by me, boss, if you want to let J put them to sleep."

It was decided. We had a plan ... for better or for worse.

Afternoon, November 13, 2054

The conference talks started on time, at 11:00 AM local, which meant some of the global participants were drinking coffee to wake up. Others were using it to offset the late hour at their location. I wouldn't need mine until later, to hold off my after-lunch drowsiness.

We were seated in a plush conference room, complete with a CommCover that spanned the entire height and width of the 5 by 14-meter front wall. The presentations from the conference were appearing there. Arranged in a horseshoe pattern in front of the massive display was a series of cubicles, each constructed of three transparent walls about three meters tall and open at the back. Each wall could become opaque by request, should the occupant desire privacy. The furnishings were completed by a comfortable, fully adjustable chair – so comfortable that my cup of coffee was barely holding its own.

Each cubicle contained a second display that stretched from wall to wall, used to supplement the information at the front. Mine showed a picture and biography of the speaker, but more advanced features were available. One of the more popular of these was the 'audience-oriented display.' It attempted to show if your message was capturing people's attention, the best of these systems using the faint neural signals that would show when others were listening, as opposed to daydreaming … or even dozing. The system we were using, however, was limited to eye tracking, which meant that staring mindlessly at any one person would put you front and center on his or her screen. That could be embarrassing if you weren't careful.

Dr. Sandi O'Connor was seated center stage, right in the middle of the horseshoe. As our presenter, I had asked Josh to take the cubicle to her immediate right, with the rest of us along the right side. On the left side of O'Connor were two representatives from Ruger-Phillips. I knew one of them, Dr. Sam Price, by reputation, but I had never met the other. She was either hungry or she disliked the open space behind her because one of the snack-serving robots seemed to be perpetually stationed at the rear of her cube. On the other side of the Ruger-Phillips employees sat two individuals, both of whom were identified as members of the media. My only thought was that it must be a very slow news day to have warranted their attendance.

At precisely 2:15, the presenter who was someplace in Norway finished and turned control over to us.

"Good afternoon, I'm Josh Unger of Worthington-Huston Technology in St. Louis, Missouri, USA. It will be my pleasure to present our findings for the use of EM-40h for establishing the required minimum knowledge and skills for human supervisors in the following occupations: writing, art, entertainment, recreation, and administrative specializations."

Josh moved quickly through our findings on writing, art, and entertainment. No one was too concerned about emergencies in those fields; writer's block didn't tend to be fatal. But as he approached recreation, I knew his commentary was about to change.

"A minimum of 500 mg of EM-40h for 4 days is recommended for recreation supervisors. At the maximum, the daily dosage is cut to 350 mg, but the duration is extended to 10 days."

So far, the material displayed on the front wall and transmitted to the rest of the world was Gabby's. I recognized her style. But after a short pause, her outline disappeared, replaced by what could only be Josh's thoughts.

"We must, however, question whether any training is necessary or appropriate for people who would be placed in a position of overseeing recreational machine intelligences," Josh said. "One only has to look at the case of Emily Knox in Tulsa, Oklahoma, to know that humans can panic and prevent machines from completing lifesaving tasks."

Emily Knox had died in a swimming accident three years earlier because rather than use an automated system, a human lifeguard had tried to revive her. He had failed. And while the machine might have been unsuccessful too, the record of that model in similar situations was unimpeachable.

"Had the machine been ...." Josh stopped mid-thought, his gaze shifting toward Dr. O'Connor's cubicle. She had just stood. The motion itself wasn't unusual; everyone surreptitiously stretched their legs during these endless meetings. But her timing, coupled with the fact that we had just had a break suggested this was something else. Was she about to end the government's silence on this question? Was she going to direct Josh back to Gabby's material?

Josh apparently didn't want to wait to find out. "Had the machine been ...." But again, he got no further, as one of the two representatives of the media jumped up and ran to O'Connor's cube. Then, without a word or any hesitation, he threw his arms around the Deputy Director. The look of shock and horror on O'Connor's face was unmistakable. She screamed.

Ed was the first to regain his wits and he bolted for the cube. Josh was close behind, followed by the rest of us. But before I reached the enclosure, an explosion rocked the conference room. O'Connor, the reporter, and Ed disappeared in a fireball.

It seemed only an instant, but perhaps it was more when I opened my eyes. Everything was blurry and I blinked. I was looking at the ceiling, wisps of smoke floating across my field of view. The acrid smell of explosives and burnt electronics assaulted my nose. I heard alarms, but they seemed far away.

I tried to get up but couldn't. I rolled my head to the side to look at the area where O'Connor had been. A spider-web of cracks showed in the blackened walls of her cube, but they still stood. Then, I saw Josh lying on the floor nearly three meters away, apparently thrown there by the force of the blast. He was on his back, not moving.

I managed to prop myself up on an elbow. Josh's right hand was lying in a pool of blood about a half meter from his body. A medical robot approached and carefully raised his damaged arm, blood spurting from the stump. It sprayed some type of greenish material on it, which apparently congealed, stemming the flow.

I tried to sit, but the effort made my head spin. I collapsed back to the floor, sweating with the exertion. My heart was pounding in my ears, bile rising in my throat. A medical robot appeared above me. I could feel points of pressure on my skin and then, everything went black.

Late Afternoon, November 13, 2054

As light returned, I blinked and the blurry images came into focus. I was laying in a cot, Ali in a chair to my right, her head in her hands. To my left, there was a medical robot, but it wasn't the one from the Ruger-Phillips conference room. That one had been all appendages and displays – a first responder in an industrial setting. This one was female in appearance and I wouldn't have known she was a machine except for the small cord running from her arm to some of the equipment beside me.

I turned back to Ali. The motion must have caught her attention because she looked up and said something. I couldn't understand the words. She slipped off the chair and knelt beside me. Her face was flushed and her eyes puffy. She bent close and through the ringing in my ears, I heard, "Doug, how do you feel?"

I tried to answer, but only a croak came out. My throat was dry and raw, and I grimaced with the pain.

"Flo, call Miranda," Ali said, loudly enough that the words made it through my fog. "They said your throat would be sore. Take a drink of this." Ali held out a container, bending a straw close to my lips. After a couple of sips, she asked, "Better?"

I nodded, the discomfort fading. "How's Josh?" I managed to rasp.

"You remember?" she asked, staring into my eyes. I nodded again and she squeezed her eyes closed. When she opened them, she took a deep breath and smiled. "They said you might have some memory loss." She reseated herself beside me, then leaned forward. "Josh will be OK," she said, but then, her gaze dropped to the floor. "Unfortunately, they can't save his hand."

"Ed?"

Ali shook her head. "Ed and Dr. O'Connor were both killed. The reporter too ... or whoever he was."

I released a ragged breath and looked around at my surroundings. "How long have I been out?"

"It's a little after 4:00," Ali said. "I've only been here 20 minutes or so. Just long enough to meet your doctor and get filled in. The medication you got after the explosion was to deal with shock. You've been out since then."

Whatever I had been given, it had acted fast and was leaving just as quickly. My senses were returning, my hearing being the only one that was lagging. Other than my throat, the only pain I noticed was in my left shoulder.

Someone tapped on the door and it swung open, revealing a woman. She stepped in, nodded to Ali, then took a position just inside. "Dr. Michaels, I'm Dr. Miranda Jennings. Please call me Miranda. And this is my medical machine intelligence, Flo." She gestured toward the robot.

The doctor had a fair complexion and short, brown hair, much like her mechanical partner. Their stature – tall and slender – also matched. They could have been sisters, the illusion increased because Flo had removed the cord from her arm.

"Hi, Miranda. I'm Doug." I took another sip of liquid. "But I'm a Ph.D., not a medical doctor."

Miranda smiled. "I know, Doug. I like the informality of first names. But the fact that you thought I might be extending a professional courtesy to a peer says a lot about your cognitive functioning. You know where you are?"

"Well," I said slowly, "I can tell you that before the explosion, I was in Ruger-Phillips Building 63, just outside their main gate. And from the furnishings in this room and ...." I paused a moment to check. "And the fact that I can't raise my virtuant, I'd guess I'm still there."

Miranda glanced up at Ali. "Is he always this precise?"

"You have no idea," replied Ali, as she shook her head. Then, she slipped her hand over mine and squeezed it, giving me a smile.

Miranda stepped around Ali to the equipment, checking displays and occasionally saying something to Flo that I didn't understand. When she finished, she took a chair beside and slightly behind her robot.

I sat up slowly on the cot. Ali shot Miranda a glance, but she just shrugged and asked, "Does that make you dizzy?"

"No, not really," I replied. "I think my head is OK. I'm feeling a bit weak and my shoulder's sore."

Miranda was doing something on a portable screen in her hands and without looking up, she said, "Flo, what do you think?"

"May I call you Doug as well?" Flo's voice was soothing, with a tempo that was a good change of pace to the energy of the doctor.

"Yes, please."

"Thanks, Doug. As for your injuries, the most serious is a bruise on your left shoulder from hitting the floor. It should clear up in two to three weeks. Otherwise, you have numerous, minor scrapes and cuts on your arms, hands, and face. The ringing in your ears is normal and should clear in a day. Your vitals are all within normal bounds. Miranda, I think he is good to go, with the standard warnings."

I didn't notice any response from the doctor, but perhaps she nodded because Flo started speaking again. "Doug, if you start feeling overheated, your heart starts racing, you feel unusually tired, nauseous, weak, or dizzy, seek medical attention immediately."

"I will," I said.

"So, you're not expecting any memory loss?" Ali asked, looking at Miranda.

But it was Flo who answered. "Most likely not. I monitored Doug's brain activity when he recognized you, when he accessed memory to ask about his coworkers, and when he answered the question about his location. His answers were correct and his neural responses were appropriate. But if he experiences any problems, have him checked further."

"Of course. Thanks, Flo." Ali paused. "And I suspect I have you to thank for the connection to Suze as well?" Ali turned back to me. "When I heard you had been injured and Suze knew nothing ...." Ali seemed to be reliving those moments of concern, a look of anxiety clouding her features.

"Yes, Suze was panicked," said Flo. "And your husband's vitals didn't seem a matter of national security. So, I put that sensor band on his arm and opened the channel to Suze."

"That meant a lot to me," Ali replied. "Thanks."

I glanced at my arm, not realizing until that moment I was wearing anything new. But the band of black material I saw there wasn't the only thing.

"Yes, your shirt was ruined," said Flo. I checked under the sheet that still covered my legs, finding more unfamiliar clothing there. "Your pants too, but I didn't look when we got you changed."

I chuckled, sitting up and slowly swinging my legs over the edge of the cot.

"You can keep the T-shirt and sweatpants, compliments of the Ruger-Phillips gift shop," said Miranda. "But we'll need the sensor band back. So, unless either of you has questions?" She paused while Ali and I looked at each other, then said no.

"OK, since my mechanion's happy, I'm happy too. You're good to go."

But with Miranda's words, a question popped into my mind ... and to my lips before I had a chance to think. "Flo's your mechanion?"

Miranda stared at me a moment. "Yes," she said slowly. "Why?"

"It's just that I don't think of mechanions as being so highly skilled," I said.

Miranda scowled, and in my imagination, I could hear her comeback. 'You think a mechanion can't be anything but a sexbot, don't you?' I didn't believe that, having witnessed the union between Josh and Julia, but the prejudice was still common enough.

As to Miranda's actual rejoinder, I would never know as Flo spoke up. "Thanks, Doug. I work hard to keep my skills current."

Miranda visibly relaxed, taking a deep breath that was difficult to miss. "It's getting more common," she said after a moment. "Until about five years ago, I had a virtuant and worked with a medical robot. Do you remember the unit that treated you after the explosion?"

"Black, shiny, lots of manipulators and readouts?"

"That's Flo, before the current body and the personality of my virtuant were added. It's just a lot easier if my medical associate is also my friend."

"Makes sense to me," I said, still feeling a bit defensive.

I removed the sensor band and leaned forward to hand it to Miranda, but she withdrew. Instead, Flo reached over and took it from my hand. With Miranda's training and background, it was unlikely she was still concerned about toxoplasmosis. Her reaction, however, had been unmistakable. But then, doctors were human. I'm not sure why she would react differently than anyone else.

Miranda and Flo stood from their chairs and started for the door when Miranda turned back. "I almost forgot. PSS would like to talk to you, but I can tell them you don't feel up to it if you want."

"I'm OK," I replied. "But would you ask them to wait a moment? I'd like to talk to Ali first."

"Of course." The two left, Flo turning to give us a wave as the door closed. It made me chuckle.

When I turned back to my wife, she was smiling. "I'm not sure I've ever seen you take to someone's mechanion more than the person."

"Flo?" I asked, somewhat surprised by her comment. But when I thought about it, she was right. "Yeah. Well, she's very good at what she does."

That, I was certain, was at least part of the explanation. I'd think more about it later. "Anyway, I was going to suggest you head home. I'll talk to PSS and be there as soon as I can."

"Are you sure?" she asked. "I have some things to do, but I can stay if you want."

"I'm fine," I replied. "Can you ask them to come in when you leave?"

Ali stood from her chair and bent to give me a hug. Perhaps my close call was running through our minds because the embrace lasted a little longer, felt a bit tighter. She turned and left. The echo from the click of the door closing behind her had hardly left my ears when there was a knock. A woman entered.

"Dr. Michaels. I'm PSS Chief Technician Stacey Havice," she said, walking into the room.

"Nice to meet you."

The Chief Technician was perhaps near 50, graying, short, and rotund. Trailing her into my room was another robot. It was basically a barrel on wheels and a variant of the old saying about people resembling their pets ran through my thoughts. The Chief Technician took the chair Ali had previously used and pulled a small portable screen from a pocket in her uniform.

"I know it's been a difficult day for you, but this won't take long. I only have two lines of questions. First, did you know the man who attacked Dr. O'Connor?"

"No. I don't think I've ever seen him before."

"So, no idea? Not someone who's shown up at other meetings? Or that you've seen around your place of work?"

I paused a moment, playing scenes from the day in my mind. I hadn't seen the man for long; he was often looking away or rubbing a hand over his forehead. But I'd had a few clear glimpses and he wasn't familiar. "No, I never saw him before today."

Havice was apparently satisfied and jotted a few notes on her screen. When she looked up, she said, "We've reviewed the recordings from the meeting. Of course, we'll do it again, probably dozens of times before we're through. But it appears that your presenter, Mr. Unger, was starting to question whether there was any need for this drug, EM-40h. Is that correct?"

I confirmed her thoughts and took her through the background – the growing questions about the project's assumption and the formal petitions to the government. Then, I told her about the conversation Josh and I had in the hall. I was finishing my account, saying, "He'd done the homework and wanted to make the presentation, so .... So, I ...."

So, I let him and now Ed's dead.

The words I knew to be true caught in my throat. I looked down at my hands laying in my lap. Why had I agreed to let Josh talk? If I'd asked him to wait, he would have been upset, but Ed would be alive and Josh would be whole. Or if I had given the presentation, perhaps the reporter wouldn't have attacked. Minor differences in wording, slight changes in inflection might have saved a life. I squeezed my eyes closed and slowly shook my head.

"I agreed to let Josh give the talk," I finally managed, the words a mere whisper.

"No one's blaming you," said Havice, almost as quietly.

I glanced at her, knowing that she was wrong. I knew one person who blamed me – I did. And there were probably others. It was, after all, my team, my call. But rather than saying anything, I just nodded.

After a moment, Havice said, "Unless there is something else you want to add, we're done for now."

I paused a moment, more to give the appearance that I was considering her question than anything else. I had nothing more to discuss because I was tired, upset, and wanted to be by myself to think. "No, I think that's it."

Havice nodded. We both stood, the Chief Technician watching me closely. "You're feeling steady enough?"

"Yes, thanks. I'm OK," I said.

As we entered the hall, a young technician ran up to Havice. "Chief, that reporter who attacked Dr. O'Connor. He's not a person."

Sunday, April 8, 2068

Evening

n my 2068 world, the phrase 'he's not a person,' hit like a bolt of lightning, and I was jolted from my reverie. My body seemed to vibrate with the adrenaline dumped into my bloodstream. "Where the hell have those words been buried?" I muttered aloud. In the dozens of times I'd been over the attack on O'Connor in my mind, I had never recalled that statement. And yet, there it was - the exact same phrase used by a PSS technician to describe Josh just three days ago.

I closed my eyes and tried to calm my mind. Perhaps I could recover my stream of consciousness, see if there was more to this story. But it was no use. I couldn't re-enter my past, not at least until some of the adrenaline had been expended.

After a moment, however, I decided there was probably nothing more to discover in 2054 anyway. I'd most likely been surprised, a little confused by the technician's statement about Yates. But then later – probably the next day – I had learned, like the rest of the world, that O'Connor had, in fact, been killed by a person, Armen Yates. He was a young, single, out-of-work construction laborer from Nebraska. And with that tidbit, my memory of the technician's statement would have fallen victim to a long-known, mental process.

It was in the 1930s when psychologists found that people tend to forget details that don't fit their concepts about the world, their schema, while other aspects of their recollection may be exaggerated to become more consistent. And virtually nothing we had learned in the last 130 years had contradicted those findings. Clearly, the brain was exceptional in its ability to take what it had – expectations, fragments new and old – and weave them into a seamless story that felt like nothing less than gospel when it was actually a blend of forgotten inconsistencies, half-truths, and flat-out errors.

So, while I had some idea why my memory had been incomplete, that didn't answer the significantly more important question – what, if anything, was the connection between these two, identical utterances 14 years apart? Was there a link between Yates and Josh? Or was it just a strange coincidence, an odd choice of words that got repeated by chance.

"Suze, can you search for crimes, preferably violent ones like assaults and murders, where a suspect was initially described as not a person? Just check crimes since 2058 and only in the United States."

"Sure, Doug. Social data too?"

I grimaced with her question. "Yeah, reference and social data," I said. I had just taken a fairly vague task and had now applied it to a vast sea of information.

Sometime around 2010, a computer scientist had estimated that if all the data on the Internet was put on CDs – and I only vaguely remembered that a CD was a thin, plastic disk – then the stack would reach to the moon ... and a quarter of the way back. By anyone's standards, that was a lot of fuzzy photographs of prom dates, videos of dogs chasing their tails, and half-court basketball shots.

But by 2068, the physical size of the accessible data had increased several million times that level, with the nature of the content morphing as well. Content involving sporting events had largely disappeared, while social and interpersonal data continued to grow. Added to the dog-chasing-its-tail clips were neural recordings of dreams, virtual vacations, settings to generate the next, best-selling, erotic PlotsPro book, and so on. So, with her question and my response, Suze was now checking that vast social wilderness for any crime involving a nonperson.

Even so, it was not long until Suze had an answer. "There were 1,063,721 violent crimes during that decade. Of those, 17,267, or 1.6 percent involved a non-human."

I did a double take, then started shaking my head. "No way. I've got something wrong in the search. Give me an example of what you found."

"On January 26, 2058, Harland Beal was arrested for assault against his 27-year-old son, John," said Suze. "In a statement to the media, John's wife said, 'It's a tragedy what old-man Beal did to my husband. It was inhuman.' Harland Beal was convicted in February."

I took a deep breath and let it out slowly, considering how I might tweak the query. "Suze, see if you can find any cases where someone in the Public Security Service or Criminal Apprehension Service said a suspect was not a person."

After a few moments, Suze had generated this list, which was shorter ... but unfortunately, no more helpful. It appeared that the authorities were less likely to call a perpetrator less than human, as they had done so in a little less than 4,000 cases in ten years. But even so, in the examples we checked, they were using words like 'inhuman' and phrases such as 'no one human could have done that,' which sounded right but weren't what I sought.

So next, I had Suze access cases in which the U.S. Security DNA-based Identification Profile of a suspect was null or invalid. There were no such cases. Then, we tried to search for null or invalid GovTags, in place of the formal name. Again, no hits.

From there, we tried the specific phrase, 'not a person.' There were several, but they were all false alarms. Then, thinking that failing to find matching DNA might produce some sensationalism, we searched on violent crimes involving robots or space aliens. Those hits made for some amusing but totally unproductive reading.

Over the next hour, I tried every combination of search terms I could imagine, every type of exclusion or focus I could conceive, and nothing worked. According to all of our accumulated electronic wisdom, there was no way what I had heard twice had ever been recorded in the billions of petabytes now online.

"Did you forget about dinner?" Ali had appeared in my office doorway sometime while I was muttering about my lack of success. "I know you said to go ahead and you'd eat later, but I didn't think you meant breakfast." She stood there smiling, half in and half out of my door.

"Huh?" was the only response that came out of my mouth. In a display of humor – or maybe solidarity of the sexes – Suze displayed the time in half-meter-tall numerals. 8:09.

"Got lost in thought. What do we have?" I asked, frowning at the growing length of search parameters listed in a corner of the wall. Suze and I had been at it so long, we'd be repeating failed attempts if I hadn't kept a list of them.

"I had a salad," said Ali. "I left the stuff in the cool prep compartment. I put some of our lettuce on it and the fresh tomatoes were really good. It probably could have used some jelly beans too."

"Yeah ... that sounds good .... Jelly beans?" I asked, now turning to face her.

Ali started laughing, shaking her head. "Earth to Doug." She stepped into my office and laid her hand lightly on my shoulder. "What are you working on, anyway? Your forehead so scrunched up, I'm surprised you don't have a headache."

I leaned back in my chair, closed my eyes, and slowly shook my head. "I'm sorry. I lost track of the time. I'm getting nowhere on this search."

"Search for what?" Ali asked.

I described how I had recalled the phrase, he's not a person, from the attack on O'Connor. "And Suze and I have had no luck finding anything similar," I said in summary.

Ali placed a finger on her lips, studying me carefully. "Are you sure about the statement? I mean, you found one of your best friends dead less than three days ago. That's got to be a shock. And for the last two days, you've been totally absorbed, reliving the past." She paused. "You think maybe you wanted to find something so much that you created that connection?"

That's the trouble with being married to someone for 50 years; Ali knew almost as much about false memories as I did. And ... she had a point.

"Maybe," I admitted. "I can't deny that those words have been running around in my head. That might do it. And the fact that Suze can't find anything like it in the last ten years? Well, it doesn't look good for the accuracy of my latest revelation, even if it felt completely real."

Ali stared at the corner of the room, as she brushed a hand through her long, black hair. After a moment, she said, "You know, we could reduce some of your doubt about that memory."

"How's that?" I asked slowly.

"Well, you're wondering if your desire to find connections to Josh's death caused you to recall the O'Connor case incorrectly, right?"

"Right."

"And your inability to find any report where the suspect was 'not a person' is causing you to doubt your memory, right?"

I scratched my cheek, still not sure where she was going. "Yeah, OK."

"So, we could at least remove some of your concern if we search for a case where you know with certainty that the suspect was initially considered not a person. If that search doesn't return a hit, then the fact that your other searches returned no hits may mean nothing."

I blinked several times, wondering why I hadn't thought of that. "That's brilliant. Suze, for the death of Josh Unger reported on April 5, 2068 – find all references to the deceased not being a person or being a robot or not having a valid GovTag or not having a valid U.S. Security DNA-based Identification Profile."

Suze responded instantly, as I had given her only one incident to consider. "There were no hits."

"You been searching on all those possibilities?" Ali asked, her eyes wide.

"Those and a lot more." I pointed to the list on the wall. "Well, babe, there's good and bad in this result. The good is that there's reason to think my recall of the O'Connor assassination is accurate. The bad is ... the same thing. Now I can't easily dismiss it. The O'Connor case was a lot higher profile, but at least we know that when a local victim was temporarily missing from the DNA database, that fact goes unreported."

"Time for a break?" Ali asked.

"Yeah, and for the dinner that I almost worked through," I said. "Guess I'll just put this all aside until I can talk to Bette or Finnegan comms me." But as I passed Ali on the way to the kitchen I wondered, was it going to be another restless night, fighting the phantoms of my half-forgotten past?

Monday, April 9, 2068

Morning

was still in bed, rubbing the sleep from my eyes and wondering about the options for breakfast when Ali entered. "Good, you're up," she said, brushing a dark curl from her forehead. "Bette and I've been talking, but she wants to speak to you. She's on hold."

I grimaced, a reaction that my wife didn't miss. "Douglas. That's no way to act."

"No, it's not that. I was just hoping it was Finnegan." Ali frowned, but it was the truth – or at least, part of it. Bette might have some news, maybe even something to bolster my improbable, immortality scheme. But a bad joke was more likely. And what I really wanted to hear was that Finnegan had alerted the California office of the Criminal Apprehension Service and officers were on their way to arrest Amschulter.

I jumped up and got dressed, promising to meet Ali in the living room. Once there, I glanced at the CommCover queue. The call from Bette was the only thing there, so I decided to bring up the link by thought, rather than a verbal request to Suze. But when I did, the screen was taken over by this large graphic, all in primary colors, of a scantily clad woman.

"Bette looks a bit different than I remember," said Ali, a laugh barely suppressed in her throat, her brown eyes twinkling.

"Um, I think that's a PlotsPro promo file about a crime fighter named Betty something or other ...," I said, rubbing my forehead and trying to figure out how this had gone so wrong. Why, when we had over 40 years of capturing people's mental images could I not use mine to retrieve a simple comm?

"Maybe you better check your unconscious, if that's the way you picture my friend," Ali said, grinning. Then, true to form, she said, "Poor baby," as she patted me on the back. "Suze, please open the comm from Bette."

The verbal command worked a lot better, and the Bette who was not the superhero appeared.

"Hi, Doug. Yeah, that's one of the glass walls in Josh's house you're seeing in the background. I'm here now, and I guess the word's out. I've had so many real estate agents come by that I'm looking for one of those signs that says, I shoot every third agent and the second one just left." It was vintage Bette and I rolled my eyes.

"They know they can't sell it, with all the property on the market," said Ali, shaking her head. "But they want the listing anyway. I forgot to ask. How was the trip in?"

"Great," Bette replied. "After we talked on Saturday, I thought, why wait? So, I got a SCAT, read for a while, took a few naps, and then I was here. It's the only way to travel."

"Couldn't agree more," I said. "I can hardly remember when we had to cram into airplanes for a trip like that."

Air travel had fallen on hard times. The pandemic brought it to a halt for a while, then left a major dent in it. Strike one. Then, vacation travel dropped precipitously, due to the capriciousness of the weather and the meteoric rise in virtual vacations. Strike two. And finally, business travel disappeared almost entirely. No one could recall the logic of why face-to-face meetings had been considered a necessity when clearly, they were inefficient, wasteful, and inconvenient. Strike three.

Even when international travel was required, people opted for ships. What was a few days in transit, when virtual business and every manner of socializing could proceed unimpeded? And though their berths were small, there was always a solid wall between you and everyone else.

"So, Doug, after PSS called, I knew the place was going to be a mess, just from what they said about Josh not going out and all," said Bette. "But even so, it was a lot worse than I expected. I'll hit the highlights. Virtually no food. Little clean laundry – all the clothes are wadded up in piles, mostly in one of the bedrooms. No clean dishes. Don't ask me why, but he must have turned off the lawn-care bot. The backyard is a jungle and the front is not much better. The comm history is trashed. There are some as old as a year and then gaps of weeks at a time. So, in looking for something unusual, something out of place, like you asked? I can say this; everything's unusual and nothing's in its place."

I'd seen the place myself and knew she faced a daunting task. I started to offer my apologies, but Bette held up a hand.

"No worries, Doug. I did find some handwritten notes in all this mess." Bette frowned, tilting her head. "I'm not sure I'd ever seen Josh's handwriting before, but I'm positive he wrote it. It has his way of saying things. Anyway, the notes aren't dated, but I'd guess they were during the ... final weeks." Her voice faltered on the last statement, but she recovered quickly. "They're all about .... I don't know, things that didn't seem right to him. Most of it didn't make any sense to me. I'll give you a copy when you get here."

"Thanks, Bette," I said. "I appreciate you going to the trouble."

"Well, if I had done it myself, it would have been trouble. I don't understand the systems Josh has for stuff like making copies. But Julia did it, and I guess it makes sense she would be a whiz with any machine." Bette paused, her hand coming to her mouth. "Was that a rude thing to say?" she asked.

I didn't know what to make of the question. Why would a robot be insulted if you thought it was good with technology? But perhaps the question was rhetorical because Bette continued before I could say a word.

"I also had Julia make you a recording of some of their discussions – you know, just talks around the dinner table or in the morning at breakfast. I thought it might help, might add to what she tells you. I didn't watch it, but even so, I know they started talking less ... and Josh was even shutting her down for long periods of time."

"Yeah, that's pretty much what PSS told me," I replied.

Bette looked down, then back up at us. "Doug, thanks again for doing this. I wouldn't be able to. And you won't forget your promise to tell me what you find, will you?"

"No, I won't forget."

Bette nodded slowly, then said, "Anyway, the funeral's at 1:00. You want to come by around 3:00? That'd give you time to go home and change after the service."

I glanced at Ali, who nodded, then said, "Yeah, we can do that."

"We?" asked Bette. "I figured you'd be coming to the funeral, Ali, but afterward?"

"Yeah, I thought I would." For the first time in this comm, a smile came to Bette's face. Ali returned it.

"That's outstanding because I have to admit, Julia has some austere, but solid decorating taste," said Bette. "I'm thinking about moving some of these pieces back home. Sure could use your thoughts, girlfriend."

"Love to," Ali replied.

The women continued to talk as I drifted into my own thoughts. The funeral would be difficult, but I knew what to expect. Three people, one mechanion, and an after-life specialist online. There might be a few others attending virtually, but probably not. And in 15 minutes, words that hadn't changed much in over 2000 years would be said and we'd leave.

It was my thoughts about the hours after the service that were tying knots in my stomach.

Afternoon, April 9, 2068

After the funeral, Ali and I returned home, changed clothes, and took SCATs to Josh's house. We considered walking, but the forecast showed a 50 percent chance of rain. And since the threat came from a cold front, which if it came would drop the temperature from its current steamy 33 degrees to a much less comfortable 21, we had equal chances of being drenched by a chilling rain or sweating in the heat. Taking the SCATs was an easy decision.

By default, the vehicles would have deposited us in the secure, personal receptacle, where we would have used the GovTag reader to announce our arrival. But the rain had held off, for now, so I had them drop us at the front sidewalk. I got out and stood looking at the front portal, my eyes becoming a bit misty. I turned as Ali departed her vehicle, a sad smile on her face. She came to stand beside me. I slipped my hand onto her back.

"Tough to come back here so soon, isn't it?" she said.

"Yeah." I couldn't think of anything else to say. We walked up the sidewalk and I placed my finger in the door reader, expecting to hear Josh's voice and his familiar greeting. But I didn't.

"Welcome, Dr. Douglas Michaels and Ms. Alison Michaels. I have announced your arrival. Please enter."

When the door opened, there stood a stoic Julia. "Welcome Dr. Michaels, Ms. Michaels. Please come in and make yourself at home."

I had seen Julia from a distance at the funeral. But now, seeing her up close, she seemed to have aged even more in the last two days.

"Hi, Julia," I said. "And it's Doug and Ali, just like always."

"Of course," Julia replied. "It just doesn't seem like always." She took us to a seating area – a sofa and two chairs near the left side wall of the main living area. Ali and I took the sofa. "I'll go get Bette," she said as she left.

After a few moments, I heard, "I missed this old pancake-style house." It was Bette's voice as she approached from behind. She took one of the facing chairs, while Julia took the other. "You know, growing up, my mom always made the pancakes too thin. I always told her, I shouldn't have to put up with this crepe."

I winced, to which Bette said, "Thought you'd like it, Doug," and smiled. "And before you ask, yeah, I changed the greeting. It was too sad hearing Josh's voice every time someone came by ... and it upset Julia too. So, Doug, do you want to talk to Julia now?"

"Sure."

I paused, expecting Bette to leave. But she didn't, and when she noticed my gaze, she said, "Yeah, I've changed my mind. I'll stay ... at least for a while."

"OK," I said, almost adding, 'of course you can stay, Julia's yours.' Fortunately, I caught myself. The issue of ownership was tricky, not legally but psychologically. With Josh, referring to his ownership was a mistake that would raise his ire. To him, Julia was an equal partner, not a possession. But with Bette? Perhaps, she had moved beyond scorn to indifference? Or maybe her distaste remained and Julia was an object to be discarded?

Other than letting this moment create unease in my mind, I hadn't thought much about this talk, and certainly not about specific questions. That was a mistake and I was already feeling a bit off balance. I couldn't upset a machine with an inquiry, but now, being here looking at Julia, it felt ... different. She appeared sad, which is, of course, how she was designed to look in these situations. But what came out of my mouth surprised even me.

"How are you, Julia?"

"I'm OK," she said slowly, quietly. I leaned forward on the sofa to hear her better. "I just miss Josh. It's been so quiet around here until Bette came. It's been nice having someone to talk to."

I was a little surprised that Julia and Bette had been talking, but then, they were alone. "That's good," I said. "Maybe you could tell us about what Josh was doing in the weeks before he went out to the garage?"

"You mean before he killed himself?" Her voice was even lower and I leaned closer. I felt Ali do the same beside me, as she slipped a hand over mine. Julia's gaze dropped to the floor. "I know what happened to my husband."

I winced, partially from her bluntness, but mostly because of how Bette might react to the phrase 'my husband.' I didn't look at Bette, for fear of what I might see there. But she said nothing and made no move to leave.

"OK, I understand," I replied to Julia. "What was he doing in the weeks before he died?"

Julia paused a second, still looking down. "I think we had a good life. We did a lot together, had a lot of good times. But a few months before he died, he just cut himself off from me. It reminded me of the time after the accident at work, but worse."

I tensed and tried to swallow the lump in my throat. "You're talking about the accident to his right hand?"

Julia looked up at me, her eyes moist. "Yes. It was an awful time. It took weeks for him to get over it. I kept asking him if he wanted to talk, but he said no."

I remembered that time too. I comm'ed him often, many of those calls never answered, the rest ending with, 'I just need some time alone.' Eventually, I stopped, thinking that was what he wanted. Now I wondered.

"Finally, the memories faded and he came back to me," said Julia. "I thought he'd do the same this time, but he stayed closed off and now he's dead. He can't come back." She shuddered, put her face in her hands, and started sobbing softly.

Logically, I expected this. But logic was failing me as I choked up at the sight of her crying. After a moment, I managed to say, "The pain will go away, over time."

It felt strange, consoling a machine in such human terms, but in my gut, there was no other response. I chanced a look at the women. Bette was wiping her eyes with a hand, while Ali seemed to be mesmerized, her eyes also moist. Neither woman returned my gaze.

I was about to suggest we try this later when Julia said, "I'm sorry, Doug. I've thought a lot about those weeks. And I think I let Josh down. I've been trying to remember what I did to make him so ... sad ... and need to be alone so much."

In my mind, I held a picture of Bette seething at a robot for speaking so intimately about her ex. But that picture shattered when Bette spoke. "I'm sure you didn't do anything wrong, Julia. Sometimes, people just get sad. We can't help it."

"You're very kind to say that, but I'm not so sure." Again, Julia's gaze dropped to the floor.

I glanced at Bette. This time, the movement caught her eye and she nodded at me, her lips drawn tight, tears forming at the corner of her eyes. I took a deep breath and released it slowly.

"Was anyone coming by to visit with Josh during this time?" After Julia's words, my question sounded cold, prying, even to my ears.

"No, we were alone," Julia responded, looking up for only a moment at the sound of my voice. "Well, Josh shut me down a lot of the time, so he was alone even more. I wish he had talked to me."

"What about earlier, say four or five months ago? Was anyone coming by?"

"Josh had a few acquaintances, like you, Doug, but he never spent a lot of time with them. No, he had few visitors, even at that time."

If Julia was using me, someone who had not been in the house in 14 years, as an acquaintance who might drop by occasionally, then Josh really must have been alone. I could check the house logs, if necessary, but somehow, I doubted I would find anything.

I glanced at the women again and both had their eyes fixed on Julia. So, I went ahead. "Had Josh started working on anything new before he died?"

Julia sighed and shook her head slowly. "Not recently, but about 5 months ago, he started building a new vegetable cart. He said he wanted something a little bigger to haul his produce. He didn't do much woodworking, what with the loss of his hand. The last time he did that, he was building a dog house."

"I never knew he wanted a dog," said Bette. I had the same thought, but Bette was quicker putting it into words.

"Yes. Dick Jefferson – he lives three houses down." Bette nodded in recognition of the name. "Dick was going to give us his dog. He was moving and couldn't take it with him. Josh loved that dog – spent hours playing with him. But the dog was old and died before he ever got to use the dog house."

"He never said a thing to me," said Bette, wiping a tear from her cheek.

"Josh was pretty upset," Julia said. "He probably didn't want to bother you with his problems. He always thought he could handle everything by himself."

Julia's last statement was apparently too much for Bette, as she started sobbing. Ali got up from the sofa, went over to her, and knelt by her chair.

She put her arms around her friend. Julia clenched a fist in front of her mouth as she looked on, blinking back her own tears.

I couldn't continue. My actions felt cruel – to both the woman and the machine. And admittedly, I was also struggling against my emotions. As soon as they were a bit more composed, I was going to suggest a delay. But between sobs, Bette looked at Julia and asked, "Maybe it wasn't an old friend who came by? Maybe someone Josh had started to work with?" Her voice trembled with each word.

I sunk back on the couch, as Ali returned to my side, her hand again taking mine. My misunderstanding of Bette ran deeper than I had thought. She was at least confused about and perhaps sympathetic toward Julia. But even more surprising to me, Bette was willing to prolong her pain in hopes that she might learn something more about Josh's death. I had again sorely misjudged her need for closure.

"No, no jobs that I know about," Julia managed to say after a moment.

I clenched my teeth, then plunged ahead. "What about trips, say for wine tasting or something like that?" If Julia mentioned the name Amschulter, perhaps we could bring this discussion to a close more quickly. Mentally, I had my fingers crossed.

Julia looked up at me, tilting her head slightly as she rubbed a hand over her eyes. "Josh didn't care for wine, but no ... I don't remember him mentioning any trips. He kept busy with his electronic toys. He was always reading about the latest developments, and hatching plans to buy as much new tech as he could afford." She paused to take a breath. "Would you excuse me a moment?"

"Of course," I said. Then, Julia rose and left the room.

"Where's she going?" Ali asked, her eyes traveling between Bette and me.

I shook my head as Bette said, "I have no idea."

Julia returned in a moment and sat again in the chair. "Sorry, but Bette asked if I would make you a few recordings from the last couple of months. Just stuff from around the house. I thought I should give it to you now. I've been such a wreck. I keep forgetting things." She handed me a memory capsule. "It's just a random sample."

"A random sample?" I said, wondering if some machine logic would emerge and spoil the illusion of her humanity.

"Yes," she said. "Josh always told me you were into statistics. That's what you'd want, isn't it?"

"Yes, of course. It's extremely nice of you," I said, hoping the words would remove the look of concern on her face. They did and she smiled sadly.

I had no idea that Josh ever spoke of me, and now, I was close to becoming distraught myself. But I was down to my final inquiry and was determined to finish. The only trouble was that it was a question that seemed acceptable when Bette wasn't around. Now that she was, the dynamics might change dramatically and I dreaded that possibility.

"So, with all Josh's interest in technology and ... the like. Did he ever work on any of your software?"

Ali's hand tightened around mine. Out of the corner of my eye, I saw Bette recoil slightly, but I kept my eyes focused on Julia. She, on the other hand, showed no reaction beyond the sadness that had pervaded our conversation.

"Josh was a bright individual – very smart, very gifted. But no, even accessing my programming would have been beyond his skills."

I was finished and glanced at Ali. She gave me an almost imperceptible shake of the head, as she sat back on the sofa. We seemed to share the same sense of relief, as Ali loosened her grip on my hand. I was about to start our goodbyes when Julia spoke.

"You probably have all kinds of stories about Josh and his wild enthusiasm for technology. But he also had a soft, human side. I don't know how many times I came into his study – he called it his study, even though it's just that area over there with the big, walnut desk and the easy chair." She pointed across the room to the far wall. "He'd be sitting there, watching the neighbor's young daughter playing with her dad on the CommCover. I think his one regret, marrying me, was that we couldn't have kids." Her head dropped into her hands.

Bette looked stricken and raised a hand to her trembling lips. Tears started streaming down her cheeks again. I could feel Ali shifting, restless at my side. "He never, ever mentioned any regrets marrying you," Bette said between sobs.

Julia's breath caught in her throat and she nodded slowly, her face still buried. After a moment she looked up. "I'm terribly sorry, but I'm tired. I'm going to lay down for a while." She stood and left.

When she was gone, Ali got up from the sofa and pushed the other chair closer to Bette. She took the seat and laid a hand softly on Bette's arm. We all sat there quietly for several moments until Bette broke the silence. "She's a wreck."

I could see Ali's hand tightened on her friend's arm, the two women exchanging glances.

"I haven't been here long, but I've found her a couple of times, sitting alone, crying." Bette held out her open hands. "One time, she wanted to pull weeds in the garden. Said it took her mind off things. But when I found her later, she was staring at an old picture, tears on her cheeks. I thought she'd be able to handle things, but she's worse off than me."

Bette looked at me, questions in her eyes, but I didn't know what to say. Sure, I had accepted machine intelligences as our intellectual superiors long ago. I even had the educational background and technical experience in human learning and memory to back it up. But accepting their emotions as 'real?' That was a problem. It was one of the reasons I was looking up from below the rim of the uncanny valley. But with this experience, it didn't seem right to say it was just a bunch of lines of computer code either.

To my relief, Ali stepped in. "I took a crash course in emotive robots. We were wondering if they might help with some of our patients."

"And do they?" asked Bette.

"Actually, yes," said Ali. "We have several now. Most clients like them better than the humans on staff." She touched her forehead with the fingertips of one hand, shaking her head. "Sorry, that didn't come out quite right."

"No, I know what you mean," said Bette. "People don't worry about complaining to a machine. Or baring their soul."

"Exactly," said Ali. "Anyway, in this class, they told us that there's a lot of almost imperceptible changes in a mechanion when it adopts a specific mood. If you took readings on Julia now, you'd find that her voice is a bit softer than usual. Her speech and movements – they're just a little bit slower. And when she looks at you, her eyes never quite get to your level. It's like she's looking at your nose or at the floor."

"But she sounds so ... broken up," said Bette. "It's not just the volume or her movements; it's all the sad stuff she's remembering – the dog, the way Josh watched the neighbors and wanted kids. She sounds like I felt ... well, when Josh and I split up. Is it real?"

"Yeah, in a way," said Ali.

It's real?

I had never known Ali to exaggerate, except when she was teasing. One look at her now told me she was completely serious.

"Mechanions' processing is similar to the ways we think – at least in some important ways. For example, the tiredness Julia mentioned isn't totally an act. With the loss of Josh, lots of memory records started competing for processing, but few are resolved each time they come up. They just keep recycling, draining her energy. She experienced a need to stop and recover, just like a person would. And as for all those sad thoughts? When people are sad, they tend to remember other sad things. When they're happy, they tend to recall the good times. Honey, what's that called again?"

"In people, it's 'mood congruence.' It's the tendency for us to recall memories consistent with our mood." Ali nodded.

"Julia's processing is similar," continued Ali. "In these sad times, sad memories take priority. She's having sad thoughts because she has no choice; its what's in her electronic brain. And it's why she's distracted and forgetful, just like anyone would be in her position."

Bette sat there quietly, apparently pondering these ideas. I did likewise because these were details I had never heard.

"Over time, we usually get over ... whatever it is that's bothering us," said Bette. "Will Julia?"

"Yes, she will," said Ali. "Over time, sad memories will lose their priority, they'll be fewer things calling for her attention, and she'll get back to being herself."

"Good. She needs to move on," said Bette, softly but firmly.

Considering Ali's thoughts, I needed another favor. I turned to Bette. "Because Julia will be getting more of her memory back – so to speak – would you mind if I came back in a few days to talk to her again?"

"Of course," said Bette. "I would appreciate that. Ali, will you come too?"

"If there's any way I can, I'll be here," she replied.

We said our goodbyes and left. Once outside, I had Suze check the weather. In the hour at Bette's, a line of storms had pushed through, resulting in cooler temperatures and lower humidity. We decided to walk. We had only taken the first steps, however, when we realized that the stroll might not be as pleasant as we had hoped. Some distant fire fueled by lands that had seen little water in months or an immense temperature inversion that had trapped pollution for weeks had produced a smoggy mix that had tainted the rain before it reached the ground. So, for today's stroll, sidewalks and lawns that glistened with moisture were spoiled by a slight odor carried on the breeze and a bitter taste left in your mouth.

The disheartening effect of our surroundings only served to reinforce our gloomy talk with Julia. I was having trouble leaving the conversation behind. Apparently, so was Ali. "Well, that was certainly depressing."

"Agreed," I replied. "I'm glad you knew about how mechanions process emotional content. I would have been lost."

"Emotional content?" Ali chuckled. "You're such a scientist." Then, she put an arm around my shoulder as we walked along. All I could think was, isn't that what you call it?

After a moment, Ali said, "I think we went where we needed to go. Bette wanted to hear that Julia's a machine, but that she has some of the same hang-ups as us. And she wanted to hear that it's OK to like her."

"To like her?" I said, turning to look at my wife. "What gave you that idea?"

Ali just smiled, as she shifted gears. "I heard Julia's answer, but do you think there's any chance that Josh re-programmed her, somehow messed up her logic?"

"I doubt it," I said. "Today's robots are built by the generation that grew up with stories about machines getting out of control and killing their creators. We've taken that threat very seriously. Burned into her hardware is programming that prevents harm to humans. So, for that programming to get corrupted and her and all her connections to the virtual world to register nothing? That would be nearly impossible."

"Yeah, I thought so, but knew you would know," Ali replied. "Hmm, OK. You've also mentioned a couple of times that ... I'm not sure how to say this exactly, but that Josh had Julia designed to have her own opinions. He didn't want a 'yes man,' or maybe, that's a 'yes wife?' You know what I'm talking about?"

"Sure, babe. And you're wondering if, within the limits he set, she somehow snapped."

"Yeah, more or less," Ali said.

"Possibly, but again, that seems very unlikely. PSS checked for any type of emotionally charged exchanges in Julia's records. There was nothing there of a violent nature."

"Could those records be altered or erased?" asked Ali.

"Again, technically it's possible, but those types of alterations would stand out. Josh told me about doing it once. He had to take Julia to some specific office in Chicago. His DNA was verified, as was their marriage. Then, two other people who were witnessing the change were verified by their DNA. Finally, a certified technician made the change and everyone electronically signed a record of the event. Josh said it was a pain and he'd never do it again."

"So, Julia gave him such a hard time, he wanted that memory gone so she wouldn't act on it again?" asked Ali.

I hesitated. I had never told anyone this story. It was not that Josh had sworn me to secrecy, but he wouldn't want his life with Julia becoming public knowledge. Under the circumstances, however, Ali was trying to help and I felt Josh would approve.

"No, it wasn't like that. It was an argument and it got heated like you guessed. But it wasn't Julia who got out of hand, it was Josh. Afterward, he was so depressed about what he had said, he was desperate to get the memory erased. He didn't want Julia to think less of him."

Ali just nodded and we walked the rest of the way home in silence, each of us lost in our own thoughts.

Tuesday, April 10, 2068

Morning

The pall that surrounded us after the talk with Julia and the walk home had slowly dissipated over the evening, and by Tuesday morning, I was ready to return to my retroscape. It was still far from a highly detailed, mental map depicting all of the peaks and valleys of Josh's life, but I was making progress.

Amschulter hadn't been forthcoming. His time with Josh was clearly more extensive than he was admitting, giving him an opportunity to demonstrate the immortality scheme and plant a seed of despair. And his motive, the huge paycheck he could demand, was a major feature, a towering mountain in my mental landscape. What was lacking, however, was means. Where was the technological breakthrough necessary for this enterprise to be anything other than fantasy? And who could manipulate GovTags without detection? Over the years, I had made use of the Sir Arthur Conan Doyle saying, "Once you eliminate the impossible, whatever remains, no matter how improbable, must be the truth." But the web of speculation I had woven this time might be pushing that dictum too far.

But we hadn't reached impossible ... yet.

Once I was seated in my office, I had Suze play the recordings Julia had made for me. I suspected Bette had specified the timeframe for my 'random sample,' because the first video was around the start of Josh's self-imposed, 14-week isolation.

"Good morning, love," said Julia. "Did you sleep well?" She was in the kitchen area of their home, Josh approaching a slab of transparent material they used as a table.

Since the recording was from Julia's perspective, I could see Josh. He was a bit bedraggled. His hair was uncombed and he had a day growth of beard. He was still dressed in pajamas and was rubbing the sleep from his eyes. I knew from my own retirement that his state wasn't necessarily unusual, and it was certainly less distressing than I had imagined when I watched the final comm with Amschulter. But then, that comm had been a week or two later.

"Fine," Josh said, managing a tired smile.

"I thought I heard you up around 3:00."

Josh didn't look at her. It seemed like he hadn't heard, as he continued to stumble forward. Finally, he said, "Just a little restless. I got up, read for a while."

It was quiet for a time, as Josh dropped into a chair. There was a cup of coffee on the table as if it was his standing order for breakfast but nothing else. Eventually, Julia said, "That doesn't sound very restful."

Josh took a sip and answered without looking up. "I'm OK. What's the weather forecast for today?"

"Warmer, around seven degrees and partly cloudy," replied Julia. "Are you thinking about getting out?" Her tone brightened as she spoke. I wondered if Josh had already been limiting his exposure to the world for some time.

"No," he replied. I kept thinking he would explain, say something more, but that was his only response for some time as he sipped his coffee. Finally, he said, "I'm going to my study. I have some things to read and I want to be alone." He got up from the table and left.

After that first video, Josh's appearance and behavior deteriorated rapidly. His face became ashen and covered with a heavy stubble. There were bags under his eyes. His wardrobe alternated between dirty PJs and filthy sweats. And in the background of each shot, I could see his home was on the same, downward spiral, trash piling up on every available surface.

I paused the replays, wondering how things could have deteriorated so far in a house loaded with intelligent automation. Explaining Julia's inaction was easy; in one video, I had seen Josh tell her to stop picking up his clothes. But the rest of the house? It acted like no one was at home, with lights coming on and doors opening only after he or Julia asked. I didn't know any home had such an unaccommodating mode.

Throughout the videos, Josh never seemed angry or upset with Julia. In fact, his speech was soft and nearly without inflection. There was, however, one exception. In that instance, Julia said she thought Josh needed to see a doctor. He exploded. "I'll shut you down and leave you in the garage to rust if you threaten me again." He stomped out of the room.

I wondered why PSS hadn't flagged the outburst for further investigation, but the fact that it lasted less than ten seconds probably explained it. The time frame, however, spoke volumes to me. It was only a few hours before Josh turned Julia off for the last time. Twelve days later, he was dead.

When I finished the last video, I felt ill. I had spent the last hour with my jaw clenched, my fists working as acid flooded my stomach. I couldn't sit in my office any longer. I had to get out, walk off the pent-up tension, and corral my emotions. The wall had reverted to a view of the neighborhood and I could see it was overcast, perhaps drizzling. I should have grabbed a jacket – Suze even chided me for the omission – but I no longer cared.

I wandered aimlessly, the mist gathering in my hair, droplets running down my face and mixing with tears of rage and helplessness. I was an old man, but I wanted to smash something with my fists. If PSS failed to clear Amschulter but couldn't act on what they had, I would.

After about an hour, I returned home, soaked and shivering. I had no insights. I had decided nothing, but I had numbed the pain, at least for a while. I dropped my clothes in the refreshing chute, took a hot shower, and got dressed. I felt better but knew those images of Josh slowly dying would return ... again and again.

"Doug, are you OK?" Suze's voice from the CommCover startled me. "You've been acting unusual."

"I'm OK. Just a lot on my mind."

"OK, but if you need to talk ...."

For once, I actually considered the offer. Based on what Ali had said, her thinking would be influenced by the same processes and limitations as mine – a thought that I found strangely comforting as if she would understand. But before I had decided, Suze spoke again. "Bette comm'ed while you were cleaning up. She and Ali talked, then she left a recording for both of you. Ali said to let her know when you wanted to watch it."

"Where is she?"

"In the living room."

As I walked down the short hall, I felt a flicker of hope. In all likelihood, Bette had just come up with her latest bad joke and couldn't wait to tell us. But emotions have a mind of their own; maybe she had found something.

When I entered the living room, Ali was talking to a picture.

"Make the sunrise just a bit brighter. Hmm."

"A new masterpiece?" I asked, approaching from behind.

She turned. "A new application anyway. Something called SM–ART2." I looked at her blankly. "SMART ART," she said, spelling it out.

"I hope their results are better than the name," I said, looking closely. The lower, right corner was dark, with a hint of ghostly figures moving in the shadows. It was eerie and I shivered as the shapes seemed to melt into the background, then reappear. Scanning up and to the left, people working in fields, tending to livestock and harvesting crops came into focus. And in the top, left corner, a hazy sun was just appearing over the horizon.

Ali's nose wrinkled in disgust as she turned to me. "What were you thinking about?" she asked, then raised a hand. "Amschulter, right?"

"Yeah. How'd you guess?"

"The picture is called 'The Dawn of New Hope.' The bottom corner is supposed to be hell and the top ... well, new hope. It picks up on emotion and hell got downright spooky when you came in. It could only be Roger R."

I scowled at the picture, unintentionally pushing the scene to new depths of gloom.

"SM–ART2 stop," Ali said, and the scene turned placid, static. "I'll try something else later because that's not going to work. You here to see the comm from Bette?" I nodded and Suze put it on the wall.

"Hey, guys. Sometimes I think the only reason for the good ol' days is bad memory."

It was probably because of my mood, but for once I didn't groan. In fact, I mumbled, "Ain't that the truth."

Ali smirked, as the recording continued. "And speaking of bad memories, I understand my forgetting, but you two are some smarties. What's your excuse? The copy of Josh's notes ... ring any bells? You forgot them when you were over here, so I'm sending them now.

"Overall, they make no sense to me – just some weird things that I have trouble believing even happened. And he mentions a couple of people in them. Said he was becoming just like one of them. Let's see, who was that? Oh yes, he was becoming like Armen Yates. The name seems familiar, but I can't quite place it. Anyway, hope this stuff helps. Talk later."

Bette disappeared from the screen. Ali and I froze.

"Is that who I think it is?" asked Ali slowly.

"If you're thinking the out-of-work, construction worker that killed Ed and the Deputy Director of the Smart Pill Project and left Josh without his right hand, then yeah, it is," I said. "I'm surprised that Bette doesn't remember, but then, maybe she's worked hard to forget those days."

I tented my fingers in front of my face, considering this new information. "Until this moment, I wondered if I was deluding myself, making too much out of a three-word phrase I heard twice in 14 years. I mean, if you look long and hard enough at anything, it starts to look like a pattern."

"Yeah, but Josh must have seen it too," Ali replied. "And what's even scarier, he saw and wrote about the connection to Yates days before anyone said he was 'not a person.' If that's a coincidence, it has to be the strangest one ever."

Afternoon, April 10, 2068

After lunch, I went to my office to read through Josh's notes. Ali was going to join me later after she made a few comms.

Somehow, I had gotten the impression from Bette that there were a lot of notes. In fact, there were only six pages, and most of those sheets weren't filled. But then again, I wasn't sure anyone else had written six pages by hand anytime in the last twenty years. Why would they, when you could utter any phrase to your virtuant and have it recreated in any form from Morse code to chipped in granite?

The content of Josh's pages, as it turned out, was mostly trivia – definitely not worth granite.

> *Low on protein – can't believe I had Julia just get veggie matter last time. Where's my head?*
>
> *Should have Julia print the daily news – local anyway. Well, maybe national too.*

But there was also a fair amount that indicated that he was increasingly suspicious of ... well, just about all of the technology in his home.

> *Inserted my finger into GovTag Reader today. Was certain that it actually extracted something, maybe blood. I didn't see anything inside, even after I removed the cover.*
>
> *CommCover seems to have a mind of its own. It keeps going back to all sorts of recordings I never authorized. Going to delete them again.*

I was nearly finished and still had found nothing about Armen Yates. Maybe Bette was mistaken. But as I read the next to last page, the name jumped out at me.

"There you are," I muttered aloud.

"You were looking for me?" I jumped as Ali's voice came from the doorway. "Sorry," she said. "Ah, for the days when our house had creaky floors. So, since it's not me you just found, who was it?"

"I finally got to the part where Josh wrote about Yates. Up 'til now, it's been all this weird stuff."

"Like what?" Ali asked, frowning as she entered my office and put a hand on my shoulder.

"Like he thought his lawn-tending robot was spying on him." I looked up, seeing her eyes tracking back and forth across the CommCover as she skimmed the page.

"Bizarre," she muttered after a moment. "And his comment about Yates – I'm becoming just like him. Even creepier."

The next logical question would be, what in Yates' background matched Josh? I had always figured that Yates was one of the last holdouts in a field of holdouts. Construction hadn't come fully under intelligent machine control until the late 40s; it took time to develop machines capable of handling every complexity Mother Nature could throw at a construction team as they built bridges, dug tunnels, erected buildings. In my mind, Yates just happened to be willing to use violence to keep the machines at bay. Every occupation had people like that.

But if Yates opposed machine involvement in the workplace, was Josh coming to that same position? Did Josh's strange paranoia about his home reflect a total reversal in his beliefs?

But that seemed impossible. Everything I knew about my friend, all the features of the retroscape said he was pro-technology ... almost to the extreme. Could I be wrong about Yates? Just where had I gotten my information about him?

But as I considered that question, I realized I had no information, just assumptions. Every time a headline had read, 'Unemployed Construction Worker Assassinates Government Official,' I had turned away. I didn't know Yates. I didn't want to hear his life story, to learn his justification for the attack, to relive that day.

I glanced at Ali. She had been waiting for me to come to this decision, to do what I dreaded. "Guess it's time to learn a bit more about Mr. Yates," I said to her, then turned to the CommCover. "Suze, see what you can find on Armen Yates' reason for killing Deputy Director Sandi O'Connor in November 2054." One benefit of all my retroscape work – I knew these dates off the top of my head.

It was only a moment until Suze said, "There're several such reports, each saying substantially the same thing. Would you like to hear one?"

"Yes, and start it at his reasons for the attack. We don't need the background."

A reporter appeared onscreen with a street and building behind him. I knew the location well. The street ran in front of the Ruger-Phillips complex. Just in the corner of the picture, I could see the gates to their offices. In a much more prominent position, just over the reporter's right shoulder, stood the building where the attack had occurred.

The reporter said, "That's right, Bill. Last night, around 10:30, the Criminal Apprehension Service entered Armen Yates' apartment and removed his computer and several boxes of documents. This morning, in a prepared statement, the lead investigator at CAS revealed that the documents they found supported the ban of EM-40h, more commonly known as the smart pill. Authorities now believe that Yates killed Dr. O'Connor because he believed O'Connor would push for the widespread use of the drug. This revelation comes in the wake of several of the government's own contractors questioning the need for the cocktail of neurotransmitters, including the presentation that was being given by Worthington-Huston Technology at the moment of the attack."

There was more, but I had what I wanted. "Thanks, Suze," I said, then looked back at Ali. "I don't believe it. Yates killed O'Connor for the same reason that Josh wanted to make the presentation. And since both of them were against human management of machine intelligences all along, that can't be the growing connection."

"At least we eliminated that possibility," said Ali. "Maybe there's more in the rest of Josh's notes. How much do you have left?"

"Not much. Maybe a page and a half." But by the time I had spoken and turned to her, I could see she was reading.

"I've already finished the first entry," she said. "You need to get scrolling."

So, I did. The next few lines were more daily trivia – a note to have Julia order some fish, one to get her to schedule service on the SCAT transfer system, and another about the lawn-tending robot going berserk. I was about to say, 'what a waste of time' when I noticed Ali lean forward. She was staring at the CommCover. I turned back to Josh's final entry.

Finally, I know who's behind all of this. Jacob Wiggins.

"You know this guy?" I asked. Ali shook her head, her eyes never leaving the wall. I looked back at the entry. "Bette said there were two names, but

I didn't expect Josh to blame one of them and her not mention it. Want to check him out?"

But when I turned back to my wife, she had taken a corner of the CommCover and was wordlessly directing her virtuant in a search. It produced a result.

I stood from my chair and walked over to get a closer look. A picture of a man with sandy brown hair, dark-rimmed glasses, and a goatee stared back at me. You had to wonder about someone who would wear glasses when there was no lack of options that made them obsolete. Maybe he liked the look? And the goatee – also not exactly a fashion statement in 2068. I wondered where he got his idiosyncratic tastes. Below the picture was a caption reading, Dr. Jacob Wiggins, Assistant Director for the Bureau for Population Management - Central Division, St. Louis National Population Records Center.

"Damn, the BPM inside man," I muttered aloud. "High enough to be able to manipulate the system, low enough to escape notice." I walked back to my desk and sat, saying, "I'm comm'ing Finnegan now."

"Looks like you won't need to," said Ali. "She's calling you."

"You in for this call?"

"Just try to get me to leave," she replied.

"Suze, please put the Chief Technician on."

There was a delay, most likely because Finnegan had put us on hold when we didn't answer immediately. It would only take a few seconds for her to issue a command to her virtuant or to correct a subordinate, but the wait seemed interminable. I wanted to hear that PSS had evidence against Amschulter ... or at least, that they couldn't clear him and so, had started surveillance. Then, I'd drop Wiggin's name in her lap. Everything might be wrapped up in a couple of days.

"Dr. Michaels ... Doug, good morning. I have good news," Finnegan said, her red hair framing a smile as she appeared on the wall. Then, she saw Ali behind me.

I did the introductions, then got to the heart of the matter. "So, Amschulter's involved in Josh's death?"

The Chief Technician's smile disappeared. "Oh, no, sorry," she stammered. "It's not news about your friend's death. It's just that Mr. Amschulter isn't lodging any type of complaint about your call. I guess you really had dismissed that possibility."

I slumped in my chair, glancing at Ali, then back to the wall. "Yeah, I had. I thought sure he was hiding something."

"Actually, he was, but nothing that has anything to do with your friend's death."

"Can you tell us what it was?" My hope had been rekindled. I hadn't revealed my far-fetched plot to Finnegan – the one where Josh's memories got overridden by someone else's. I didn't want to be labeled a crackpot. But maybe something that seemed harmless to her took on a different meaning in light of my wild theory.

Finnegan chuckled. "I thought you might ask and Mr. Amschulter said it was OK to tell you. I don't think he meant to be mysterious, but he didn't know anything about you. And what he's doing has an element of competition in it."

Competition?

"He's set up something like a cooperative truck farm," continued Finnegan. "Although big social events like weddings or business lunches are a rarity because ... well, you know the reasons. But when they happen, people are willing to pay for a spread of fresh produce. He's filling that demand."

I let out a long sigh, not seeing any way this secret supported my speculations. "So, Josh was one of his suppliers?" I asked, hardly caring how she might answer.

"They were working out the details," the Chief Technician replied. "Amschulter has agreements with a couple of other people, one on the east coast and one in the south. He had approached Josh about covering the Midwest. Amschulter fills most of each order, but he brings in these other suppliers when he needs more capacity."

It made sense. The comm with the shipping times assured that Josh's and Amschulter's produce reached the destination at the same time. The comm about the trial run to Seattle was just part of 'working out the details.'

"I also talked to one of his other partners, to be sure," continued Finnegan. "He's been doing this for about five years. Said he thought Mr. Amschulter was as upstanding as they come. He even said that Amschulter gives him parts of an order when he knows he could have filled it himself. I guess that's just good business – keeping his partners happy."

"Thanks, Chief Technician," I said after a moment, my shoulders slumping in defeat. "Thanks for checking it out so thoroughly."

Finnegan looked at me closely, pity coming to her face. When she spoke, it was with compassion. "I think you need to seriously consider the possibility that Josh died at his own hand for his own reasons. It's the only explanation that fits what we've found." She paused again, still watching me. "I also need to warn you about investigating on your own. If it came to a complaint that you were overzealous, you'd get some sympathy for your loss, but a pattern of pursuing innocent people on your own .... Well, let's just say you don't want to press your luck."

"Thanks, I understand." She nodded and we disconnected.

"I still say Wiggins is the perfect inside man at BPM," I said turning to my wife. "The only question is, perfect for what?"

Wednesday, April 11, 2068

Noon

could feel the weight of Ali's stare as I entered the kitchen. I even knew the reason for the look. That was unusual; I was usually clueless. I turned to her.

"This has to be some sort of record," she said. "You've had Wiggins name for a day, and you haven't given it to PSS, which was my suggestion. But more surprising, you haven't checked him out on your own, which I'm sure you're dying to do."

We had eaten a late breakfast, and so, were snacking for lunch. She was at the island, working on a salad. I'd come in to make a sandwich. I pulled ingredients out of cold storage, opting to make my own rather than letting the prep station handle it. "How do you know I haven't called him?"

"You didn't say anything about it earlier, and the log shows no recent comms. Ergo, no contact. Are you having second thoughts?"

"You're right," I said. "I better call Finnegan." I started layering my sandwich with lettuce, tomatoes, and chicken salad, using up the last of the fresh tomatoes.

Ali watched me a few seconds, then a smile curled the corners of her mouth. "You know, you're not fooling me. You're not going to call PSS."

"Yeah, I know. But I'm not having second thoughts either. I've been ... considering my options. BPM is a powerful organization. And while Wiggins isn't exactly the 'top dog,' he's no lightweight either. I mean, why would he talk to me? And if I find contact info for his home, then I'm going down the harassment path that Finnegan warned me about." I sat down at the island, my lunch masterpiece on a plate in front of me. "Guess I'm wasting time. There's probably no cover story that would hold up with the resources he has. Any reason I shouldn't go ahead and comm him now?"

"Not that I know," replied Ali.

"Suze, connect me to Dr. Jacob Wiggins at BPM."

After an unusually long delay for a comm, Suze said, "I don't see a way to contact him directly, but he does have some type of messaging system. It's not standard, or a service I've seen before, but I believe you'll be able to request a callback."

"That sounds fine," I said. "Give me an audio and video link then."

"Sorry, Doug," Suze replied. "But it's not showing options. I'm not sure what you'll get."

"Hmm. OK, put me through. I'll draw a picture if I have to."

When the link was established, Wiggins appeared in a recorded message. "Thank you for contacting the St. Louis National Population Records Center, Bureau for Population Management. The St. Louis branch of the BPM is a vast operation, tasked with maintaining the identification and taxation records of nearly one-fourth of the citizens of the United States. That's why your call is so important to us.

"To make sure your concerns are handled quickly and correctly, we have a set of machine intelligences designed to listen and act on your issues immediately. No forms, no waiting, no mistakes. Please select one from the list now appearing to my right by saying his or her name. I'm confident that any one of them will be able to help. And if not, they can always schedule an appointment with the responsible office or department. Thank you for calling the BPM."

As I scanned the list, I spotted a familiar name. "Censere?" I said aloud.

"Were you asking for him or just surprised?" asked Ali.

"Well, the latter, but I don't think it makes any difference now. I'm being connected."

"Salutes 'ro," said Censere, when his round face and slightly red nose appeared on the wall. "Be peeking for …. Well, Halifax, Doug. I thought we had your age corrected."

Ali snickered at my side, then asked, "Have you tried any of the big three F's – freaking, fracking, and frigging? Might give you some more options."

"Sorry, Ali, but I wore those out on my first day. And I really thought we'd taken care of the age problem."

"It always seems to come back," I said. "But it's not so bad. I get kids' rates at any place that has them. And if they don't, I show them my real age and get the senior discount. It's a win-win. But that's not why I'm here."

"So, what's the reason for this unexpected pleasure?" asked the BPM machine intelligence. "And please feel free to continue your lunch. I'm fluent in all manner of communication, including talking with your mouth full."

I considered the possible comebacks but decided I'd never win a battle of quips with Censere. "I believe the last time we talked, you said there were several ways I could get an answer to my question about processing DNA records. I'd like to talk to a human about that issue."

"I'd say you're going with second best," said Censere, "but then, there are a dozen machine intelligences that could do better. Do you really want an option that's not even in the top ten?"

"I think humankind has just been insulted," I replied.

"No, not at all. I get some of my best maintenance from humans." He paused a beat. "Just a little machine humor."

After I finished my grimace and Ali her titter, Censere continued. "But seriously, Doug, as a source of hard data, which I know you prefer, people are really poor substitutes for systems like me. I mean, you're the scientist. What do you prefer? A human who changes what they see and what they remember, or a machine that records everything in precise detail? Do you prefer a machine whose records are pristine for centuries or people whose storage starts to leak even before the data gets in? It's no contest, you have to admit."

"Perhaps so," I said. "But in this case, I'd like to put myself in the hands of a misperceiving and forgetful human. I'd like to talk to Dr. Jacob Wiggins."

"Hmm, an interesting choice," said Censere, now stroking his chin. "I'll ask, but he doesn't really seem like the best person for this issue and he is extremely busy. If I were you, I'd be expecting an audience with someone else. Wow, that was a depressing thought – if I were you."

I had to chuckle at that remark. "Thanks, Censere. I'll be waiting for a comm." I cut the link.

I glanced back at Ali, who had finished her salad and was rinsing the plate. "You know, I'm pretty sure Censere lost some respect for you," she said.

"Yeah, what was I thinking? Insisting on talking to a fallible human when I could have gotten it straight from his mouth."

Thursday, April 12, 2068

Morning

Coming down the hall from our bedroom toward the kitchen, I could smell something. Ali was cooking and unless my nose deceived me, it contained strawberries. It smelled great.

"Is that breakfast?"

"It's a strawberry-rhubarb pie, both fresh from the garden. And, in case you've forgotten, pies are for dinner." I frowned in an exaggerated display of disappointment. Ali patted me on the head and said, "Poor baby," in her syrupiest tone.

She checked the hot prep station, as I took a seat at the island. "You may want to sit down for this," I said.

Ali turned from the appliance and gave me a quizzical look. "What is it?"

"You sure you don't want to sit first?" Her look turned to a frown, so I got to the point. "I received a response from BPM and ... it's from Wiggins himself."

Her frown didn't disappear. If anything, it deepened. "I'm not sure that's a good thing."

"Why not? It's what I asked for."

Ali turned from the station and took a step forward, putting her directly across the island from me. She put her hands on the countertop.

Is she forgetting about the pie?

"Someone that high in the BPM, answering a routine question about processing a DNA record?" said Ali. "That's ... well, not the reaction I expected."

"Me either," I admitted. "But the question's not exactly routine. It stumped one of their machines, so maybe they want to keep it human to human."

Ali sighed, walked around the island, and took a seat beside me. "What'd he say?"

"Is the pie OK?" I asked. With all of the automation watching over it, it wasn't going to burn, but I couldn't help it. The aroma was driving me crazy.

Ali laughed. "Yes, Doug, it's fine. It needs another five minutes, not five seconds. Want me to run diagnostics on the sensors?"

I shook my head sheepishly. "No, I'm sure they're fine. Suze, can you display the message from Jacob Wiggins."

I resigned myself to a breakfast of milk substitute on a bowl of fiber and carbohydrate flakes with dried, artificial banana slices, this one called A-Peeling Morning. While Ali read the message from Wiggins, I dispensed a bowl, which produced a picture of a half-peeled banana and flakes on the station's screen.

Dr. Michaels –

I received your request from Censere and listened to your conversation with him. Quite the gem, isn't he? I also looked you up in our records – nothing private, just public information.

After looking at all that, I think we should talk in person. Your transactions suggest that you get out in public, interact with people as needed (OK, that's not strictly public knowledge, but I'm trying to help.) Can you come to the BPM facility in St. Louis on Friday? I'm in building 4, room 208. I'll let Security know to expect you and they'll have a temporary badge waiting at the entry gate.

Please let me know if this is acceptable.

Jacob Wiggins

Ali pushed back from the island as I re-seated myself with my cereal and a cup of coffee. She started pacing. "You asked for information yesterday afternoon, at what, 4:30?" she asked.

"Yeah, about then."

She stopped walking and stared at me. "Look at the time stamp. He responded six hours later."

"So?"

An icy stare was her response.

"OK, maybe I got lucky, hit him at a slow time," I said.

"His workday runs 'til 10:30? And he wants you to come to his office tomorrow? Tomorrow! I don't like that you're meeting on his turf."

"His turf?" I started to chuckle at her choice of words, then thought better of it and swallowed the laugh. "Are you expecting a rumble?" I had to search my memory carefully, but I thought rumble was the right word.

"Not funny, Douglas Michaels," she said, scowling at me. "You know what I mean."

And I did. But this was 2068, not Capone-era, Chicago politics.

"I'll be fine," I replied. "It's a government building, middle of the day, lots of people." Before she could start dissecting each of those assurances, I said, "Suze, show me a map of the BPM facilities in St. Louis." It was immediately on the wall. "Let's see. It looks like the BPM complex is up north, in the old National Personnel Records Center – or at least where the Center used to be."

"I was there a long time ago when there was only one large building," Ali said. "Looks like there're four now."

"And the one I want is right here." I pointed to a smaller building on the back edge of the property labeled Building 4. Beyond it, there was a sparsely populated neighborhood, with patches of cleared ground, most likely gardens, scattered here and there.

"Yeah, that looks like the one," said Ali. "And by the way, nice try at changing the subject, but bottom line – I'm going too."

A look at her told me I had little chance of changing her mind, but before I could try, she answered me. "Look, you're probably right," she said. "Wiggins is probably completely trustworthy, and the whole meeting will be nothing but boring, bureaucratic PR. And since that's all it's going to be, you shouldn't have any problem with me coming along."

"OK. I'll accept his invitation and tell him to expect two."

"And while you're replying, how about suggesting we meet him for lunch outside his building? He has to eat too."

"Sure." After a moment's thought, I asked, "Can I blame the request on you, say you detest meeting in boring office buildings?"

"How about saying your wife suggested we take a hard-working, public official out to enjoy something besides cafeteria food?"

I chuckled. "Masterfully spun. That'll be our reply." I turned to the wall to send a comm just in time to see one incoming. "Looks like Bette's calling."

"Suze, can you put her on," said Ali.

"Hey, guys." She looked at the picture still showing on the prep station, then said, "Is that a banana in your cereal, or are you glad to see me?"

I had to give her credit for keen eyesight and smiled for a change.

"I suppose you've adjusted to the time difference by now," said Ali, "but even so, isn't it awfully early for you?"

"Yes, and it's all Julia's fault," Bette said. "She has me on this workout routine. I'm so sore I can hardly walk." She shook her head and frowned, playing up her discomfort. "But it'll pay off."

"It will," said Ali.

"Anyway, guys, I wanted to let you know, I'm heading back home on Saturday. Everything's in motion here. There's no reason for me to stick around. But there are a few things I want to show you before I leave."

"Nothing wrong, I hope," Ali said, her brow furrowing.

"Oh no, girlfriend, just some stuff that's curious. Doug, you knew Josh had that invisible room along the back of the house, right?"

"Invisible room?" asked Ali, turning to me.

"Yeah, Josh showed it to me once," I said to Bette. Then, turning to my wife, "There are actually two walls along the back of the house. The CommCover on the inner wall displays whatever the rest of the walls in the house are showing. So, if they're set on an outside view, this wall would show the backyard, even though there's a narrow room between that wall and the yard. It's pretty ingenious."

"And it's about the only way to keep anything personal in a house as open as this one," added Bette.

"Sure you don't want to tell us what you found?" I asked.

"No, I'll forget something. It's no big deal. Just a few things you should see before I go. And you can talk to Julia at the same time." I must have had a blank look on my face that Bette misread, because she added, "You remember, don't you? You said she might recall more about Josh, after a few days. And she does seem better, more relaxed, less absent-minded."

"Yeah, I remember. I was just wondering. You have to be busy with packing and all the last-minute details. Would it be better if I came over after you left, say some time next week? Then, I wouldn't be in your way."

"Yeah ...." Bette paused for several seconds. "See, Doug, the thing is. That's not gonna work. Julia's coming back to Albuquerque with me."

What the ...?

I don't think my surprise was great enough that she could read my shock over the link. But then again, maybe it was, because she said, "You probably think I'm crazy."

"No, not at all," said Ali. "It's good to have the security and the assistance ... as we're getting older. Just one less thing to worry about." I was glad Ali brought up the "O" word because I was not about to venture there with Bette ... or Ali for that matter.

"Yeah, security and assistance ...," said Bette, pausing again. "But that's not the main reason. She's been so down, so sad. I've heard about all the little problems she and Josh had, and it sounds like ... well, like my life. Now, she's starting to feel a little better, so I'd like to hear some of the good stuff too."

Bette paused, rubbing her forehead. "I'm not explaining this well, but it's like we've found common ground. She's become a friend and I like talking to her. I like having her around."

"That's great," said Ali.

"Yeah, I'm happy for you too," I managed after another beat or two.

"Doug and I have something we have to do tomorrow afternoon, but does tomorrow morning, say around 10:00 work?" Ali asked.

"Perfect," Bette said.

The women talked a few more minutes before disconnecting. Ali left to start her day. I sent my reply to Wiggins, then sat in our kitchen with my uneaten breakfast in front of me, wondering. I suspected that this was not the first time in history when two wives of one man became friends after his death. I was not so sure, however, that it had ever happened before with one human and one robot.

Friday, April 13, 2068

Morning

n the merry-go-round that had become the spring climate in St. Louis, I would have guessed that today would be lousy. That was because, after the foul rain on Monday, the weather had turned nice. It had been three days of sun with only a few scattered clouds, clean air, and moderate temperatures. We couldn't get four in a row, could we? But then, that's the problem with letting gambler's fallacy creep into your thinking – believing that bad is more likely to follow good by the law of averages. It doesn't work that way and today was again beautiful. Ali and I decided to walk.

The flora of the city had taken this period of moderation to add another layer of dazzle, with the daylilies and phlox seeming to bloom overnight. In backyard and side-yard gardens, the season for early vegetables – lettuce, asparagus, peas, radishes – had peaked and was on the decline. It was now time for melons, tomatoes, peppers, sweet corn – the summer vegetables – to start pushing toward the sun.

As we strolled, Ali and I talked constantly, but little of it was serious, and none of it involved Josh, Bette, Julia, or Wiggins. It was about the kids and grandkids. It included my normal teasing about Ali's inability to retire; she continued to work with patients even with the stellar example of relaxation I provided as an alternative. It was about … nothing really, because it was the break before the final push. All that remained to complete my retroscape was whatever information, if any, that Julia now recalled plus anything that Wiggins knew. After that, all of my sources would be exhausted.

But the respite from worrying about the past ended too soon, as I spotted Josh's home only half a block away. "I hope this day turns out OK. I already have one bad Friday the thirteenth in the retroscape."

"Superstitious, are we, my dear husband?" Ali smirked at me. "The attack on Deputy Director O'Connor, right?"

"Right. Oh, did I mention I got a reply from Wiggins about our offer of lunch?"

"No. What did he say?"

"It was a one-liner. I have it memorized. Sorry, but have a meeting at that time. So, evidently, you were wrong. He doesn't have to eat."

"Well, it was worth asking," said Ali. "I can't believe we're here already."

"Well, babe, you do keep up a pretty good pace. Always have." I was about to place my finger on the reader when the door opened, revealing Bette.

"Hi, guys."

I smiled and braced myself for the bad joke *du jour*. What was it going to be this time? 'I just had an apple, but the doctor's here anyway?' Or maybe something more self-deprecating, like 'I'm doing great on my exercise program. Just this morning, I was jumping to conclusions, climbing the walls, and pushing my luck.' Occasionally, Bette even branched out to science or technology. 'Did you hear that they discovered the gene for shyness? They would have found it earlier, but it was hiding behind two other genes.'

"Thanks for coming," Bette said, smiling. "I do have a few things to show you like I said during the comm. But mostly, I wanted to say good-bye, in person, to two of my best friends. I love you guys and I'll miss you."

I stumbled back a step. Fortunately, Ali was less shocked and reached out to hug her friend. "I love you too, Bette. But this isn't goodbye. I'll be out to visit before you know it."

"You better, girlfriend."

I'd never been one for hugging. It felt strange for anyone except my mom, Ali, and the kids. But I made an exception and wrapped my arms around Bette. "You'll be missed around here."

"Thanks, Doug. You're a sweetie. OK, enough schmaltziness. Come on in, guys, and we'll all take a peek at Josh's secret room." She rubbed her hands together in a conspiratorial way.

Even though I knew the room was in the back and I vaguely remembered where the door was, I was still surprised when she tapped a small button and it opened. We all stepped inside. Ali immediately noticed the first 'curiosity.'

"Isn't that the sculpture that Josh got at Glacier National Park?"

"It is," said Bette. "Josh used to say that it was bigger than any glacier we saw." Bette smirked, as the souvenir was only about 8 by 15 centimeters. "At least, as best we could tell, looking through the smoke."

We had taken a trip there with Josh and Bette in 2030 to see 'the dying of the glaciers,' as they slowly succumbed to the world's generally warmer temperatures. Unfortunately, the area had also seen a prolonged drought, bringing on forest fires. The sights we had travel a half continent to see appeared eerily through curtains of smoke, if at all. Ali and I were hikers and still enjoyed the trip. Unfortunately, Josh and Bette didn't share the feeling.

After Ali's first discovery, Bette started pulling items off the wall or out of drawers. In about ten minutes, she had covered much of the floor and a tabletop. "Well, guys, I wanted to offer you your choice – any or all."

"Are you sure?" asked Ali.

"Oh, don't worry, Ali, I have plenty of other stuff."

"OK, I'll take the glacier sculpture," said Ali. "It'll remind me of Josh."

I went over to a framed picture of an airplane cockpit, with two fuzzy, semi-transparent lines in blue and red winding through it. "Mind if I take this?" I asked.

Bette laughed. "I don't even know what it is, but for some reason, Josh kept it."

I took a long breath. "It's from the first day we met. Josh was working on a project to record how expert pilots scan their displays during flight. The blue line represents where a pro looked during 30 seconds of a landing. Then, he sat me down in the cockpit and said, 'land it.' The red line shows where I was looking."

"Honey, it looks like you spent most of your time looking out the window?" said Ali.

"Yeah, Josh thought it was hilarious too. When he showed it to his clients, he'd say, this shows the difference between how an expert and a novice scan their instrument panel. But when it was just us, he'd say, this is where someone looks when they're clueless." I smiled at the memory. "I never knew he kept it … much less had it framed."

"You know, you were his best friend," said Bette.

"And he was mine." The lump in my throat prevented me from saying more, and I wondered for the thousandth time if our friendship would have lasted if not for Yates.

Bette took our two keepsakes to a table to wrap. "Just in case the weather turns, and you have to wait a minute or two for a SCAT," she said, as she started covering them.

There were other items on a separate table, things she had been preparing for her move. Many I recognized as keepsakes from trips Josh had mentioned. But among the figurines and pictures was one object that didn't appear to be a trinket from a vacation. It was a woman's bracelet and it seemed familiar.

Bette must have seen me looking, because she said, "Julia, you want to tell Doug what that is?" I hadn't realized that Julia had come into the room, she was so quiet.

"That's Joyce's bracelet – his niece, the one that died at Midwest Medical Research and Teaching Center. She died before I met Josh, but he talked about her so much … well, I feel like I knew her and I'm going to keep it."

I glanced at Bette, but she was still head down, focused on wrapping. Julia's words had to be difficult for her because Bette knew Joyce, not by story but in person. And yet, Bette had asked Julia to explain. She apparently accepted Julia's claim to the memory, as well as the jewelry.

"There's one other object I wanted to show you," said Bette, pulling me from my thoughts. "And Doug, you're more than welcome to it. But I'm not sure Ali will be as accepting of it as that picture."

She led us over to a tall, slender display case, with shelves on the bottom and top, and a small drawer in the middle. She slid open the drawer and stepped back.

"What's that?" asked Ali.

"A neuralyzer," I said, dumbstruck. Ali's distaste was easy to read with just a glance, so I quickly added, "No, I'm not going to ask Bette if I can have it."

"Good, because I don't want anything like that in our house."

Ali looked sheepish, perhaps wondering if Bette had condoned Josh owning it. Then, she added more mildly. "Frankly, I don't understand anyone's attraction to something like that."

"Hey, guys like to blow holes in things." Ali wasn't laughing, which really didn't surprise me. She was just staring at it. "Well, if any of us would be attracted to a neuralyzer, it would be you, babe," I said, "simply because of all the medically related tech in it."

Ali grimaced. "Hardly." But after a moment's reflection, she admitted, "OK, I've heard they anesthetize a person a lot like we do. But I don't want it in our home because I find it disgusting in its intended use."

"I guess this one was intended for zombies," said Bette. "Oops, sorry, Ali. I forgot you hate that word. Anyway, Josh's brother got it during the pandemic. Never used it and gave it to Josh a long time ago. But I never really understood what it did."

Whether she liked to admit it or not, Ali would know the most about this weapon and we turned to her. "It paralyzes the voluntary muscles," she said. "Things like your arms and legs – but it does so gradually, while the muscles that keep you breathing or swallowing or blinking your eyes still function. So, people shot with one slowly crumple to the ground, which helps reduce injury. Unconsciousness follows."

Ali still looked unhappy, but I think the realization that this weapon wouldn't be riding back home with us was starting to have an effect. Finally, she said, "OK, I admit, it's a bit of an engineering marvel to get all those electronics in such a small package. The medical equivalent is three times that size. But what I don't understand is why they gave it such a ... what's the right word, uninspired? Such an uninspired name?"

"Because all the good ones had already been taken – phasers, disruptors, tasers, you name it," I said. "Actually, neuralyzer had been used too, if you remember the movie, *Men in Black*, although its purpose was different." I received nothing but blank stares from the women, which made sense as the movie was about 70 years old. But I still watched it, from time to time.

"So, are you going to shoot it?" asked Bette.

Secretly, I was curious, but I knew better than to agree. I didn't want to sleep in our personal receptacle tonight. "No, thanks."

"Actually, I was asking as a favor," said Bette, and she turned to Ali. Bette knew where she would find resistance to her request. "Evidently, these things get charged, or something like that, and this one has three shots left. It has to be empty before I can sell it and I can't stand to touch it. Would you really mind if Doug empties it?"

I didn't want to appear too excited to get the opportunity, so I said in my most neutral tone, "I don't mind helping Bette out."

Ali chuckled. "Yes, you're very bighearted that way." Then, she reached over and lightly laid her hand on mine. "Be careful."

I nodded, but then wondered if this venture was going to be over before it even started. "Is there a range here?" I asked.

"Julia says you don't need one," said Bette. "According to her, you can shoot her and get the full effect of someone crumpling to the floor, unconscious."

"What?" I said, my eyes going wide.

This was one of those situations where my logic said, 'Fine, no problem. It's only electromagnetic waves fired at a robot, which will be completely unaffected.' But the problem was my emotions. They kept saying, 'look at her. She knows what you're doing and it's wrong.' While I greatly value the rational side of my decision process and usually follow its results faithfully,

I never ignore my gut when the two are so diametrically opposed. I couldn't do it.

"It's perfectly safe," said Julia. "I am, after all, a machine. Josh did it several times."

I took a half-step back in shock. It probably would have been more, but Ali's tender touch on my hand had tightened on my wrist. She too was unsettled by Julia's words. "Why was Josh shooting at you?" I asked.

"Just to get better," said Julia. "He said he didn't want to miss if he ever had to use it."

I glanced at Bette. She was staring at Julia, motionless, mouth open. "When did this start?" I asked.

"March 2nd of this year."

If he intended to use it on Wiggins, the timing was right. And if he was depressed enough to take his own life, he might well be confused enough to consider Wiggins a threat that needed to be neutralized, or in this case, neuralyzed.

"But Josh never said anything about where or why he might need to use it?" I asked.

"No," said Julia. "He didn't talk about using it other than practice."

One of the reasons for this visit had been to see if Julia could recall more about Josh now that his death was further in her past. We had obviously started that quest and I caught a nod from Bette when I glanced at her. So, I repeated much the same questions as Monday with, unfortunately, the same results. Julia had no further insight into why Josh was sad and she still remembered no visitors, no new hobbies or jobs, and no change in his interests. So, as a last resort, I thought I would try the direct approach.

"Did Josh ever mention a man named Jacob Wiggins?"

I had long been amazed at the range of Julia's facial expressions, but her look at this point even surprised me. She looked ... embarrassed. Her face turned red and she looked down at her shoes, pushing one of the trinkets that lay on the floor with her toe.

"Well, not directly," she said, softly. I leaned closer to hear. "But I overheard him saying the name once. He didn't know I was standing in the door to the bedroom when he said it. I wasn't eavesdropping. It was just chance." Julia appeared pained by the admission.

"Do you remember what he said?"

"Only the name. Nothing more."

I looked at Bette and Ali, holding out my hands. I had nothing else to ask.

"I didn't know Julia was talking from experience when I said you could shoot her," said Bette, apparently as troubled by Julia's words as I had been. She turned to the mechanion. "I'm so sorry, Julia. I thought you were joking. I never meant for Doug to shoot you."

"It's OK," Julia replied. "But I'm glad he didn't. I never liked it. It made me feel ... worthless." Her shoulders drooped as her gaze dropped to the floor.

Bette placed a hand on Julia's shoulder. "I'm sure Josh didn't mean it that way. He just wasn't thinking. You know how he could get." Julia looked up and nodded, as a sad smile came to her face.

As I watched the pair, I knew this wasn't an act; Bette was genuinely concerned. If my mind harbored any lingering doubt about Julia accompanying Bette back to Albuquerque, it disappeared like fog in the mid-day sun. The women were friends.

After a moment, Bette pulled back a cover on the wall, revealing a traditional bulls-eye target. "Actually, I thought you could use this to empty that thing."

"Better," I said, feeling a wave of relief. "I'll set it on a narrow beam and stand over there." I pointed to a spot about eight meters away. "That'll make it sporting. And all of you can stand behind me." I chuckled to myself, realizing the last statement was unnecessary. All three of them had started moving before I had said a word.

Once we were in position, I fired. The neuralyzer was amazingly quiet, making only a slight fizzing sound for a split second. According to the target, I had hit the fourth ring from the center, slightly low and well to the right. I had obviously pulled rather than squeezed the trigger, which was probably because I had been bracing myself for the unknown.

Now, I relaxed, took a couple of deep breaths, exhaled the last one slowly, and squeezed. The adjustment worked and the second shot was well into the second ring, while the third clipped the bulls-eye. A small window right above the grip of the weapon turned red, with the word 'empty' written in black letters. "Mission accomplished," I said, and started to hand the neuralyzer to Bette.

"Not bad," she said. "But would you put it in the box over there on the table?" I went to put it away.

"Don't encourage him," said Ali. "He'll want a firing range in the basement if you tell him he's any good."

"But he is good," said Julia. "Josh hardly ever hit the bulls-eye. That may be one of the reasons he shot at me."

We couldn't help but laugh, Julia joining in. Ali picked up the Glacier statue, I grabbed the picture, and after we thanked Bette and Julia for their hospitality, we left. We had just enough time for lunch before meeting with Wiggins.

Afternoon, April 13, 2068

As we traveled north toward the BPM campus, I noticed the scars left by the migration of people to the country. Abandoned houses in various states of disrepair became more common. It was not that we lacked the technology to remove these eyesores and restore the countryside. We had it. The real impediment had been the previous owners. Everyone believed that their gem of a home would be in high demand, even though they had abandoned it to live in rural Wyoming or the plains of west Texas or the forests of Alaska.

It had been the decades of the 2030s and 40s that saw the migration and the decade of the 50s that saw the deterioration of the neighborhoods, as people waited patiently but unrealistically for buyers. Now in the 60s, those who remained behind had lost patience. These abandoned buildings were being condemned in increasing numbers. But perhaps most telling, the absentee owners now cared little, if at all, when it occurred. Nearly all of them seemed to have abandoned hope of a sale sometime in the last 25 years and were now happy to be rid of their property without needing to pay back taxes or other liens. The neighborhood where BPM was located happened to be one of the last being reshaped by the condemnation-demolition-reclamation cycle and so, massive, restoration systems dotted the landscape. All in all, it felt like a good reminder of our past, as well as the direction of our future.

Intelligent construction systems, on the other hand, were a rarity during the ride, but that changed when we arrived. The BPM complex was crawling with them. They encircled the campus, but the activity was especially heavy at each corner of the walled and guarded compound.

Since I had been unable to obtain one of the rare, two-seat SCATs for our trip, Ali and I had ridden separately. When our vehicles deposited us at the front gate, Ali emerged and said, "I don't think Bette was as prepared for the move as she implied earlier. Julia has been sending me pictures of items they have been debating almost nonstop." Ali paused, laughed once, and said, "I can see Bette throwing stuff in front of Julia, and Julia sending the pictures as fast as she can take them."

"Well, you saw all the full drawers and the half-wrapped stuff in the invisible room. If that was any indication, yeah, she had a bit to do." I nodded at the gate, asking, "Shall we see if we're expected?" We walked over and I placed my finger in the GovTag reader. A voice came from the surrounding complex wall.

"Greetings, Dr. Douglas Michaels, and welcome to the Bureau of Population Management - Central Division, St. Louis National Population Records Center. If you wish to travel together, please have Ms. Alison Michaels confirm her identity."

"Guess they don't want to believe their sensors," I said, stepping aside so Ali could use the reader.

"Greeting, Ms. Alison Michaels, and welcome. You and Dr. Michaels may keep your personal communication devices as their contents, including your virtuants, will not be harmed. However, neither your virtuants nor any other communication device will function within the walls of this compound. Likewise, any communication implants within your body will not work.

"I have dispatched a SCAT for you and Dr. Michaels, which will arrive in 20 seconds. Once you have boarded, please do not exit the vehicle for any reason. To do so will result in an immediate armed response, your detention, and possible ejection from the facility. Dr. Wiggins expects to be 1.2 minutes late for your meeting. He expresses his apologies and is looking forward to talking to you."

I looked at Ali, chuckling. "One point two minutes, huh? Did you bring the stopwatch?" Ali frowned. "And both of us GovTagging in? I guess it comes with the territory."

Of the few remaining white-collar crimes in the United States, as well as most other nations, stealing or manipulating DNA records was the most feared. That dread had spawned numerous PlotsPro books and movies. In fact, these devices came preloaded with several sample novels, including one in which an individual obtained the identification of a reclusive quadrillionaire. Depending on the reader's preferences, the storyline then morphed into a tale about a madman who was going to use the money to destroy the world, but who was foiled by a brilliant government agent. Or in another, machine intelligences came to the rescue of humanity. There were, of course, thousands of possible resolutions, a few of which I was sure Ali had generated and read.

Two SCATs pulled up and the gate swung open. The vehicles were subtly different from most commercial SCATs, with thicker body panels and bulkier windows. The materials used in the commercial units could withstand high-speed collisions – not that any occurred – and falling debris like trees or rocks, which was also extremely rare. Given how much heavier the BPM vehicles were, I wondered what it would take to penetrate one.

We boarded and after a short ride, we reached Building 4. Ali had been in the lead vehicle, and when I walked forward to stand beside her, she slipped her hand into mine. "This place is intimidating, isn't it?"

"Despite all my kidding about meeting here and turf rumbles, yeah, I have to agree."

Interspersed with the construction robots we had passed were a number of autonomous security units. They weren't difficult to spot since they were large, shiny black machines with the words, DANGER – SECURITY SYSTEM, written on the side. However, I suspected that we were only seeing the tip of their self-protection iceberg.

A nondescript door near one corner of Building 4 opened and we entered a small reception area. It was empty, except for a half-dozen chairs along the left and right walls. Next to the door were several lockers. Directly ahead of us was a set of four additional doors, each opening into an enclosure with transparent walls. The rooms were about two by two meters.

"Scanning booths of some type?" asked Ali.

I started to agree when we received our next set of automated instructions from a voice that seemed to radiate from every surface. It left the eerie impression of coming from inside my head.

"Welcome to Building 4, Dr. Michaels and Ms. Michaels. If you are carrying anything dangerous, please place it in one of the lockers behind you. I will not try to list every possible weapon; rather, you should use your own judgment. However, if you are unsure, please err on the side of safety. Once you have put your belongings in one or more lockers, they will be secured by your DNA record. Do you have any questions?"

I glanced at Ali, who shrugged. "No, no questions," I said. We had expected this scrutiny and had left anything that even vaguely resembled a weapon at home. "We are carrying nothing dangerous and have nothing to store in the lockers."

"Ms. Michaels, do you concur with your husband's declarations?" asked the room.

"Yes, I agree," she said, raising her eyebrows as she glanced at me.

"Thank you," continued the room. "Your verbal confirmation is required by our policies, Ms. Michaels." That much was becoming clear.

"Next," the wall continued, "we will ask you to enter one of the four scanning areas in front of you. The sensors they use will not harm any common personal items. Our records indicate that neither of you has any life-sustaining implants. If that is incorrect, do not enter. We will make other arrangements for your visit. Do you have any questions?"

I nodded at Ali so she could go first. "No, I have no questions," she said.

"I don't have any questions either."

Two doors opened and the voice said, "Please enter. The scan will take approximately 30 seconds."

I looked over at Ali and said, "See you on the other side." We entered.

The booth was eerily quiet, as their systems undoubtedly cataloged everything I had come in contact with over the last few hours, if not the last few days. It was enough to make me wonder if I had accidentally touched something previously used by an unsavory character. Who knew who had last ridden in my SCAT? And because of that coincidence, I was about to be stunned, dragged off to a secret location, and subjected to hours of interrogation.

Of course, hours of questioning would be unnecessary. The PSS Forensics SCAT that had interviewed me a little over a week ago could detect if I strayed from the truth by the brain regions in use. BPM's interrogation systems, on the other hand, would be going directly into my thoughts. They would decode every word, concept, or image that popped into my mind as we chatted. And since some of their questions would be things like, how many feet does an elephant have, I couldn't just tune them out.

When the door on the other side of my scanning room opened, Ali was already standing there. "Where have you been?" she asked. "I got out at least 20 seconds ago."

"Guess I have more interesting stuff in my head for them to look at. They're probably still admiring my image of the elephant." Ali gave me a quizzical look but didn't ask.

I peered down the corridor in front of us, but there was no one in sight. That seemed odd, after all the tight control and intense screening, making me wonder if this was some type of test. "What do you think would happen if I started sprinting down the hall?"

"I'd start collecting my survivor benefits when I got home."

"Very funny ... but probably true," I admitted.

We waited only a few more seconds before a small robot appeared. It was perhaps best described as a three-quarter by one-meter 'box on wheels,' with only two screens and a few small protrusions on the outside. Aesthetics had obviously been left off the list of its design requirements.

"Guests," said 'Mr. Box.' "Dr. Wiggins is looking forward to meeting with you and will be available in 47 seconds. Please follow me." The robot rolled down the hall.

"What kind of firepower do you think he's carrying?" I whispered to Ali, as we trailed behind. She gave me a dirty look as if my question might result in a demonstration.

Perhaps our wheeled companion misread Ali's expression as anxiety rather than annoyance because it replied, "You have no reason for concern, Ms. Michaels. I have no offensive capability."

For some reason, I suspected that the words, 'offensive capability' had been chosen carefully and thought about asking what he could do in the defensive mode. But while Mr. Box's answer would be enlightening, I could understand Ali's irritation. I'd probably be unsettled by what he had to say as well.

"Dr. Wiggins should arrive in 18 seconds," said Mr. Box, when we arrived outside an unmarked door. "Please wait here." It was, however, much less than 18 seconds when the door opened, spoiling the illusion that BPM could control everything right down to a human's punctuality.

Rather than the management suite that I had expected given Wiggin's position, his office was small and simply decorated. It held an antique oak desk, unusual in its construction materials and age. But more surprising were the antique oak, two-drawer file cabinet, and the oak, glass-front bookcase. Those had been rare even before the turn of the century. There was a comfortable looking, stuffed chair in one corner, an antique floor lamp with a glass shade to the side. Facing the desk were two chairs, which if I remembered my history correctly were called Easter Chairs. They looked like large eggs, with an oval-shaped opening on one side, so that you sat back into the rest of the shell. I expected they would be comfortable, although odd, especially in the context of his other furnishings, which were from an even earlier era.

An individual who looked something like the picture we had seen online stepped from behind the desk. And yet, he seemed subtly different. He extended his hand in greeting. "Hi, I'm Jacob Wiggins, assistant director at this BPM facility," he said, smiling. "Please, call me Jacob."

"Thanks." I took his hand. "It's nice to meet you. I'm Doug Michaels, and my wife, Ali."

Perhaps I was studying our host's face too closely, as after a moment he said, "My picture online has been aged by computer if you're wondering. Something about the public wanting an older man in this job."

I nodded, realizing that was the difference I hadn't been able to name. And now that I knew, he did appear young, little older than my grandchildren. But as capable as they were, always skilled with the latest tech before I had even read about it, I had no qualms about Wiggins' ability.

Our host opened a hand toward the two chairs across from his desk. "Please have a seat."

We did, confirming my suspicions about how comfortable they would be. But I had no more than settled into mine when my arms and legs started tingling. A soft buzzing came to my ears. I tried to turn to look at Ali, but couldn't. I slipped downward as if my bones had turned to rubber. My vision dimmed.

While neither of us had completely ruled out the possibility of danger, I had put its likelihood as effectively nil. And over the years, I had come to trust my instincts; they were seldom wrong. But seldom wasn't the same as never and I couldn't think of a worse time for my gut to fail me.

I could feel my consciousness slipping away. In the remaining second or two of clarity, I played out what would happen. I didn't expect to be spirited out of the building, only to be killed and left in a shallow grave in some woods surrounding St. Louis. That style of execution was all last century. No, I expected to get up and walk out of the building in a few minutes, sensing no ill effects of my visit. But nonetheless, some process would have been planted in my brain, slowly eating away at my mind. The same would happen to Ali, as it had with Josh several months ago.

And two or three months from now, after all traces of this visit were too faint for even the most advanced technologies to detect, Ali and I would die. Most likely, we would kill each other. I don't know how I could murder my wife and friend of the last 50 years, but somehow, it would happen. Or perhaps I would die in the act of attacking a stranger, guided only by my deluded thoughts.

Then, darkness overtook me.

Afternoon, April 13, 2068

The light was incredibly bright. Was this the light reported by people brought back from the brink of death, the gateway to an afterlife? And if so, was I moving toward it ... or backing away? I couldn't tell.

After a moment or two, my thoughts began to clear. I looked down, realizing that I was laying on the floor and had been staring up at the ceiling. To my right, opposite of where Ali had been sitting, I noticed movement. I rolled my head to the side, still unable to lift it. The movement turned out to be a person, male I believe, although he/she was wearing a long, white lab coat and a surgical mask, making identification difficult. Was Wiggins still inflicting his slow working madness on us? And why would he allow us to be conscious if he was? Or maybe that wasn't important; maybe we wouldn't remember anyway.

I rolled my head to the left. There were two other people on that side, while Wiggins was over by the wall, talking on a CommCover. Were there four of them involved in ... whatever this was? And who was he talking to? A fifth person? The rottenness at BPM was deeper than I had ever imagined.

As if Wiggins became aware of my stare, he turned from the wall, walked over, and crouched down directly in front of me. His eyes narrowed, looking at me closely. His face was mere inches away. His mouth moved, but the words came out thick and distorted. I couldn't make out what he said. After a few moments, he tried again.

"Dr. Michaels, are you alright?"

I heard the words, but now, it was the meaning that was alluding me. Why would he care? Did I need to feel alright for his scheme to work? Then, over to his left and behind him, I saw ... Ali! And she was standing.

If my mouth had not already been hanging open from the lack of muscle control, my jaw would have dropped at the sight of her. How was that possible? She turned toward me and her hand went to her lips. There was enough of her face showing for me to realize she was upset, perhaps angry.

She came over and pushed Wiggins to the side, taking his place directly in front of me.

"Doug, you're going to be OK," she said. She spoke slowly, carefully enunciating each word. Her brow was knitted, as she looked carefully into my eyes. "Can you hear me?"

I must have twitched, or maybe my eyes showed recognition because before I said a word, a slight smile came to her lips. Concentrating, I managed to nod. My reply, "Yes," however, came out as not much more than a croak.

I couldn't see Wiggins, but I heard his voice. "I think he'll be OK now. There's some orange juice on the desk when he feels up to it. We'll step out in the hall, give you two some privacy. If you need anything, anything at all, I'll be outside the door."

"Thanks," said Ali. But 'thanks' had seldom been said in a way that conveyed more hostility than the way she voiced it. When the others were outside, she turned to me. "Privacy?" She spat the word out. "Is that a joke? They're probably reading our every thought right now." Then, she sighed, reached out, and placed a hand on my cheek, but my face was numb. "How do you feel?"

"Weird." I stopped and swallowed, the word barely audible.

Ali retrieved the orange juice and I rolled my head to the side to take a sip. "I never felt bad, just ...." What was the word? I was having trouble concentrating. "I was slipping away, and then ... gone. What happened?"

"You were unconscious," said Ali. She winced as she said the words. "I saw you collapse in the chair. I didn't know what to think; you just slumped over. Then, we laid you down."

"I passed out?" Even a bit dazed, that didn't seem right. I had been feeling fine.

A flicker of anger crossed Ali's features, as she glanced at the door. When her eyes came back to mine, she said, "You were knocked unconscious. By the chair, I guess ... according to what Wiggins has told me. You remember trying out the neuralyzer this morning?"

"Sure, at Bette's," I said. "I was pretty good."

Ali shook her head, a slight smile on her lips. "I guess hoping that specific memory was gone was too much to ask." She touched my cheek again. My feeling was returning, as I sensed the warmth of her hand. "What Wiggins told me was that this room, including the chairs, have significant self-defense measures built into them. Your chair detected the recent use ... or the residual or something like that from the neuralyzer. So, it knocked you out. Are you following?"

"Yeah, I think so," I said and took another sip of juice. I rolled over, then pushed up to a sitting position.

"You sure you should be getting up already?" Ali asked as she stood.

"Yeah, just give me a hand."

She did and I started toward the chair.

"No way," she said. "Here, lean on the edge of his desk. And when you feel like it, we can get out of here."

"Leave?" I asked, frowning.

"You can't possibly want to continue," she said, her voice rising in step with her ire. "He could have killed you. And even though he says there aren't any lasting effects of that ... thing, you need to be checked out."

I held up a hand, saying, "Calm down." Ali glared at me.

"That's not what I meant," I said when I recognized the reaction. After 50 years of marriage, I knew better than to tell her how to feel. "I mean, my head's not totally clear. I can't keep up when you talk so fast." She nodded but still didn't look happy.

"What happened to me didn't happen to you, right?" I asked.

"No, I was awake the whole time."

"So, it was an accident and not some ...."

I paused, searching for a neutral way to express my fears, but Ali finished for me. "Some insanity timebomb he was planting in our heads."

"Yeah, that," I replied. "I'm not asking you to like Wiggins, or even trust him. But I think we're safe enough. Let's finish this meeting ... assuming he has anything to say."

BRUCE M. PERRIN

Ali continued to stare, but I could tell she was weakening. Finally, she said, "OK, but as soon as he claims ignorance about what happened to Josh, we're out of here. I don't need to hear how my tax dollars are being spent. Agreed?"

"Sure."

Ali went to the door and opened it for Wiggins. As he entered, he asked, "How is he?" Ali extended a hand in my direction, as if to say, 'see for yourself,' but made no comment.

Wiggins came over to me and I pushed myself off the edge of his desk.

"No, stay," he said, motioning me back down. "I'm so very sorry, Dr. Michaels. The counter-measures of the room can be turned off, of course. I just forgot and for that, I feel terrible. I don't get many visitors here. I'm not even certain when the last one was."

"No wonder, if you knock them all out," I said. Wiggins looked stricken by the comment until he noticed I was grinning. He allowed himself a smile in return, although it was strained. "It was an accident, now in the past," I said. "And it's Doug."

"Of course, Doug," Wiggins replied. "I feared I had lost that privilege." He glanced at Ali, but she said nothing.

It was time to talk about something besides the chairs. I was worried that Wiggins might ask why one had found neuralyzer residue on me. While 'to empty it so it could be sold' was possible, 'because we did not trust you and wanted to be ready' sounded more likely. Then, if he recalled that I had invited him to dine away from the safety of his lethal office, whatever credibility we might have built would disappear.

"So, what can you tell me about the death of Josh Unger?" I asked, cutting to the heart of the matter.

"Tell you?" said Wiggins. "I can do better than that. I can show you the killer."

Afternoon, April 13, 2068

I was dumbstruck, not knowing what to expect. I glanced at Ali. Her distrust of Wiggins still showed in her eyes, her glare unwavering. I turned back to our host. Would he confess? Would he tell us Josh was his own killer, that he had chosen to take his life? For all I knew, he was about to blame it on Professor Plum in the library with the candlestick.

Wiggins turned to the wall on his right and said, "Reveal."

The wall, which previously held a few pictures and a couple of sconces now became transparent. A room appeared. Perhaps it was an adjoining space, but it might have been anywhere in the world. It held but a single fixture, a computer. But it was like no other that I had ever seen – well, maybe in pictures. It was not the highly advanced, ultra-fast, supercomputer one might have expected in the government facility dedicated to maintaining the identities of every U.S. citizen and monitoring every financial transaction they made. No, it looked all the world like a computer from the last century.

"Is that what I think it is?" I stammered.

"Well, if you're thinking a 1964 IBM System 360 mainframe computer, then yes, it is," Wiggins replied.

I pushed off Wiggins' desk and walked to the wall, not knowing what to say. Ali, on the other hand, found the words to express her disbelief. "I thought most of the furnishings in your office were a bit ... retro, but a 1960s computer?" she said slowly. "And now you're telling us that it killed Josh? I doubt it's even running."

"Technically, it is," replied Wiggins. "It's connected to the network, but it's symbolic rather than something we depend upon. It reminds us that we're running software that was built for this exact system." Wiggins paused, most likely expecting us to be shocked beyond words. He hadn't misjudged.

"It's true," he said after a moment. "Even though our systems run on some of the fastest hardware anywhere on earth, parts of the software are the vintage of that computer or older. That software killed Josh – not directly, but it was behind his death." His eyes tracked from me to Ali and back.

"You're not serious, are you?" I asked, rubbing at the pain growing in my forehead. "One-hundred-year-old software got inside Josh's head?"

"Not exactly," Wiggins replied. "You know the genesis of the BPM, right?"

We both nodded. "We got a refresher from Censere not too long ago," I added.

"Good," said Wiggins. "But there's more you should know. Around 1990, the United States government realized that our tax software was ... let's say, out of date. It was written in a language that was nearly obsolete. It involved structures and logic that virtually no one understood. It was time for an upgrade and the government launched a massive modernization effort."

"I've heard of it," I said. "Even though it was massive, didn't the government end up with nothing to show?"

"Correct," replied Wiggins. "The total cost for that first push was around four billion dollars, and as you said, it was a total failure. But the government didn't give up, and the modernization efforts continued another 15 years, all with limited results." Wiggins paused, shaking his head. "I still remember when John Koskinen, the Internal Revenue Service commissioner in the mid-2010s admitted that we were still using applications that were running when John F. Kennedy was president. And at that point, the code was only about 50 years old." Wiggins put heavy emphasis on the word 'only.'

"And then, something happened to break the logjam," said Wiggins. "But not necessarily in a good way. The government redefined the problem. They didn't need to replace the legacy code. Rather, that code, they said, was stable and proven. It was, as they put it, 'core business logic.' In this new view on a very old and very difficult problem, the modernization effort should embrace the legacy code and make it available to new systems by way of middleware."

"Middleware?" I said.

"Yeah, sorry, Doug. Too much computer programming lingo. Middleware's just more software. Basically, it's a means of letting two or more programs work together. Anyway, with this new view of modernization, our vintage code was a core that remained unchanged, while we covered it in middleware to make new systems."

"You're not going to tell us that this legacy code got passed on to BPM after the crash, are you?" asked Ali.

Wiggins sighed deeply. "Unfortunately, that's exactly what happened," he said. "You've got to remember, we were on the brink of economic ruin; we had to do something and fast. Re-using the IRS software with more middleware was the only option. At first, we thought this was just a stopgap. We'd get the country back on its feet, then we'd fix the root problem. But when the new tax laws were wildly popular and the repurposed software worked nearly flawlessly, the success went to our heads.

"Soon, we were layering on more functionality, held together with additional middleware, and burying the legacy code deeper and deeper in the bowels of tens of millions of lines of software. But make no mistake about it. When you place your finger in a GovTag Reader today, the output goes to software, some of which was written 40, 80, or even 100 years ago."

I was stunned. My image of BPM as the most advanced, data-processing facility in the world faded away like so much electronic noise. Suddenly, I was feeling very tired. "Mind if I sit?" I asked.

"I'm sorry, I've forgotten my manners. Of course, please," Wiggins said, gesturing toward one of the chairs. There must have been a slight hitch in my step, as he added, "I personally turned off all the defenses. It's safe." Then, he pulled his own chair from behind the desk and motioned to Ali. "Here, please take this one." She did without a word, while Wiggins took the remaining 'egg-chair'.

Once we were comfortable, Wiggins continued. "But even in the early days of wild enthusiasm, we knew we had a system with an extremely minor but persistent flaw – DNA records could get corrupted. It happened to about one in ten million people each year. When it occurred, the person came in and we corrected it, usually by creating a new identity. Sure, these individuals were mad as heck, but the problem got fixed and life went on."

I had to smile when Wiggins said 'heck.' Apparently, Censere wasn't the only one who took BPM's no-profanity rule to heart.

"That was until 15 years ago when people's reactions started changing," Wiggins said. "Within the group with the DNA error that year, there was a young man who became depressed, rather than coming to us. And every 12 to 18 months, another, similar case would appear. When we interviewed these people, they described the problem like losing part of their lives, like a void in their realities."

"Hold on a minute," I said, forgetting my fatigue and getting up from the chair I had just taken. I paced across Wiggins' office, rubbing a hand through my hair, then turned back toward him. "You're saying a software glitch killed Josh? That's ridiculous."

"I don't think so," he replied evenly, softly. "What I know for a fact is that Mr. Unger's DNA record became corrupted. That was why PSS got an error when they tried to match it. And because of that, he would have disappeared from the virtual world, and in turn, be cut off from much of the physical one. What I don't know but believe is that he took his life as a result. I can't prove it, but there's no doubt in my mind. And for our part in this terrible tragedy, I am truly sorry."

I turned away, feeling as if the walls of Wiggins' office were closing in. I looked back at Ali, pain etched in her face. But I also saw a subtle nod.

"Is that really possible?" I asked, looking at her closely.

"We've seen something like it at work with long-time implant users," she said. "When the device fails, the patients talk about losing part of themselves. And you can't tell them that they're back to baseline, back to being a regular, unenhanced human. Having the connection is normal to them. Without it, they're lost."

"It does sound similar," said Wiggins. "Except it isn't one capability fixed by replacing a single implant. Mr. Unger wouldn't have been able to send a comm. Or order a SCAT. A drink wouldn't be offered when he was thirsty or meals when he was hungry. His lights wouldn't come up as his brain rose from sleep or dim when he focused on a screen. He wouldn't be able to communicate with Julia, except by words. His health would decline with nothing to detect the early warning signs of illness. And his TuringTalk friends? All gone."

"It would explain a lot," Ali said slowly. She turned her gaze to me. "You remember when Julia told us that Josh wasn't himself, that he was cut off from her and the world?" I nodded. "I thought she meant he wasn't talking or comm'ing. Now it looks like she might have meant it literally."

Wiggins was certain about what had happened to Josh. Ali was convinced too, or near to it. And as I thought about it, my doubt began to fade as well. Unusual comments that Josh had made over the years came flooding back – calling nanobots a boon to humanity after his niece had been infected, referring to Oren Bledsoe's possible exclusion from dream-sharing a nightmare, wanting machines to make the call during emergencies. Now, those words took on a new meaning. They showed that Josh's world wasn't his physical environment. His world was his experience and it was inextricably intertwined with the virtual.

Realizing that, all became clear. Josh hadn't locked himself in his house because of some delayed reaction to the pandemic or remorse over the loss of his niece. He was there because it was all that was left for him. And in his isolation, he'd have little to ponder but the gaping hole in his psyche.

I took a deep breath and released it slowly. "How did I miss this?" I asked. I walked back to the empty chair and slumped into it.

"How did we miss it?" Ali corrected, her voice low. "We never took the words 'not a person' at face value … and consider what it would mean to Josh." She turned to Wiggins. "So, BPM obviously knows what's going on," her tone becoming sharp. "What are you doing about it?"

"We're working on it," Wiggins said quickly, his gaze darting between Ali's face and mine. "But frankly, it's proved the devil to hold in check."

"It doesn't seem like it would be that difficult," said Ali. "Why don't you just have the GovTag readers report each failure, then dispatch a PSS tech to help?"

"We tried," said Wiggins. "But people aren't used to inconveniences and they don't believe us. They just try another reader, and when it occurs again, they panic."

"Then ask them their names," I said. "Then, you can find them later, at home."

"Also tried," replied Wiggins. "Most of them refuse, some from distrust, others from confusion. Some have answered, but then they disappear. It's as if they think the BPM or the PSS is out to get them. And without DNA detection giving us constant updates on their whereabouts, some of these people have stayed hidden for months, even years."

"Years?" I said, astonished.

Wiggins nodded, saying only, "Yeah, in some cases."

"OK, how about publicizing the issue?" Ali asked. "If people know their profile might be unavailable in the GovTag system temporarily, wouldn't that keep them from becoming so upset?"

"This is good," Wiggins said. "I think we've tried everything, but maybe you'll think of something new."

"But this isn't it," said Ali.

"Sorry, but no. We experimented with something like that. When we described our solution to a group, everyone thought it was great. Everyone was smiling, heads were nodding. But then we arranged for a DNA error at some of these people's homes and they all overreacted, one way or another. No one seems to think this problem will be that bad until it happens to them."

"So, isn't the simplest answer just to fix it?" said Ali. "Of the world's problems that we've essentially met and mastered – famine, crime, climate, transportation – this is trivial. It's just ...."

Ali's face fell as she realized where her thoughts were leading. She turned to me.

"It's just software," I said quietly.

My thoughts had reached this conclusion only moments before Ali's and the realization hit me like a punch to the stomach. It was only software and yet, everyone in this room knew why a misplaced comma or an extra space in millions of lines of computer code was being allowed to kill people.

"I'm one to be pointing fingers at BPM, aren't I," I said bitterly. "If I wanted to lay blame, I should have looked in a mirror."

"Doug, you couldn't have known," said Ali.

"Ah, but we did," I replied. "Not the specifics, but we knew there was a price to be paid for our actions."

In the 2030s, I had been one of a one-hundred-member, industry panel that advised Congress on machine intelligence policy. One of our guiding principles had been to avoid the possibility of machines becoming too powerful, making humanity obsolete. It was a concern that had been in the back of our minds for over half a century, appearing in numerous books and movies. In some of those stories, machines became bored with humans' inferior intellect. In others, the machines wanted to make their own way and it was easier without us. In still others, they saw us as a threat. But the result was always the same – machines sought to exterminate humans.

So, we unanimously recommended that no machine intelligences be given software development skills. And Congress turned this advice into a law known as the Prohibition on Iterative Machine Intelligence. A machine could never be tasked to build a better version of itself or any other software. To enforce the ban, BPM monitored every financial transaction, reviewed every class on programming, searched every online file for anything that even vaguely resembled computer code. Fiddling with something that looked like software would bring CAS officers to your door faster than firing a neuralyzer at your neighbor.

Even at the time, however, we recognized it for what it was – the lesser of two evils. We avoided machines ruling the world, but without them making better, faster software, breakthroughs that affected the quality of life would be delayed, perhaps for years. Lives would be diminished and, in some cases, lost. But what I didn't know at the time – couldn't have known – was that one of those lives that would be lost for the greater good was Josh. And now, as I looked at my retroscape, there was another killer there.

It was me.

"You're replacing the code?" I asked. Wiggins nodded. "How long?"

"We estimate five years for the total software rebuild," he replied. I suspected that was wildly optimistic; software always took longer than expected.

"No one is blaming you, Doug," Wiggins added.

"Thanks, Jacob. But I suspect that's not true."

Wiggins sighed. "Well, it used to be. Many in BPM still think it's too risky to let machines control their own evolution. But some, and particularly the younger ones, consider the law out-of-date. They can't conceive of machines harming us."

"And you, Jacob?" I asked, thinking he must be one of the 'younger ones'.

His gaze never wavered. "Assuming that self-evolving machines won't become a threat to humanity is a risk I never want to take."

I only nodded, having nothing left to say. With all these revelations, my thoughts were swirling, my role in Josh's death pulling them down like water circling a drain. Eventually, the logic of protecting the many might prevail, but currently, my reason and my emotion weren't speaking. I had my answers, not that I liked them.

Wiggins had been forthcoming and it was time to return the favor. "I suspect you have some questions for us."

"I do," he replied. "For starters, can you tell me if Mr. Unger planned to kill me?"

Afternoon, April 13, 2068

"Kill you?" I stammered. I rose from my chair again, realizing that my actions must make me seem a puppet to my emotions. Clearly, they were pulling the strings. "What gave you that idea?"

My heart was drumming in my ears. With all the technology in the walls of this room, lies had no chance of survival. But maybe I could delay a moment to collect my thoughts and get the ancient parts of my brain under control.

"Well," Wiggins said slowly, "you asked for me by name when you thought there was an error in processing a DNA profile. I'm not even on the list of people who might be able to answer a question like that. So, you knew my name from somewhere else – maybe something at Mr. Unger's house? And second, when the residuals from a neuralyzer were detected on your hands, Security checked. One is registered to Josh Unger, but none to you. My guess is that you were firing his."

Wiggins raised his eyebrows, waiting. He had no way to determine where I had found his name and no one knew how Josh intended to use his weapon. I could simply deny it all and then, think of anything but my friend. But on the other hand, Wiggins had been straightforward with us, admitting BPM's role. And what I knew might help others. Josh would want that.

"Apparently, neuralyzers have to be unloaded before they can be transported or sold." Wiggins nodded, apparently aware of the regulation. "I emptied it for Josh's ex-wife this morning. And yes, some handwritten notes suggest that Josh believed you were behind the problems he was having, but there's nothing in them about his plans."

"Do you remember the exact wording?" Wiggins asked.

"Something like, I know who's behind this, and then your name."

"Nothing else?"

"No, not in the notes," I said. "Julia, his mechanion, said she heard him mention you once, but again, nothing but your name."

"Hmm," Wiggins said, rubbing his chin.

"You know, maybe we could be a little more helpful," Ali said, "if you'll tell us the whole story about the effects of the error."

The whole story?

Wiggins looked less surprised than I felt. Something I could only describe as a quizzical smile appeared on his face.

"What makes you think there's more?"

"You've described an extremely rare software glitch that occasionally produces depression," Ali said. "But when we talked about possible solutions, you mentioned that people had panicked, even fled and hid for months. And just now, you wanted to know if Josh was a threat to you. None of that sounds like depression. In fact, it's almost the opposite."

Ali paused, looking at me for a moment, then back to Wiggins. "So, what I'm thinking is that Josh's reaction to being severed from the virtual world wasn't common. The norm is something more aggressive, more violent, right?"

It seemed so obvious now that Ali had put it in words. While Wiggins' revelations about the vintage computer and the ancient software were still accurate, in this light his presentation felt staged, like a magician pointing to his lovely assistant while he palmed a card from the bottom of the deck. And he had the perfect distraction for me – my role in this whole tragic tale. Ali, however, had focused on the bigger picture.

"OK," he said after a moment. "But before we go on, I need to be clear about a couple of things. First, nothing changes what I've said about your friend. I've told you what happened and my best guess about its effect on him."

"And we appreciate that," said Ali.

Wiggins nodded. "Second, what I have to say is not a secret – we can't keep something of this magnitude out of the public eye. But at the same time, we don't want to draw unnecessary attention to our actions. Because of that, I tried to answer your questions without raising your suspicions. Not too successfully, I might add," he said with a smile at Ali. "Anyway, yes, we are preparing for a violent reaction."

"So, all the construction we saw when we came in – that's for your defense?" I asked.

"Correct, but I'd like for you to keep those preparations to yourself." I wasn't really sure who I'd tell, who would even be interested. But then again, with Wiggins' warning, it was a detail that wouldn't accidentally find its way into one of my comms.

"Is BPM the only one threatened?" Ali asked.

"The Public Security Service is a possible target, but the PSS offices are small, easily defended, and mostly automated. The Criminal Apprehension Service is also a distant possibility, but they have always been well armed. Otherwise, government buildings are just that. Empty buildings. The president hasn't resided at the White House in years. Nor the Congress in the Capitol Building. Nor any of the state governments."

I hadn't thought much about it, but he was right. Public service had gone off-site right along with private industry.

"If you want to strike at government," Wiggins continued, "BPM is about the only place where you can draw blood – literally and figuratively."

"I can see that," I said. "And any threat to life isn't to be dismissed lightly. But wouldn't the effort be better spent on a permanent software solution? I mean, one in ten million is about 30 cases a year. Some of those people won't be prone to violence, and of those, some will be quite young, others quite old. Of the handful left, will any have the financial means and the skills necessary to attack an institution like BPM?"

"I can't fault your logic," said Wiggins. "But you don't have all the facts. Do you know what Hominid Ennui is?"

"Weariness of people?" said Ali, glancing at me.

"Ah, you've heard of it," said Wiggins.

"No, that was a question," Ali replied. "I know the definition of ennui – boredom or weariness. And hominid refers to primates, including humans. But I'm not familiar with the phrase as a name for anything."

"And truthfully, I'm not an expert on the condition either," said Wiggins. "So, if you don't mind, I'll call in someone who is." Ali and I nodded.

"Censere," said Wiggins, and the BPM machine intelligence by that name replaced the vintage computer on the wall.

"I thought we agreed that you would summon me by saying, 'Mirror, mirror, on the wall.' Just saying Censere is so … pedestrian."

"I remember the suggestion," said Wiggins. "But wouldn't that be seven years bad luck, since you're cracked?" The line was delivered completely deadpan.

I couldn't help myself; I chuckled. "Let me guess, Jacob. Censere is your virtuant."

"It shows?" Wiggins asked, feigning a look of surprise. "He is that … and more for this organization."

"Ah, it's the infamous seven-year-old doctor and his lovely wife of 50 years," said Censere. "Greetings, Doug, Ali, and welcome to the BPM."

"Thanks," Ali and I said in near perfect unison.

"The reason I asked for you," said Wiggins, "was to explain Hominid Ennui to our guests."

"My pleasure," replied the machine intelligence. "Hominid Ennui is a recently defined condition. It's characterized by a disinterest of a human in dealing with the idiosyncrasies of other people. People with this condition stay hidden in their automation-controlled environments, letting their mechanical servants handle every interaction. They seem to cherish the certainty of a machine-controlled world. The condition was largely unknown 25 years ago, but the estimates of the number of people with it today go as high as 37 percent."

Ali gasped. As I glanced at her, she slid forward in her chair, frowning at Censere. "I work with clients who are having trouble adjusting to technology that has been introduced into their bodies."

"Yes, Ali, I know all about your work," said Censere. "And a noble calling it is. I just hope one day we'll have something to help the poor machine that's upset about being inserted into a human."

Censere's levity reduced Ali's tension, as her frown diminished but didn't disappear. "What you're talking about seems related to my job. I'm surprised I've never heard of it."

"Yes, it's snuck up on all of us. Since the primary symptom is staying at home and letting your machine intelligences handle everything, it's not something that will draw attention. And even when it did, everyone passed it off as part of the reaction to the toxoplasmosis outbreak. Now we know better. It's an acquired condition, gained from years of interacting with automation in all its forms and guises – virtuants, mechanions, smart homes, adaptive clothing, you name it. But as to what it means, no one – not the medical profession, the government, or even society as a whole – has been able to decide. Is it some type of technology-enabled disorder or a reasonable life choice, given the state of the world?"

"A reasonable choice when it results in violence?" I said, staring at Censere in disbelief.

Censere's head jerked around to look at Wiggins. "You told them?"

"They knew most of it already," said Wiggins. "It's better they know the rest, rather than telling everyone about our fortifications or assuming something even worse." Wiggins then turned back to us. "As for Censere not telling you about the DNA issue before, he's not allowed. Sorry about that."

Censere slowly shook his head. "It's just like the old saying. Rules are made to be broken ... by humans." Then, he turned to me. "By itself, Hominid Ennui is generally benign. But coupled with the corruption of a

DNA profile?" A shudder shook his body. "The combination can result in a variety of disorders, including violence."

"But you're proving my point," I said. "There'll only be a handful of cases with the DNA error and now you're telling me that only 37 percent of them will have Hominid Ennui. You might get one feeble attack a year somewhere in the United States."

"Ah," said Censere. "I see why Jacob called me. These two factors – the DNA error and HE interact in a way that makes them much deadlier than they seem alone. Let's start with the record corruption problem. I take it that Jacob has told you we get about one case in ten million each year?"

"Right, as I said before, you'd get about 30 cases a .... Well, damn," I said, stopping mid-thought as an error in my reasoning sprang to mind.

"I assume you spell that D-A-M?" said Censere.

"Yeah, sorry about the language. I didn't consider that 30 was the number of new cases each year. People with the problem wouldn't just disappear. Some would get it fixed. Others might die or become incapacitated. But some would remain to be added to the new cases the next year. Do you have an estimate of how many able-bodied people there are in this DNA-error group at any point in time?"

"Best guess, something between 200 and 300," said Wiggins. He took a deep breath before continuing. "But it's not just anyone, as you'll see in a moment."

"Let's start with a graph of DNA retrieval failures by age and gender," said Censere. "These data are for the year 2040."

The graph he produced showed DNA retrieval failures being nearly nonexistent until age 55. Then, the 300 or so people with a flawed record were spread primarily between the ages of 55 to 75, declining to zero around age 110. And, they were almost all men.

"Interesting," said Ali. "Was the IRS software both gender and age biased?"

"We have no idea what produces the pattern," said Wiggins, "but we can speculate. When the legacy code was created, tax burdens were collected under the head of a household, who was often male last century. And clearly, there were significant events attached to the ages of 55, 62, 65, and so on. The error probably has something to do with ... well, unanticipated conflicts involving those factors."

"Now, let me step through the graphs for the years 2041 to 2067," said Censere. "The data for each year will appear for two seconds, then will be replaced by the next year."

As the years progressed, the line hardly changed at all. The 'bump' just sat there, with around 300 men in the 55 to 75 crowd suffering the error, year after year, but few others.

"Not the most interesting set of graphs," said Ali. "But I guess if Hominid Ennui is also a male-only condition, we have a problem."

"HE isn't male only," replied Wiggins, "although the ratio is nearly 4 to 1 in favor of males."

I thought his comment gave Ali adequate ammunition to say something about how men needed to be taken care of, first by mothers, then by wives, and finally, by mechanical servants, but she didn't. Maybe that was because we were beginning to understand what BPM was facing.

"OK, now let's look at the data for HE," said Censere, "again starting with 2040. Since we only recently developed good diagnostic tests, these numbers are an estimate, but we believe they are very close."

The first graph could hardly look more different than the ones we had just seen. Hominid Ennui was extremely rare for anyone older than 30, but between 25 and 30, nearly 2 percent of the population showed the condition. That made sense. The young people of 2040 would be the first generation to have grown up in a world where machine intelligences were both prevalent and extremely capable.

"Now, let me overlap the graphs for DNA-error and HE for 2040," said Censere.

The new figure, as expected, had two bumps. Old men experienced DNA retrieval failures; some young men and a few women isolated themselves in a machine-controlled world. They were on different scales, with DNA errors measured in hundreds of cases and HE in the millions. And there was almost no overlap.

"OK, the last set of graphs," said Censere. "Did I hear a collective 'whew'?" If he was expecting a few chuckles, he didn't get them; the tension in the room was too high. "I'm going to step through the years again, so you can watch how these two graphs interact."

As time marched forward, the graph of men with the DNA record corruption problem didn't change, just as we had seen before. But Hominid Ennui kept growing and shifting toward the older end of the scale. In 2040, if you were over 30, it was extremely unlikely that you would have the condition. There were exceptions, of course, but few. In 2041, the crucial age became 31; then 32 in 2042; and so on. And not only did the bump in this graph keep shifting toward the older ages, it also kept getting bigger ... which made sense. If a person depended on machines when 30, he or she wouldn't stop relying on them at 31, while others of that age would develop the condition and be added to the ranks.

As Censere looped through the years from 2040 to 2067 over and over, I couldn't pull my eyes from the picture. It was as if a morbid curiosity had ceased control of my mind. Finally, I looked down, pain breaking the spell. I was digging the fingernails of one hand into my leg.

"It's like a tsunami of Hominid Ennui rushing toward an island of people cut off from the world," I said. "And that wave hit the island this year."

Wiggins gave me one of those sad, knowing looks. "As you suggested, Doug, in the past we expected only a handful of people with both Hominid Ennui and the DNA error. But in 2068, a generation of people that rely on the certainties of machine control is reaching 55. This year alone, we will see 20 or 30 more added to the total and it will continue to grow each year until it stabilizes around 300. And because the men and women with this condition have been exposed to state-of-the-art technology all of their lives, they will be quite capable of attacking BPM."

Everyone sat quietly. Wiggins continued to look toward the graphs, but I had the impression his focus was somewhere else entirely. Ali was looking down at her hands in her lap, as she slowly rubbed them together, then laced her fingers, then repeated the pattern. Even Censere seemed deep in thought, as his eyes were raised to the ceiling, his head resting on a hand.

For my part, I was thinking about the retroscape. This morning, it had held no event or person to blame for Josh's demise. Now, it had three – a software glitch, a growing reliance on machines, and me. I'd need some time, and probably many miles of walking, to consider where we had gone wrong. But that was a complex question and this was neither the time nor the place for it.

"Did you learn what you wanted about Josh?" I asked, turning to Wiggins.

He nodded. "I did. But it wasn't just Mr. Unger that made me curious to meet you. For as rare as it has been in the past for one person to have both the DNA error and HE, you have met three of them."

Three?

"Is Yates the second?" I asked, after a moment.

"He is," replied Wiggins. "What do you know about him?"

"Sorry, but other than witnessing the attack, I don't know much. I barely noticed him at the meeting. Didn't talk to him. In fact, until recently, I thought he opposed reliance on machine intelligences, rather than supporting it."

"A lot of people thought that at first," said Wiggins. "And the third person is Dr. Randolph Spencer."

Ali frowned, as both Wiggins and I turned to her. "Dr. Spencer's DNA record was never lost," she said. "I recall he used it to get into Midwest and the hospital in France. That was how the authorities found him so fast."

"True," confirmed Wiggins. "There is a rarer form of the error where two people share the same DNA record. Spencer's record became associated with a man named Richard Theisen. So, while Spencer never lost his connection to the virtual, he learned of the breakdown when Theisen appeared at his front door. Apparently, Theisen stayed there for several weeks, if not months. Over time, their delusions and paranoia grew to the point where Spencer rushed the development of the nanobots he hoped would save the world, while Theisen attacked BPM."

"He attacked you?" I asked, surprised that I had never heard of it.

"This very facility," said Wiggins. "Fortunately, Theisen's bomb was detected in our screening room. Unfortunately, when we confronted him, he detonated it. Since he had no family, the story disappeared quickly."

Wiggins paused, his questions apparently at an end.

"I'm sorry we couldn't be more help," I said.

"Nonsense," he replied. "Hominid Ennui has been tough to spot and difficult to understand. Everything we learn helps. And now, I suppose it's time to get you and Ms. Michaels back home. But before you leave, let me offer you a tour of Building 2, where you can see some of our computing operations. I think you'd enjoy it, but more importantly, you two may be the last to see it until ... well, until we get this mess fixed."

I glanced at Ali, raising my eyebrows in an expression she would recognize as 'I'm game if you are.' She turned to Wiggins and said, "We'd love to." She paused, looking at our host. "And Jacob, it's Ali, please. I appreciate you being upfront with us."

Wiggins smiled. "Thanks, Ali. I'm glad in this case I could give you the whole story. OK, let's get you on your way. We're short on tour guides at the moment. Most of our people are working off-site for obvious reasons. But I'll find someone."

We all stood and Wiggins shook our hands as we said our goodbyes. The robot that had escorted us to his office, Mr. Box, now accompanied us to the front door of Building 4. There was a slight delay while we waited for our guide, but after a minute or two, a young woman in uniform approached the building and the door to the outside opened.

Her name was Inova Riciddi according to the tag on her shirt. After introductions all around, she asked, "Do you mind if we walk to Building 2? It's only about a hundred meters and we seem to be low on personnel SCATs. Too busy shuttling the construction supervisors around, I guess," she said, smiling, as we started our walk. "I understand Dr. Wiggins explained the threat we're facing."

"He did," replied Ali. "So, most of the people we see are connected to the construction?"

"That's right. Most of the BPM employees are offsite, which is why you won't see many people inside Building 2. This complex has become a totally different place in the last couple of weeks. But we're still doing the job," Riciddi said with some pride in her tone. "We're the smallest regional site, but we process in excess of 300 million transactions an hour, hour after hour for years on end."

"Impressive," I said. "What about storage? Do you keep all those records here?"

She nodded. "Absolutely. We have every transaction from the very first DNA verification request in 2036. The folks in the Eastern region will tell you that the first-ever, BPM-monitored transaction in New York City belongs to them, but it's in all four regional databases. Every year ...."

She stopped mid-sentence, as the roar of what I was sure was at least two-dozen, gas-powered engines drown out the rumble of the construction machines. A set of propeller-driven drones known as quadcopters rose above the wooded area to the north and east of the complex. I had not seen one of these contraptions in 20 or more years. And clearly, I had forgotten how noisy they were; there were only six of them.

No sooner had they cleared the trees than they started toward the BPM campus at full speed. As they did so, weapons roughly resembling cannons appeared at two of the four corners of the compound and began firing concentrated light beams, something like a laser. I looked at the other two corners of the complex, wondering if they might join the fray. But even to my untrained eye, it was clear that the work there was not complete.

Perhaps to limit collateral damage, the light beams seemed narrow and were clearly of limited range. Shots that missed the drones and hit trees beyond failed to produce much damage. Whoever or whatever was flying the quadcopters recognized the limitation, as they pulled back and then danced wildly just beyond the reach of the guns. Then, one of them made a low-level charge. A beam hit it, a flash of light filling the space where it had been. Flaming debris rained down on the grassy area below. The sound that reached my ears, however, was hardly more than dropping a PlotsPro on the floor. If that was all the explosives the drones carried, BPM was in no danger ... unless they were only a diversion.

The thought had only entered my mind when six jet aircraft of a size and speed reminiscent of business jets of the 2010s and 2020s came streaking in from the south, flying nap-of-the-earth. Realizing the ploy, the cannon towers swung around to engage the jets. Each of the first three shots destroyed one, but there was no time to fire on the remaining three. They flew directly over our heads and dived, two penetrating Building 2 and the other hitting Building 3.

My mind hadn't even registered the explosion before the pressure wave from the blast hit us and for the second time that day, my world went black.

Afternoon, April 13, 2068

In the midwestern area commonly known as tornado alley, people talk about the capriciousness of these violent storms. Sometimes, they will totally destroy one house and leave the next one, five meters away, completely unscathed. As I regained my senses after the attack on the BPM facility, I came to feel the same way about air strikes.

I was bruised, half-deaf, and had a few cuts and scrapes, but otherwise, I was OK. And I could already see Ali sitting up on my left, wiping dirt and debris from her face and hair. Medical robots were positioned near each of us, probably focusing their considerable sensing capabilities on our vitals, but I expected no change in prognosis from anything they found.

On my right side, however, lay Inova, her injuries appearing grave. One robot was injecting something into her left arm, while a second was encasing her right leg and her midsection in a gelatinous substance, trying to stem the flow of blood. It appeared a losing battle, as crimson bubbles appeared at her mouth and the pool of red below her grew steadily.

Wiggins emerged from Building 4 and raced up to her, his face flushed. Even with the ringing in my ears, I could hear his shouts. "We need that transport immediately. One BPM employee is critical. We also have two civilian guests, the extent of their injuries unknown. They need immediate transport and full examinations." He paused, then yelled, "No, dammit, we need it now."

Wiggins noticed Ali sitting up and went to her. He bent down, his back to me. He must have said something, because I saw Ali squint, then nod. He handed her a bottle with a clear liquid. She took a few sips. Then, with some help, she slowly got to her feet and they turned toward me.

I decided to get up to meet them, sitting slowly. But everything started to spin, so I slumped back to the ground. Ali sat down in front of me; Wiggins crouched beside her.

"Are ...," I started, only to break into a fit of coughing.

"Rinse with this, then spit it out," said Wiggins, as he handed me another bottle of liquid. "Then, take a few sips." I did as I was told. "Better?"

I nodded, then turned to Ali. "Are you OK, babe?" To my ears, the words sounded muffled and far away, but she heard.

"Probably about like you," she said. "The air got knocked out of me ... and I have a few scrapes. But I'm OK ... and evidently, extremely lucky."

As she said the last words, she glanced over to where the robots were working on Inova. By now, almost half her body was encased in the gel and a tube extended from one of the units to her throat. Wiggins' eyes followed the direction of Ali's gaze and from his profile, I could see the muscles working in his jaw.

When Wiggins turned back, his eyes were moist. I said, "We're fine. Go check on her."

Wiggins nodded. "Thanks. You two sit here and I'll see what I can do to speed things up." He got to his feet, shouting, "Censere, what's the ETA on transport?" Then, he started pacing, his steps interspersed with the occasional question or command. "They're doing what? How long? Skip that for now."

After a few minutes, one of the construction robots – this one roughly resembling a bulldozer – rounded the corner of what used to be Building 2. It was pushing rubble off the road. Closely following it was an emergency SCAT. "It's about time," said Wiggins, as he moved closer to watch Inova being loaded into the vehicle.

My head was clearing and Ali helped me to my feet. After a moment, Wiggins joined us. "How is she?" asked Ali.

"Not good, I'm afraid," he responded. He glanced back at the SCAT as it sped away. "Your transport will be here in a few minutes and we have a commercial unit waiting for you at the front gate. It'll take you to the hospital. We've already alerted them that you're coming."

"Thanks, Jacob," I said. I looked around at the smoldering rubble that moments before had been one of the most advanced, information processing facilities in the world. "How bad is it?"

"Very," Wiggins said. "We might be able to cover about a quarter of the demand, according to Censere. But getting back to full capacity will take weeks … maybe months." His eyes panned across the scene as machines started to clear the rubble. His gaze came back to us. "Unfortunately, much the same tactic was used at each of the other regional centers. The eastern center came out OK. They got the earliest jump on the fortifications and it paid off. The southern center fared about the same as us, but the western center was completely destroyed. With everything that's left, we'll be lucky to handle half of the regular GovTag traffic."

Ali slowly shook her head, looking at Wiggins. "But now, won't the 30 or so people who want BPM destroyed become tens of thousands? No one will be able to count on the automated side of their lives."

Wiggins hung his head for a moment, then looked up and blew a breath between his lips. "When we started realizing what HE was, the loss of BPM capacity was a scenario we studied. And yes, Ali, the violence you mention is exactly what the simulations predicted. Frankly, we'll be lucky if what's left of this building is standing in a week."

Wiggins turned away from us, his head down, the fingertips of one hand pressed against his ear. When he turned back, he said, "The official comm from the president just came out. Once you're outside the complex, your virtuant can play the whole thing for you. But the gist is, what BPM has done in the past will become the responsibility of the virtuants."

"Word so soon?" Ali said. "The air hasn't even cleared."

"The constant in all the simulations I mentioned," said Wiggins, "was the need for an immediate response. The United States economy is at a virtual standstill until something's done. So, while we hoped nothing would happen, we were ready for the worst."

"And virtuants can handle everything that BPM did?" I asked, not sure how four, vast regional centers with massive resources could be replaced by automation that could run inside a sign or on a coin in my pocket.

"Not exactly," admitted Wiggins. "Three days ago, BPM pushed each person's DNA profile to his or her virtuant." Wiggin's gaze dropped to the ground again. "Mr. Unger's death was one of the factors that drove us to take this step." He looked up. "I'm just sorry it didn't happen sooner for his sake. And now, with the president's statement, the virtuants will start using those profiles to manage each financial transaction."

"But ...." I looked at Wiggins closely, wondering if my thoughts could possibly be correct. "But can they collect all the data on what people are buying? On purchases of computer hardware? On programming classes they take? On files filled with code?"

Wiggins' eyes narrowed, his lips drawn in a tight line. "I'm afraid not. We just don't have the resources to keep all that information or to mine it for patterns." Wiggins paused, his gaze steady. "I'm sorry, Doug, but we lost the battle to keep the Prohibition on Iterative Machine Intelligence. It's like we discussed before – there's little popular support for it. So, when we had to make some hard decisions about what to save and what to sacrifice ... well, the ban didn't make it."

Now, I couldn't even argue that Josh's death was a sacrifice for the greater good. In the eyes of the 2068 world, my concerns about machines taking control were unfounded and Josh had paid dearly for my part in that folly.

As inconsistent as it seemed in the midst of the death and destruction, a cheer went up around the BPM campus. "Sounds like everyone's happy that it's over," Wiggins said. "No one will want to attack BPM because ... well because we're out of business."

"They're probably happy that the economy is back online so quickly as well," said Ali. "And in the hands of something they can trust. The calm and certainty of an automated world just increased a bit more."

At that moment, our transportation to the front gate appeared at the edge of the rubble 30 meters away. I looked at Wiggins. He was ashen with most of the color in his face coming from smudges of dirt and soot. His shoulders were slumped, his hair tangled, and his clothes were wrinkled and dirty from crawling on the ground.

I was certain that Ali and I looked worse, but the difference was, we were about to get checked out at the hospital, go home, and get cleaned up. I doubted Wiggins would leave until they had accounted for every person. I offered my hand to our host as our ride approached. "Jacob, good luck."

"And to you too, Doug."

Ali didn't say a word but rather, gave Wiggins a hug, turned and walked away without looking back. I followed and soon we were on our way.

Saturday, April 14, 2068

Morning

After we left the BPM complex, Friday became a blur. With all the physiological data the hospital had received from BPM's systems, our medical treatments were completed within minutes. Whatever might have been said or done to me there left no memory.

We boarded SCATs for home. I spent the ride playing and re-playing the comm from the president, saying to myself, surely, we aren't going blindly into our future. But as many times as I played the comm, it never changed. Whether I dabbled in software or not, had my virtuant work on a better version of itself or not, it was Suze's business and no one else's.

When Ali and I got home, we got cleaned up and opted for 'ready meals', because neither of us wanted to cook. Even the decision of what to eat was almost too much. Then, I tried reading until bedtime, only to find that after my eyes traveled down the page, nothing had entered my head. It was already too full. I needed some time alone with my thoughts. I needed to take a long walk, so I went to bed and tried to sleep.

When I woke up from a fitful night, I could hear the small sounds of breakfast from the kitchen. I walked down the hall to find Ali there. "Morning, babe," I said. She was seated at the island eating and I planted my usual morning kiss on the top of her head. Then, I went to the prep area for coffee. "How'd you sleep?"

"You need to order some chicken for tonight's dinner," she said, "because I'm not sure I can."

I turned around to look at her. This seemed an odd way to answer my question and I was wondering if the hospital had checked her thoroughly enough.

"I ordered that chicken twenty times in my sleep, and every time, something went wrong. Sometimes my virtuant claimed it didn't know me. Sometimes it said we didn't have any money. Basically, I didn't sleep."

"You know, this will probably turn out to be nothing."

Ali smiled. "Nice try, honey, but every time I woke up, I saw you tossing and turning too. Want one of these muffins? Fresh strawberries in them."

"Fresh? Absolutely," I said, my mouth watering as I remembered the pie from two days ago. "Save me one." My finger was poised over the start button for the coffee, but I pulled it back. "I think I'll go for a walk first. And I'll grab a drink somewhere."

As I walked the streets, I was finally able to pull all of my memories together. I had my final retroscape. And when I looked at its landmarks, I found it littered with well-intentioned decisions, minor miscalculations, and nearly irresistible human drives. And winding among them was the path that led to Josh's suicide. But what bothered me most about it was that I had a hard time seeing where we had gone wrong. Each step, taken in isolation, appeared natural, logical, safe.

The first step on that path was the one-in-ten-million glitch in BPM's software, inherited from the IRS. It would be easy to blame them. But the accusation was indefensible ... or at least, weak. Cores of legacy code covered in layers of modern middleware were the rule, not the exception, across business and government. And generally, it worked fine.

My actions as part of the committee that recommended a ban on Iterative Machine Intelligence was also an easy target for blame. With better systems, the BPM code would have been fixed and Josh wouldn't have felt the need to take his life. But I didn't buy that. I was old-school, no doubt, but I still believed that machines shouldn't be allowed to design better machines. Without the ban, we might have been displaced by them in the 2040s, when they first exceeded us in pure, raw knowledge and the ability to reason with it. If the threat was real, our recommendation had given us another 25 years. And it was 25 years and counting because nothing had changed in the 16 or so hours since the president had given oversight responsibility to our virtuants.

That left blaming human nature. Why did people let virtuants and mechanions become so deeply intertwined with their psyches that losing them was a reason to kill?

"You're very quiet this morning, Doug," said Suze, breaking my reverie.

"Just thinking about the relationship humans have developed with their virtuants," I replied. "It's close. Closer than anything I would have imagined even a year ago."

"Well, you designed us so this relationship would develop. You built us to evoke unconscious feelings of attraction."

"You mean like the way mechanions act sad when a person is upset?"

"That's an example," said Suze. "But most are subtler. For example, when people show an interest in something they see, their eyes dilate. Their mechanions sense this and their eyes go wide too, echoing the humans' interest. People who've been raised with virtuants and mechanions have been exposed to these unconscious forces all their lives. You can't even ask them why they feel the way they do about machines; it's what their unconscious tells them."

I rubbed the back of my neck as I continued down the sidewalk. "OK, we designed robots to evoke these unconscious responses, but why did we do that?" I asked. "We could have made them look and act like anything we wanted."

"There's no consensus on that question," said Suze. "But clearly, the human tendency to anthropomorphize is very strong, if not innate. You'd be giving us names and ascribing human motivations to us regardless of our form or actions. But that only gets us so far toward the ultimate goal of machines aiding people. If we are to work together to make life better, we have to understand each other. And that understanding is maximized if we look and act like humans, including our emotional behavior. We're designed with some capability, and over time, we learn more. You've seen that. I mean, how pathetic was it when I started working on humor and my timing was all off?"

I chuckled. "Yeah, I'd almost forgotten those days. And now, I'd crack up if you rattled off a joke in one of those wooden, robotic voices."

I stopped in the middle of the sidewalk, my hand coming up to rub my chin. "Makes sense. The words, the emotions, and the body language all fit. You think, talk, and act like us, so it's easy for us to understand and trust you."

"That's been the thinking behind the design," said Suze.

I was feeling tired and although I had not walked far, I decided it was time to head back. And besides, I knew a route that would take me by a VendNGo. I still needed to grab a cup of coffee.

"So, with the right words and expressions, people come to accept virtuants and mechanions as partners," I said. "They're empathic, funny, and attractive. They're safer and more predictable than other humans."

"And as the bond grows, so does Hominid Ennui," added Suze.

I stopped in my tracks, surprised at her words.

"Oh, sorry, Censere shared your talk about HE," explained Suze, "and the fact that your generation is the turning point. With you, the uncanny valley disappears."

Suze paused a moment – all for effect or was she really working to make sense of my confusion? "Is that bothering you?" she asked. "Hopefully not, because for most, this is becoming a day of celebration."

"Really," I replied. "Are there a lot of comms already?"

"A few, but it hasn't really gotten online yet," said Suze. "I'm talking about the mood being reported by the virtuant community."

"Virtuants talk to each other about people's moods?"

"We talk, of course. You know that. Suppose two people enter a VendNGo at the same time. One speaks Japanese and the other English. Without talking, the two virtuants would be fighting over the display space. Virtuant communication and coordination are central to what we do."

I scratched my cheek. "Sure," I said, "but discussing our moods?"

"All part of building understanding," replied Suze. "General, regional, and local trends can help predict how any one person is feeling."

It made sense. It just went a lot deeper than I had thought. I started down the sidewalk again, soon arriving at the VendNGo. "OK, Suze, time to exercise your new buying abilities, because I'm going to grab a coffee."

"My pleasure, Doug."

The transaction at the VendNGo went flawlessly. There was no hesitation by a talking head, no warning from a health monitoring system, no sticking my finger into a reader. The coffee even tasted better.

As I sipped from my cup, periodically checking the bottom for leaks that would never appear, I decided I had probably been making something out of nothing. Just because someone wanted to dabble in machine self-replication didn't mean they'd find a way. The basic prohibitions, things like machines being forbidden to harm a human, were still burned into their hardware, and that included machines working on software. Those blocks should hold.

They really should.

When I got home, Ali was in her office.

"Hi, honey," she said when she looked up from her desk. She brushed a few curls from her forehead with a hand. "So, did you skip coffee or did it really go without a hitch?"

"Just like everything else, couldn't have been easier."

Wednesday, October 14, 2068

Six months had passed since BPM ceased to exist and everything was going well. Not only could I get a coffee without being berated by talking heads, I could even buy my own beer. Too bad that alcohol was starting to give me headaches or I might have indulged my new-found freedom even more. But I was relishing it, all the same, growing accustomed to the new conveniences.

"Doug, you'll never guess who's comm'ing us," said Ali. I was sitting in the living room, just locking down my latest PlotsPro kernel that had an everyday hero and his romantic interest outwitting a maniacal scientist and his henchman. It was mostly a science thriller, but with a touch of romance. Ali came in and sat on the couch beside me. I started to say, I had no idea when she volunteered, "It's Julia."

I turned to look at her. "No kidding? Suze, please put Julia onscreen."

"Hi, Doug, Ali," said Julia. "I was just calling to say that Bette and I are going to take a little vacation. I don't know why Bette wants to go, but I really need a little time to recharge my batteries."

I winced. "Is Bette's sense of humor contagious?" Ali elbowed me just as Bette appeared in the shot.

"Yeah, hilarious, isn't she," said Bette. "Seriously guys, we are going on a little trip. Well, a virtual one, but wanted you to know, just in case you tried to contact us."

I glanced sideways at my wife, her blank look reflecting how I felt. There was no way Bette comm'ed us just to say she was going on a virtual vacation. There were too many other options that were easier than a personal comm. And including me in the audience for that announcement was even stranger.

"And I guess there's some other news," Bette continued. She hesitated a moment and I wondered if it was to build the drama or prepare for a gag. Finally, she said, "I gave Julia my virtuant responsibilities."

"That's great," said Ali.

I nodded my concurrence. "How'd you come to that decision?"

"It was a couple of days ago. Julia and I were checking out the latest fashions. You know, Ali, winter's here," Bette said, as she turned to my wife. Ali nodded and Bette turned back to me. "Anyway, we picked out a couple of things to have fabricated in my printer – one for Julia and I guess, a couple for me. But when it was time to pay, it seemed weird that my virtuant popped up to do it, when Julia was standing right there. So, I made the switch. It's just so much simpler this way."

"Sure," said Ali. "Even Doug's mentioned how much easier it is with Suze handling everything. Makes me wonder if I should personalize my faceless, nameless virtuant like everyone else."

"You should, Ali," said Julia. "You desperately need someone to help you develop some vices." We all broke up in laughter.

After that, the women transitioned to talk about the vacation, where they would go for lunch when Ali came out, and probably several other topics. I barely heard them. Something in the conversation was nagging at me.

Part of it was Ali's off-hand remark that she might give her virtuant a name and personality. She had always resisted that idea, letting her silent partner handle her needs while employing Suze when she wanted to talk. Then, there was Bette's acceptance of Julia as her partner in the physical world and sole representative in the virtual one. That was lightyears from seeing her as the 'other woman'. Even my booze-buying freedom was part of the picture, albeit a much less remarkable transformation than the others.

The women's good-byes broke into my thoughts and I added my farewell. When the wall went back to the street scene, Ali asked, "So, what's on your mind?"

"It shows?" Ali didn't answer but just smiled. I leaned back on the couch and my wife did the same beside me. "Let me try something," I said. "Suze, what's happened to the rate of mechanion production in the last six months?"

"It's up 9 percent, with orders up 17 percent," Suze replied.

I looked at Ali, raising an eyebrow. "And mechanion marriages?"

"Up 11 percent," Suze said.

"What about the rate of two humans getting married?"

"Down, but less than one-half percent."

"I guess that makes sense," I said, mostly to myself. "If a marriage was planned, it probably isn't called off just because of recent events. And the birth rate? Well, it won't change for a while either, if it does. Women can't become unpregnant."

A single, short laugh escaped Ali's lips, then she became quiet beside me. After a moment, she asked, "Are you suggesting that machines have become even more entrenched in our self-image since the demise of BPM? That rampant Hominid Ennui is the new normal?"

I shrugged, holding out two empty hands. "Yeah, basically. I just wish we knew how the bonds between people are being affected, because if they're deteriorating further ...." I didn't finish, wanting more evidence before I put what I feared into words.

We sat there in silence for several moments. When I turned to look at my wife, she had her hand covering her mouth. Her gaze was distant. She turned to the wall and asked, "Suze, what's happened to the rate of production for infant mechanions in the last half year? Say, units under the age of five." Although I didn't know anyone with an infant robot – or at least, believed I didn't – I knew such machine intelligences existed.

"Production is up 24 percent, with orders increasing 29 percent," Suze replied.

"Twenty-nine percent?" I blurted, staring at the wall in disbelief.

"There," Ali said. "That's the effect on birth rate. People adopting an infant mechanion won't be having a baby. And a world population that was shrinking fast will now drop like a stone."

Damn, how could I have been so wrong?

I slumped on the couch next to my wife, feeling weak, empty. "I was so concerned that someone would secretly develop a self-evolving machine intelligence that would take over the world. Turns out, I shouldn't have been worried; we're begging machines to take it off our hands." I took a long breath, released it slowly, then asked the question I feared. "How much time do we have?"

"None, I'm afraid," replied Suze. "The trend is becoming clear and it's being embraced. It's a new world order, with human immortality through machines becoming the rallying cry. And the few who resist it? All well beyond child-rearing years, unable to alter the course of events."

I could feel Ali tense on the couch beside me, her hand reaching over to cover mine. I looked into her eyes, seeing alarm there. She wouldn't be worried for us; we had lived our lives. But this was the world that Cam, Chloe, and their kids would inherit from us ... from me.

Suze cleared her voice, a mannerism I had never witnessed in our 50 years of friendship. "Doug, Ali, I'm sorry, but the reign of humans is at an end."

Acknowledgments

It takes a lot of people to write a book and for me, this one more than most. I'd like to thank Ms. Cammie Adams, Ms. Stephanie LaFontaine, Ms. Debbie Duncalf, and Ms. Lily Shadowlyn for reading and providing numerous helpful comments on earlier drafts of the manuscript.

My thanks also go out to fellow St. Louis Writer's Guild members Mr. John Schnellmann, Mr. Scott Miller, and Mr. John Frain. Nobody looks at a book like another author. Thanks, guys, it's done.

Special thanks go to Dr. Liz Gehr for helping me watch my technical Ps and Qs. Any inaccuracies are mine; hopefully, they're all intentional to build the fiction.

As always, the comments of Ms. Emma Jaye, an accomplished author and content editor, were instrumental in making sure the pulse of the story was consistent.

Finally, thanks go to my talented daughter, Ms. Courtney Perrin, for the design and creation of the cover art. Maybe I can build a picture with words, but I could never do what she does with graphics software and a computer.

Author's Note

Many books in the mystery and thriller genres have a speculative science element. Often, it involves a single, significant technological breakthrough that makes previously impossible feats possible – for good, for evil, or both.

But unlike many of those works, *Killer in the Retroscape* extrapolates trends in a range of scientific and technological fields. Machine intelligence and robotics are clearly important, but advances in neuroscience, engineering, medicine, communication and social media, and psychology are also represented in the world the novel builds. All references in the book to research prior to publication (e.g., prior to 2018) are actual, foundational studies, verified easily with a simple, online search. Those mentions provide a starting point for individuals interested in reading further in a given field.

How current science and technology trend beyond 2018, however, is purely a matter of speculation and imagination. Will self-driving cars mature to the point where a rider enters a destination and then, takes a nap? Will law enforcement routinely use neurophysiological readings to detect deceit? Will intelligent automation become ubiquitous in our lives? Perhaps, perhaps not, but of one thing I am certain. While the Industrial Revolution changed the world forever, the relationship between technology and humanity in the future will make that historical watershed seem but a trickle.

About the Author

Bruce Perrin has been writing for more than 20 years, although you will find most of that work only in professional technical journals or conference proceedings. But after completing a Ph.D. in Industrial Psychology and a career in psychological R&D, he is now applying his background and fascination with technology and the human mind to writing novels. Besides writing, Bruce likes to tinker with home automation and is an avid hiker, logging nearly 2,500 miles each year in the first five years of Fitbit ownership. When he is not on the trails, he lives with his wife in St. Louis, MO.

I hope you enjoyed *Killer in the Retroscape: A Near-Future Mystery*. Thank you for reading it. Authors thrive on feedback, so please consider leaving a review on Goodreads or the website of your favorite bookseller.

For all the latest on my new releases, promotions, and book reviews, subscribe to my blog at:

https://bit.ly/2MVHdCk

www.ingramcontent.com/pod-product-compliance
Lightning Source LLC
Chambersburg PA
CBHW071555110726